THE WINTER CRONE

ALSO BY NATASHA BACHE

'Waiting for the West Wind' in *Everyday Kindness*,
a short story anthology by L.J. Ross

Sister of the Moon

(coming in 2023)

THE WINTER CRONE

THE ARCANE TALES OF TAMSYN PRIDE
Book 1

NATASHA BACHE

WHINBERRY
PRESS

www.NatashaBache.com

First published by Whinberry Press 2022

A catalogue record for this book is available from the British Library

ISBN: 978-1-9164198-1-0

This novel is entirely a work of fiction. The names, characters and incidents portrayed in it are the work of the author's imagination. Any resemblance to actual persons, living or dead, events or localities is entirely coincidental.

Typeset in Adobe Garamond by Stuart Bache in Vellum.

In loving memory of my wonderful sister, Tanya.

CONTENTS

PART THREE

PART ONE

When summer gathers up her robes of glory, and like a dream of beauty, glides away.

—Sarah Helen Whitman

PROLOGUE

pring was in full bloom at Rosemount. Sylvia's
beloved garden was awash with May flowers. The
white anemones and deep burgundy tulips swayed in
the cool breeze, indifferent to the panic rising in Sylvia's
chest. Her heart pounded as she hurried to the Poison
Garden, as fast as her old bones could carry her. She wheezed
as she fumbled in her apron for the kitchen scissors.

Her mind raced as she looked back over her shoulder
towards the house. Rosemount was bathed in crystalline blue
light with a clarity you could only see when the winds of
spring blew. Yet inside the cottage there was darkness. That
morning, an egg had slipped out of her fingers into the pan,
shell and all. The yolk broke, and as she slid it into the bin,
she'd called Bridie, informing her she wouldn't be going to
the Maypole dance. She'd better play it safe and stay indoors.
Sylvia would have laughed at the irony, had she not been so
terrified. How she wished she was there now, watching the
young girls, hair streaming, weaving their ribbons in and out

while the Morris dancers hopped, waving their white hand-kerchiefs.

Her back stiff, Sylvia stooped down to the most lethal plant she nurtured. The bulbous purple flowers of aconite bobbed as she gingerly touched the leaves. The cardinal rule, one that had been drilled into her as a child, and one she had reminded her daughter and granddaughter of nearly every day, was 'Never, ever, go into the Poison Garden bare-skinned.' Now, however, she had no time for gloves.

Holding the scissors, her gnarled hands shook as she care-fully snipped off the leaves. She was shaking so much the scissors fell to the ground. Sylvia shoved the aconite leaves deep into her apron pocket and turned back to the house. Taking a deep, calming breath, she stood for a moment, composing herself. Without thinking, her hand travelled up to her neck, to touch the locket she had taken to wearing.

With a sudden resolve and a deft yank, she pulled the chain, snapping it. She dropped it amidst the foliage, where she hoped it would not be found. On creaking legs, she made her way back to the house, pulse racing in the knowledge of what awaited inside.

1

THE MASKED APPRENTICE

The moon provided the only source of silver-white light for the flock and its spring lambs. September had seen little rain; the parched earth was cracked and uneven as a cloaked figure ran swiftly across the meadow. He caught his boot on something hard, sending him tumbling into the dried rushes. Crouching where he fell, he squinted into the dark, barely able to locate the woolly mounds lying prone on the ground. He strained his ears for any sign of disturbance caused by his foolish fall. Save for his own heavy breathing and the blood rushing in his ears, the valley remained silent.

It was sheer genius on his part that he had chosen the night of the Horn Dance. Most of the townsfolk were watching the stag heads snake through Abbots Bromley, and the one-thousand-year-old celebrations were set to continue late into the night. No one would miss him; that he was sure of.

Further down the field, Farmer Bradshaw's house sat in

darkness. He crawled over to a ewe, not daring to pull out his torch for fear of startling it further. He worked deftly, his pale dagger leaving a shallow cut on its hind leg. As he sprinted from one animal to the other, his breath fell hot and sweet inside the mask, his hood quickening the perspiration on his brow and lips.

Despite his earlier precautions, the flock was beginning to get agitated. The lambs had already succumbed to sleep, but some of the ewes were taking longer than he had calculated. Their plaintive cries disturbed the silence as the moon disappeared behind black clouds and lightning lit up the whole valley. He paused, knife in hand, as a light came on in the house below. Thunder rolled over the hills, reverberating in a deafening clap.

Three minutes and forty-five seconds. He had attempted the sprint from the house only once, about a week ago. Surely he was faster than old Pete? How many sheep could he mark in that time, to ensure he could still put enough distance between them?

The front door burst open; a dog was barking insistently, silhouetted against the light. Adrenaline coursed through his veins, and sweat poured down the back of his neck as he realised Bradshaw must still have his old sheepdog living in the house. How did he still have that old mutt? Surely it must be twenty years old by now. Hopefully it was as decrepit as old Pete. He was also fairly confident that he had a gun, and if pushed, would not be shy to use it. He had marked only a small percentage of sheep, perhaps seven or so; he hoped that would be enough to cause significant outrage.

'Oi! Stop! I've got a gun!' Bradshaw yelled.

He appreciated the warning. However, he was certain the farmer wouldn't risk a shot from so far away, not with all these sheep lying around. Perhaps he had a little time. He ran to the nearest white mound. It breathed heavily, the tongue lolling out of its mouth, gleaming in the moonlight.

Patting its thick coat, he whispered, 'This will only hurt a little.'

The knife was poised, cool and heavy in his sweating palm, when he heard the bark of the dog much too close for comfort. He had taken care of the one outside, who was now heavily drugged and snoozing in its kennel – he had shoved enough valerian root into its bowl to put half of Battersea Dogs Home to sleep. How could he not have thought to ask if the man had any pets in the house? It was mistakes like this that kept him from progressing on to bigger and better things, but he would have to chastise himself later.

Another flash of lightning exposed his position. He heard a gunshot. He abandoned the ewe, the symbol half-carved into its upper thigh. Clumsily, he rose from the ground. As he ran for the nearest gate, the barking was almost upon him, and he laboured to catch his breath through the thick black cloth covering his mouth. He risked a glance over his shoulder. The farmer was making rapid progress, the torch in his hand flailing wildly from side to side as he sprinted up the field. Thunder bellowed. Finally, after weeks of drought, the thick, static air was cut with warm raindrops.

The black shadow of the dog caught up with him. Pain sliced through his left ankle as its yellowed teeth pierced the taut skin. He yelled and fell heavily to the ground. The jaws locked around his foot. Grinding and thrashing wildly from side to side, the old sheepdog snarled and dug its hind legs into the coarse grasses, pulling backwards. The man cried out in frustration through gritted teeth; he must have dropped the dagger as he fell. His hands searched wildly in vain, and the dog's teeth clamped more tightly, digging into the bone.

He turned onto his back and kicked the dog away with his right foot. Scrambling up, he almost fell again at the hot, shooting pain emanating from his leg. He ran to the nearby gate regardless, hurling himself over it as the dog stood on its weary hind legs, trying in vain to jump the gate after him.

Running into the night, he decided Gavin Hardcastle didn't need to know about the incident with the dog. His pulse quickened as he thought about what Gavin would say to him. A broad smile, a pat on the back, and when Gavin was head of the council once more, he would be invited in, with a seat of his own at the table.

2

ROSEMOUNT

Hidden behind hedgerows, entangled in bracken and shrouded between mossy mounds, the stones of Rosemount Cottage had become a living, breathing part of the earth. Over centuries, daughters of the Pride family had inhabited the thatched cottage that lay on the outskirts of the village of Much Wenlock, their spirits and knowledge seeping into her walls and timber frame.

October's golden light was fading through the leaded windows as Tamsyn padded over the cold flagstones to the refrigerator. Cranking open the lever handle that threatened to snap off each time she touched it, she felt her stomach growl with hunger, anticipating food she knew wasn't there. Winnie, her grandmother's cat, stood on her hind legs, front paws flexing on the sideboard, her amber eyes half-closed expectantly. Arching her grey and black striped body in a luxuriant stretch, she gave a curt mewl.

'You can't be hungry too?' Tamsyn scolded. 'You've already had a tin and a half of tuna. Your teeth will rot.'

9

Surveying the fridge's scant innards, Tamsyn found a brown carrot, pulled from the garden who knows when. Eight cans of Diet Coke. Essential. Half a tin of tuna. Several opened packets of cat food that Winnie now refused to eat since realising that Tamsyn would relent and give her tuna or precooked chicken. Grapes that purported to taste of candyfloss. A packet of brown sludge that she suspected was once coriander.

Tamsyn shrugged at Winnie, before tugging on the small door at the top of the fridge. It was frozen shut. She cursed as she yanked the freezer open, ice creaking and shattering onto the floor. She reached in for the tub of ice cream, grabbing the half tin of tuna with her other hand.

'You're getting a bit chubby,' she said as she slopped the contents of the tin into Winnie's bowl. She lovingly scratched the cat's paunchy tummy and bent down to give her a hard kiss on the head.

'Pretty soon, the mice will be the ones chasing you. The rest of the week it's dried food only.' The vet had warned Tamsyn that she would have to pull out Winnie's teeth if she didn't start eating her dried food. She had also remarked on the cat's fuller face and rounded belly. Tamsyn looked down at herself. Wiggling, she smiled as she felt her stomach jiggle with a satisfying wobble underneath her sweatpants and baggy shirt.

'Don't listen to what the vet said. You look better than ever, Winnie.' The cat pushed her cheek along the side of her leg as Tamsyn added more dried food to the mound in the second bowl.

'But you do have to eat this. Trust me, you don't want to be slobbering everywhere when your teeth are gone.' Winnie looked at her as if she understood, and couldn't care less, before licking the tuna hungrily.

Tamsyn considered for a moment whether she was going mad, spending her Friday night talking to a cat and eating ice cream for dinner. Tamsyn was loath to spend money on groceries. As much as she loved food, the task of venturing into the village with its miniature supermarket was a chore she would avoid at all costs. The side-eying and awkward condolences about the loss of her grandmother irked her.

Placing the crystallised ice cream into the microwave, she absently watched the cardboard cylinder turn under its orange-yellow glow. The microwave and TV seemed ill at ease in the cottage, and she could almost feel Rosemount repelling their presence. Tamsyn had even been forced to walk to the village to get enough signal to look up how to fashion an aerial from a wire coat hanger. Her grandmother, Sylvia Pride, was abjectly intolerant of all mod cons and the cancer-inducing waves she proclaimed they emitted.

Other than the TV, microwave and a few clothes, Tamsyn had left everything in her flat in London. Or Dominic's flat, to be precise.

It had been a week or so after Sylvia's funeral that she'd told Dominic she was leaving. A gnawing, dragging sensation had taken hold of her from the moment she watched her grandmother's coffin being lowered into the ground. Her insides had churned when she heard his keys in the door, her hands almost shaking with the knowledge of the blow she was about to inflict. He had turned pale and asked her if there was anything he could do to make it right. There wasn't, she'd said. She just needed time alone. And then what had happened? Her head hurt as she tried to remember. Glass on the floor, blood on her palms.

When she'd told her work friends she was thinking of leaving, they told her on no uncertain terms that they thought she was mad. Tamsyn quickly learned that everyone adored Dominic. Sitting in a bar, she'd listened as they relayed all the reasons she was mad to leave him: he had good prospects, a good education, a great job, and an even better salary. All the perfect building blocks for the future. More than this, he was hilarious, her friend Sarah had said. He brought an energy to any get-together, while Tamsyn could be found sitting quietly in the corner. He was, they all agreed, a great guy.

That night she had returned to the flat, convinced by the broad-stroke picture they had painted, and believing that she was indeed making a terrible mistake. She waited up for him. At 1:30, she heard the familiar turning of the key in the lock. The click-clack of his perfectly polished work shoes in the hallway. He burst into the bedroom, and a second or two later, a thick cloud of bourbon hit her nostrils.

He was swaying slightly, and he asked her what time she had got in, and who she'd been out with. She felt her blood run cold, and told him she'd talk to him in the morning. The next moment, his hands were gripping her arms, his breath reeking as he shook her and demanded whether she was making a fool of him. She warned him to get his hands off her. Then there was the sound of something shattering.

She had no idea how she ended up in her car, the steering wheel shuddering in her palms as she sped up the M40.

The microwave's shrill beeping snapped her out of her reverie. Removing the half-molten ice cream, she settled down with Winnie to find something to watch. The muted images on BBC West Midlands showed aerial footage of the local villages of Shropshire. Cars floating off in car parks, and the tops of trees in a sea of water where crops and fields used to be.

She flipped through the channels, landing on her go-to. Reruns of *Poirot*. She couldn't help think that her grandmother might have loved watching them with her, if she'd ever sat still enough to watch. On the other hand, the idea of an abundance of murders in small villages would have been too far-fetched.

Although she had been with Dominic for five years, she had never introduced him to her grandmother. Initially, Dominic had been inquisitive, asking when he could meet her and asking Tamsyn what she was like. She had lied and told him that she was very frail, ill of health and too fragile to receive visitors. His curiosity had waned after two years. She despised lying, but there was not a chance in hell Sylvia would ever have entertained meeting a boyfriend.

The fact was, Sylvia knew nothing about him, nor would she care to know. The topic of men had never been a subject that was discussed in Rosemount, nor had a man ever stepped over the threshold. When Tamsyn asked why, her grandmother simply replied that men were good for absolutely nothing other than providing the seed to make babies.

All Dominic knew was that Sylvia lived in a small village

somewhere in rural Shropshire. When he asked what she did, Tamsyn thought about it for a while. Sylvia was an avid gardener, collecting the produce she grew and storing it in Rosemount's impressive pantry. She remembered that the medicine Sylvia produced was so popular in Much Wenlock that people paid her for it, so she'd told him that her grandmother brewed holistic remedies. And at the mere mention of 'holistic', his desire to meet Sylvia completely died away. Eventually, the questions ceased, and if anything he seemed relieved that he would not have to make the effort to impress.

It suited them both that they did not have to alternate Christmases as their friends had to, and Tamsyn was certain Dominic wouldn't have approved of the way she and Sylvia celebrated it. She had learned quickly when she went to university that others thought she was odd for referring to Christmas as Winter Solstice, and they certainly did not practise the same traditions that were customary in Much Wenlock. When she had asked her grandmother why other people did not build a yule altar, make wassail or spend the night by candlelight, Sylvia's eyes filled with sadness and she seemed to think carefully about what to say. *Much Wenlock is different*, she had said at last. *We remember the old ways. Outsiders will never understand you like we do.*

Now, it was incredibly painful for Tamsyn to see her grandmother's belongings lying exactly where she had left them. All those years of living alone while Tamsyn had been in London, rarely calling or coming home to visit. Too busy living her life in the smoke bubble, worrying about her job title and being able to afford a better flat in a better area. It had been an illuminating experience, to say the least, leaving her old life behind. Once she had left London and no longer had access to reliable internet, in the eyes of her friends and colleagues she might as well have been dead.

Her first weeks back hit her like a hangover. She had felt dazed and confused. A migraine held her in its vice-like grip as vague memories of living here as a child crowded in on her, vying to intrude into her mind all at once. She lay in bed, curtains drawn, as she tried to stave off the persistent headaches. She stared at the peeling wallpaper of her youth, its cream-coloured background adorned with pastel pink and blue butterflies, the pattern interlaced with bees and delicate flowers. Sometimes, if she stared long enough, the bees and butterflies would flutter their wings, or the flowers would sway in the breeze.

At night, the walls seemed to whisper as they released the heat of the day. At first, she had simply lain there, terrified. The next night, she invited Winnie to sleep at her feet, and as she heard the faint voices, she peered down at the little lump sleeping soundly at her feet, her ears twitching.

Her dreams were fragmented. A blonde-haired girl running down the hallway. A disinterested teenager with light brown hair sitting at the dining table, while Sylvia made her recite the tinctures required for gallstones and tinnitus. One morning, as light poured through the thin bedroom curtains, Tamsyn rolled over, squinting through her pounding head and bleary eyes, to look at her phone. The brusque text from Dominic read *Where's my microwave?*

She tried hard to remember what had happened after the cracking and shattering of glass. She looked down at her forearms; the faint bruises where his fingers had been were still visible. She took her time to reply. The initial anger that arose within her needed a few hours to subside, but she also wanted desperately to remember.

The next morning, she'd replied in the most matter-of-fact tone she could manage.

Sorry, just saw your message. Re the microwave, we bought the toaster and microwave together. I left you with the toaster, and as my gran doesn't have a microwave, I thought I would take it. Hope that's okay with you.

Thankfully, she had bought the television herself, so he couldn't lay claim to that.

He texted back after work that night. She thought the mention of her grandmother might have reminded him that she was grieving, and that maybe he might back off for a little while. But no. A text arrived in his lunch break.

You took the extension cable. That's my extension cable. You owe me eight quid.

Tamsyn stared at the message before flinging her phone across the room. She understood that he was hurting and felt bitterly rejected, but the person who had raised her was gone, something that clearly didn't register on the scale of *How dare you leave me and take my extension cable?*

The angry texts and calls from Dominic had subsided after a few months. Once she had stopped replying, he had changed tack to pleading. He left countless voicemails.

'I thought you said you'd be coming back to London at the end of summer?' And another: 'Sarah told me you've handed in your notice. I just want to know that you're okay. Please call me.' And her favourite: 'Everyone is worried for you, Tam. We think you may be depressed and need to talk to someone.'

The truth of it was, maybe she *was* depressed. She certainly lacked any and all motivation.

Finally, after a month of doing nothing, she began forcing herself out of bed, gingerly brushing her teeth, getting herself into clothes. Slowly, she began tentatively exploring the cottage.

She ran her fingers over the dust on the sideboard, stopping in momentary surprise when she felt a spark of energy interlaced in its knots and grooves. Perhaps it was static, she told herself. But in that brief moment, it felt like much more than that. A longing, a deep nostalgia, burst through the shell of the seed lodged in her stomach. As she walked through the cottage, she thought she heard faint murmurings in the walls, directions to the chores that needed to be completed in order for the kitchen to run as it should. She found herself pulled towards the pantry, where the dried roots and herbs lay in bottles covered in tiny flecks of dust, undisturbed since Sylvia's gnarled fingers had touched them last. In the kitchen, Tamsyn carefully examined the jars of herbs, roots and leaves gathered from the garden. Many had already dried out beyond use, while others had succumbed to mould without her grandmother there to use them.

When she had first arrived at the cottage, everything was exactly as Sylvia had left it the day she died. A pot-bellied teacup, with its gold rim and pink and blue lacework pattern, was sat on the kitchen table, the blue and white forget-me-not teapot still stationed beside it. For weeks she had walked past them, averting her eyes. There was a comfort, while they sat there, as if her grandmother had just nipped out and would be back at any moment. The loose tea leaves, once sodden, were now a dried clump in the strainer.

She found various notes scrawled on pieces of paper and stuffed into drawers. A diary of appointments. She took it out and gently opened the cover. When she saw her grandmother's elegant, looping handwriting, the darkest pit of despair opened deep inside her. She felt herself teetering on the edge, willing herself to look down into the black hole, but the enormity of it threatened to tear her apart and she withdrew. She shut the diary carefully, placing it back into the writing desk.

After a few weeks, the comfort of seeing Sylvia's things where she had left them began to fade. Tamsyn knew that the slippers in front of the armchair, the cup and teapot and the coat hanging beside the door needed to be moved before someone dropped by unexpectedly and informed everyone in the village that Tamsyn had assimilated Miss Havisham.

She delicately touched the edge of her grandmother's teacup. An imperceptible electric buzz dispersed through her body. She tried touching it again, this time holding the handle gingerly between her fingers. She ran her finger around the rim, but could no longer feel anything. With great effort, she carefully washed it in the sink, putting it away on the dresser where Sylvia always kept it. The migraine that had been growing inside the base of her skull began to work its way to her temples. She trudged back up the stairs, the echoes of the house fighting the hardened synapses in her brain. Voices, which in the early days of her arrival had whispered softly, now sounded like angry admonishments as she drew the curtains in her bedroom against the early autumn sun. She crawled back into bed, the dark hopelessness clawing at her to give it attention.

Maybe I am going mad, she told herself before falling asleep.

3
A COUNCIL OF CROWS

Crowding into the wood-panelled room of Shrewsbury's Old Library, the members of the Grove of Druids and Shropshire Covens began to assemble for their monthly coalition council meeting. The attendees begrudgingly accepted the dilapidated yet cosy room, primarily because the more spacious room with its fancy projector screen was booked by the 'new mums reading group', but also because most of them didn't like to draw too much attention to themselves. If any civilians asked—meaning people without magic—their chairwoman, Celia Mosely, would tell them they were a bridge club. She did not like to be caught off guard, so in the event that a library employee should pop their head around the door, she always carried around several packs of playing cards in her large handbag, just in case.

Celia whipped off her soaking polka-dot rain mac and placed it onto the back of a chair. Roy, her rather loveable but completely useless assistant, traipsed in after her.

'You all right, Roy? How's Gladys feeling?' Celia always asked about Roy's wife, although she knew the answer would always be the same.

He shook his head slowly, looking at her with his sad, hooded eyes.

'Not stepped a foot out of bed.' He continued shaking his head this way and that like a toy bulldog on a dashboard. Celia had never even seen, yet alone met Roy's wife, Gladys. She had suffered from health issues for as long as Celia could remember. Celia had once called round to offer them a lasagne to help Roy out while he cared for her. As he stood at the door, Gladys had screamed down at him from upstairs to enquire who was at the door, and to inform him that the hot water bottle on her feet had gone cold.

'Oh, I'm sorry. Has Dr Palgrave been?'

'Yep, yep. Still no answers,' he said, folding his coat neatly on the back of his chair.

'It's just terrible. I am sorry, Roy. Speaking of terrible, getting this room booked was a total nightmare, again! Those women in the big room are a group of eight. Eight! We are thirteen. Okay, we don't always get thirteen in attendance. But that's beside the point. We have been holding this meeting since this place opened, and we can't get a look in!'

Roy nodded and grumbled something inaudible.

As the members shuffled in through the doorway, it struck Celia how impossibly old and frail some of the council members looked. She had appealed several times to encourage more younger members to join. However, when it came to who sat on the board, the rules stipulated that the group could not exceed thirteen. She had a grim thought; she would be staring at the same twelve faces until they died off, decided to step down (which, as yet, had never happened), or were voted out. She could be stuck for another twenty years with these grave dodgers.

Two of the younger members, Dr Anita Palgrave and Leila Ahmadi, came in last. They huddled together, both dressed head to toe in black and scowling, as usual. The two women had made an unfortunate reputation for themselves as the biggest gossips and misinformation spreaders in Much Wenlock. Little did they know that everyone referred to them as the vampire bats.

The smell of herbal sweets, rain on wool, floral soap and mothballs pervaded the room as they all settled into their usual places around the table.

Gavin Hardcastle, former chairman and the constant thorn in Celia's backside, always made sure he arrived last, so as to make an entrance. She was sure he waited around the corner until he saw that they were all in the room. Like clock-work, he stood in the doorway now, trying to make his portly figure as imposing as possible. Peeling off his soaked flat cap from his shining head, he flipped it onto the hat stand and took his seat at the opposite end of the long table.

'Nasty weather, this. Haven't seen rain like it since that storm in eighty-seven!' Gavin bellowed.

Roy slowly and clumsily handed out the agenda and the minutes from their last meeting.

'Let's get on with it, shall we? I have a phone call at eight that I don't want to miss,' said Gavin.

Celia ignored him as she waited for Roy to sit back down. 'I have apologies from Gwen, Peter, Joan and Bridie,' she began primly. She waited a moment, then tapped Roy's notepad with her pen to indicate that he should note down the absentees.

'First on the agenda,' said Roy in a thick Black Country accent, 'the young Wiccans at Shrewsburys Girls' School would like funding for their theatre production.'

'How much are they asking for?' said Gavin.

'Err.' He squinted at his pad. 'Five hundred pounds,' replied Roy.

'Excellent.' Celia nodded in approval.

There was murmuring, while a few members looked back and forth across the table.

'As the treasurer, I'm sorry but I feel I should say something. How on earth could a school, a private one at that, justify five hundred pounds? For a play? If you ask me, we should let their rich parents foot the bill. This council is not a charity.' Gavin's tone was even, but dripping with condescension.

'As you are aware, Gavin, the school has yet again been hit with flooding this year. A great deal has been spent already on repairing the damage. Sets, props and costumes are extremely expensive,' Celia said as patiently as she could manage. 'I doubt five hundred pounds will cover even a quarter of what they need. Plus, it's going to be big this year. It's in the pavilion, for everyone in the town. We have allocated money for theatre and the arts,' she reminded him as politely as she could. Celia could not bring herself to look at Gavin; it was more of an appeal to the others, none of whom would give you the shirt from their back, even if they were wearing three.

'Like I said, I think their parents should pay.' Gavin crossed his arms and looked around the room for back-up, while the members shifted uncomfortably in their seats.

'Did your mother pay for your school plays, Gavin? When you were at the grammar school?' Celia said sweetly. He liked to pretend he was like the others, and Celia's favourite pastime was to remind them that he wasn't. She sighed. 'What about two-fifty, then, as a show of goodwill? They are putting on a production of *Doctor Faustus*, after all. I do love that play,' Celia said in as soothing a tone as she could manage.

Gavin's puce complexion deepened.

'I will have to go over the accounts. Find it from somewhere. I take it we will at least get a special mention in the programme?'

'Oh, for two hundred and fifty pounds they'll roll the red carpet out for us, I'm sure,' Celia replied.

Anita Palgrave raised her hand.

As an ex-headmistress, one of the things Celia had implemented was the raising of hands when a member wished to speak. This had infuriated them, but it was essential to stop them talking over one another and to keep the meeting on track.

'Yes, Dr Palgrave?' Celia asked.

'What about what happened to Peter Bradshaw's sheep? I don't see it on the agenda,' Anita said. Several members nodded enthusiastically. Here was the real flesh they wanted to rip into.

'Unfortunately, Farmer Bradshaw could not be here today to give us an update. As I said in last week's email, he and I are working directly with the West Mercia Police in order to catch the culprit. Currently, there are no leads. However, he will be in attendance next session, and I'm sure we can discuss more then.'

'This is a matter that we should all be working to get to the bottom of,' Gavin barked, leaning forwards and addressing the attendees directly. 'We have the means between the thirteen of us to get to catch the depraved little wretch that killed his sheep!'

'Please, would you raise your hand if you wish to say something, Mr Hardcastle?' Celia said. 'We all know what happens when members of this council decide to take matters into their own hands. Mistakes are made. People get hurt. Sometimes innocent people.' She stared at him coldly.

'I have it on good authority that one of the suspects is Tamsyn Pride,' interjected Anita. 'Can you confirm if this is true?'

Heightened whispering ensued. Gavin interlaced his fingers and sat back in his chair; Celia could see he was doing his best not to smirk. He was watching them whisper, revelling in the expressions on their faces. It was tiresome how much he openly detested the Prides.

'Please, please. It is not a time for speculation. There are a few suspects at this time,' said Celia, sighing inwardly. This was what they had come for, and Gavin had definitely served it up to them on a decorative plate, with a complimentary biscotti for good measure.

'So, Tamsyn Pride *is* a suspect then?' asked Leila Ahmadi. 'You don't deny it?'

'I am not obliged to discuss who is and who is not a

suspect in an ongoing case. Some of you might also be suspects. We do not want to jump to any conclusions,' Celia replied, picking up the minutes and tapping them on the table nervously. 'Everyone here has an explanation for their whereabouts that evening. Most of us were at the Horn Dance. And those who weren't have verifiable alibis.'

'I find it very funny that not a few months after she arrives back in Much Wenlock, odd things start happening again,' said Leila. The others nodded in agreement.

'The last time I checked, maimed sheep was not the issue,' replied Celia curtly.

'Who knows what perverse magic these youngsters are into these days?' Daisy Cartwright's high, shaking voice cut through the rising din.

Celia pulled a gavel from her huge bag and banged it three times on the table.

'Enough! In case some of you have forgotten, Tamsyn underwent the Binding Spell. She has no memory of magic, so how and why on earth would she carve ancient runes into animals? As far as she knows, this is some weird little village that dabbles in a little Pagan worship. There is no reason to suggest she had anything to do with it—'

'Bit funny that nothing happens around here until she's back though, isn't it?' said Leila.

'I ask that all malicious gossip and tittle tattle be kept to a minimum.' Celia's face grew hot as she saw Gavin's supercilious expression from the corner of her eye.

'You can't deny, Celia, that we have yet to see the effect of the Binding Spell when a subject returns to the village,' he said smoothly. 'How do we know that her being here for a longer period of time isn't reigniting those memories? So far, everyone who has undergone the Binding has returned home to their family for only a few weeks at a time. It has been months now. Perhaps the spell is wearing off? I'm just playing devil's advocate here, of course. Even if she still has no memory of magic, what happens if she sees something magical occur? The longer she stays here, the more likely it is she will start to notice things.' Gavin's brow was furrowed with concern.

Celia didn't know what to say as they all sat and stared at her. Finally, gathering her wits, she said, 'I have it on good authority that Tamsyn Pride means only to stay until the sale of Rosemount goes through. She will be gone soon enough. Now, let's stop with the speculation and move on, shall we?'

4
THE POISON GARDEN

After months of languishing inside the house, Tamsyn found that spring and summer had passed with a monotony and drudgery that only made her lethargy stronger. She had not realised that Samhain had come to Much Wenlock until she left the cottage to collect groceries and noticed the windows in the high street were decorated with squashes, gourds and pumpkins.

Walking through the village, she was greeted by people who knew her well. Some she had not seen since she had lived here before she left for university. An elderly man, whom she half-recognised from the social gatherings her grandmother would drag her to, greeted her with such warmth she was too embarrassed to ask his name. He invited her to his daughter's home for dinner so that she could honour the memory of her grandmother on Samhain with some familiar faces. Tamsyn thanked him for his kindness but said she had friends coming over.

He nodded, his eyes darting down to her bag of groceries, holding just enough for one.

'Ah. *Hel bwyd cennad y meirw.*' He pointed to the bag, smiling, and gave her a little wave as he hobbled away.

Tamsyn looked down at her bag. Although she didn't speak Welsh, she understood exactly what the old man had said. She had collected food for the messenger of the dead. She had nutmeg, cinnamon, saffron and a bag of currants. Absentmindedly, she must have been picking the extra ingredients she needed for soul cakes from the shelves. She flushed with embarrassment, feeling a little silly, but she missed the odd little rituals her grandmother would perform.

Walking home between the ash trees that lined Rosemount's long driveway, Tamsyn noticed a white car through the trees ahead. Feeling her pulse quicken, she hastened towards the house. As she neared, she saw a police officer sitting in the driver's seat, unaware of her presence. Looking down at his phone, he laughed as he chewed on a sandwich, still half-wrapped in cling film. She stood there, feeling nervous. After a few moments of waiting for him to notice her, Tamsyn knocked gently on the window and waved, hoping not to startle him.

Rummaging to cover the sandwich, the officer stepped out of the car.

'Good afternoon. Are you Tamsyn Pride?' His voice was soft, a warm mixture between a faintly Welsh and West Country accent, with a hint of West Midlands.

'Yes, that's me,' said Tamsyn. Her mind raced; she heard the shattering of glass, saw her bloodied hand. Had Dominic called the police?

'I'm PC Thompson from West Mercia Police. I was wondering if I could ask a few questions?' Tamsyn's insides fizzed. Sylvia would not want a man stepping foot inside Rosemount.

'Yes, of course. Please come in.' Tamsyn went to walk towards the front steps. 'Although… I've been cleaning the house, but it's still a real mess. Would you mind if we sat on the veranda? It's probably warmer out here than it is in there.' Tamsyn hoped she sounded breezy; inside, her mind was racing.

'Not a problem,' he replied, following closely behind her. 'Didn't carve any pumpkins this year?' he said, looking around the porch.

'Not this year, no. I forgot all about Halloween, to be honest.'

'Ah, I've carved two. I love this time of year. It's the best time, in my humble opinion.'

They took their seats on the faded and crumbling wooden chairs. Tamsyn could see Sylvia sitting here on a summer's day, pen in mouth as she did a crossword.

'Could you tell me your whereabouts on the evening of the twelfth of September?'

Tamsyn frowned, fighting through the rolling fog in her brain. 'Twelfth of September. Wasn't that the night of the Horn Dance?' she asked.

'Yes, that's the one. Were you there?'

'No. It's not my sort of thing. I was here, watching TV. I don't really do much else.'

'I see,' he said, pulling out a slim notepad from his top pocket and jotting something down. 'I know what you mean, about the Horn Dance. Bit weird, if you ask me.' PC Thompson paused, quickly looking in through the window of the cottage. Tamsyn's heart skipped a beat.

'Can you talk me through what you do remember doing that night? Did you see or speak to anyone? Do you recall what you watched on TV?'

'I can't remember exactly. But I probably would have made microwavable macaroni cheese and watched reruns of *Poirot* with my cat. Oh—actually, yes, I did speak to someone. I spoke to my friend Sarah on the phone.'

'And what time was that?'

'Around eight-thirty. We spoke for an hour or so.'

'Could you provide me with a number for Sarah?' he said, jotting the details down.

'Sure. Here.' Tamsyn held out the number on her phone. 'Can I ask what this is about?'

'Ah, you know Much Wenlock. Every now and then people get silly ideas in their heads. Farmer Bradshaw, just over the field here—some nutter carved his sheep up. Left 'em for dead.' He pointed his pen towards the back garden of the cottage. 'You didn't happen to see or hear anything untoward that evenin'?'

'Oh my God. No, I'm afraid I didn't. That's absolutely awful. Carved them up? Why on earth would someone do that?' she asked, horrified.

'Gawd knows. There are some real weirdos round here. Farmer says the ewes must have been drugged. The carvings alone shouldn't have killed 'em, but—' He stopped, realising too late that he had divulged too much. 'Anyway, I'm doing the rounds. Got loads of people to see. Thanks for your time.

Please contact me if you remember anything.' He handed Tamsyn his card.

'Yes. I will. Thank you.'

As the evening drew near, Tamsyn thought that she should at least make an effort to mark the eve of Samhain. She lit candles around the house and replenished the dried flowers in the bud vases next to the pictures of her grandmother. Setting two places at the table, she placed a serving of chicken, mushroom and leek pie, with colcannon and gravy, at Sylvia's seat.

Throwing three soul cakes into the fire, she batted away thoughts of what her grandmother would say about making chicken pie for Samhain. What had the officer meant about the Horn Dance being weird? That people got 'funny ideas into their heads'?

She assumed that anyone who lived here would be used to the Pagan celebrations. Shrugging away the thought, she placed a mug of wassail on Sylvia's coaster. The steam from the mulled cider punch curled in the air, lingering. It invited a memory that batted beneath the surface of Tamsyn's mind, fighting to break through. The steam, and the memory, floated away uselessly. This would be the first mug, Tamsyn reflected, that was destined to sit. Growing cold, without Sylvia there to drink it. She thought of all the Samhain dinners her grandmother had prepared and eaten, sitting here alone in candlelight, while Tamsyn staggered around bars in London dressed as a cat, vampire or SpongeBob.

As she retrieved her plate from the kitchen worktop, she

heard a commotion outside. The steel lid of the bin crashed onto the paving stones beside the house. Peering through the diamond-shaped pane, she saw an orange flash, blurred by the dirt-stained window. It zipped across the garden, and then a bushy tail tipped with white disappeared through the hedge, most likely in hot pursuit of the rabbits that burrowed throughout Rosemount's lawns.

As she opened up the French doors to the back of the house, a gust of wind blasted her in the face, whipping through the yews and the gnarled fruit trees. She stepped down onto the wild grass; the garden was completely over-grown. Apples and plums mouldered where they fell, a reminder of how long she had sat festering inside the house. She shook her head when she thought of all the preserves she had let go to waste. No one made blackberry jam on toast like Sylvia had, with hand-churned butter on homemade seeded bread.

A wave of sickening guilt washed over her. Guilt—and anger. Maybe things would have been different if her grand-mother had been... just a bit nicer. Maybe she would be more willing to look after Rosemount if Sylvia had shown just an ounce of love and warmth for her. She chided herself immediately, forbidding herself to entertain the futility of blaming someone else for the fact that she had been too depressed to get out of bed and batch-cook preserves for the winter ahead. Especially when said person was six feet under. Besides, this was only ever meant to be temporary. Eventually, she would sell up, move to somewhere like Norway, Canada or Reykjavik, and work for herself. She half-laughed at the thought. She would never have enough money to live in places like that.

Tamsyn neared the west wall of the garden. In the golden light of autumn, the last blooms of honeysuckle ambled over the crumbling brickwork. She plucked one, inhaling the last of its orange-yellow heads. It made her dizzy with its thick, sweet scent. Hearing a familiar trickling sound, she looked up again. Amidst the dried stems of spent alliums, delphiniums and anemones stood a moss-covered statue of a woman. The sun was setting on her face. Her arms stretched up to the sky, cupping a bowl from which spring water cascaded down her arms and torso, leaving brown stains where it trailed over her face and breasts. It spilled onto her bare feet before disappearing into the earth.

Tamsyn's head began to throb as her mind filled with an unwelcome vision of a little girl, crouching in the dirt next to Sylvia's familiar, broad back.

'Is it true about the water, Grandma?' she asked, looking up at the older woman and shielding her eyes against the sun, a small trowel in her hand while she helped to weed.

'Is what true?' replied Sylvia, vigorously digging at the hardened earth.

'That the water from our statue comes from the Frog Well. I read it in *A History of Rosemount*. It said that the water from our fountain flows from a nearby village. That Satan and his imps live in the well, and that they take the form of frogs. It said the largest frog is Satan himself, who hides at the bottom of the spring. Is that true, Grandma?'

Sylvia laughed. 'No. I don't think Satan would bother hiding himself away as a frog. But the legend helped to keep people away from the spring. It flows from the Devil's Causeway, by Acton Burnell. The water has healing properties. It heals, and it nourishes this land. That's why your great-great-great-grandmother, Prudence Pride, chose this land to build our home. If the normal folk got wind of what the water can do, they would get scared. They're suspicious of everything. You wouldn't want them blocking it up, or wasting it. Or, God forbid, selling it for profit.'

The images in her mind juddered, like an old video cassette that had been damaged by too many dirty fingerprints. Tamsyn stood staring at where the two figures had crouched, now a barren patch of earth. What had they been planting that day? Her grandmother had spoken of 'normal folk', and she had nodded in complete understanding. She massaged her temples, trying to iron out the ache that had descended once more. This was not the first time she had had one of these visions; she had begun to wonder whether they were even real, whether she could trust her own sanity.

She wished she had asked her grandmother so much more. How would she find out all the things she'd always thought she had infinite time to ask about? All the small things, all the important things that she was too embarrassed or too scared to ask, like *What really happened to my mother? Tell me more about Prudence Pride and my ancestors. Do you really believe the water has healing properties, or are these just tales you tell a little girl?*

Tamsyn walked on through the sprawling garden. The sloe berries on the blackthorn trees were almost ready to pick. To her relief she saw there were still damsons and blackberries that could be salvaged. Just like Sylvia, she had an aversion to waste. The grass between the ancient yews lay fettered with huge spiked weeds, whose roots would by now have grown so deep they would have truly taken hold. Every plant, fruit and vegetable at Rosemount grew at an exponential rate. Her grandmother would spend all day tending to the garden, and still she could not tame its wild growth. Vegetables swelled to monstrous sizes if left unpicked, their bloated skins bursting in the summer sun, before being usurped by the next in line.

As she approached the east wall of the garden, the density of weeds grew. Tamsyn's heart sank. The jewel of Rosemount, the Poison Garden, had succumbed to shoulder-high nettles. She let out a cry of frustration as she paced up and down the gravel path next to the beds, her eyes searching for anything that might be saved.

'Enough is enough,' she said aloud, scolding herself. 'Quit moping.' That was something Sylvia always said to her. Making her way inside, she threw on her jeans and waxed jacket, and went to find her grandmother's gardening gloves under the sink.

Outside, resting against the east wall, was a shovel. Grabbing it, she headed back to the garden and attacked the weeds and overgrown brambles with a voracious anger, mercilessly digging out their roots until her back and legs grew hot with fatigue. As she grabbed handfuls of vegetation, some of the spikes pierced through her gloves and stabbed into her hands. Undeterred, she hacked at their roots feverishly.

On and on Tamsyn worked, not noticing that the sun had set until she was forced to find a torch in the shed. Returning to the garden, she shone the light around and was pleased to discover that she had made a large enough clearing.

Bending closer and illuminating the leaves with torchlight, she could identify the plants stubbornly surviving in the midst of the gargantuan invaders. She recognised some of them: Brugmansia, *Strychnos nux vomica*, belladonna, laburnum, *Ricinus communis*, oleander and, near the back of the bed, the hemlock, still managing to grow triumphantly to dizzying heights.

Tamsyn breathed hard, realising how foolish she had been to go into the patch without wearing more protection.

'Enough,' she said out loud. Breathless and perspiring, she wiped the sweat from her brow with her sleeve. Making her way back through the carnage she had created, she made sure to steer clear of the leaves strewn on the path behind her. She looked back, eyeing her work and scanning the beds once more. To the far right, she spotted the long-speared seed heads of monkshood. In the light of the torch, something glinted among the dried brown leaves at the base of the deadly plant. Stamping her way carefully over to it, she used the shovel to make a clearing around it. The memory of the name swam inside her mind: *Aconitum Napellus*, also known as Devil's Helmet, monkshood, and wolfsbane.

She shone the torch directly at the thing: it was silver coloured, glinting dully in the light. Using the tip of the spade, she gingerly dragged it through the soil towards her. It was a pale silver locket, smeared with dirt. Tamsyn's eyes widened, not quite comprehending how or why her grandmother's necklace could possibly be at the roots of one the most dangerous plants in the garden. Seeing something else glinting, she cleared away more decaying debris and found Sylvia's old kitchen scissors, enshrouded by long weeds.

Stooping to retrieve the locket, she ripped off her gloves and began to wipe away the dirt with her fingers. She used her nail to open it. On the inside left, the beaming smile of Tamsyn at around six years old. On the right, a sepia-toned image of her mother as a teenager, with her dark, shoulder-length hair and her full lips pursed in a half-smile.

Tamsyn felt panic rise at the absurdity of the locket being in this place. She tried in vain to imagine how the necklace could have come to be there: Sylvia had never taken the locket off. Tamsyn had had no idea that it contained a picture of her and her mother; it was always just something that Sylvia wore, and Tamsyn had never dared ask her what was inside. As a teenager, Tamsyn had wondered whether it contained the picture of a man, maybe her own unknown grandfather. Perhaps Sylvia had been jilted at the altar, she'd thought, and that's why she'd always had such an aversion to men. She never dreamt it would be a picture of her own mother, Annalise Pride. Her grandmother had always made clear to Tamsyn, and to anyone who asked, that she saw her daughter as nothing but an ill omen. To keep a photo of Annalise in her locket would mean acknowledging her existence.

Tamsyn looked back at the scissors; how odd that they had been discarded on the ground like that. Tamsyn's head was still groggy, but she knew one thing. Hell could freeze over, and Sylvia would still be setting everything back in its place at the end of the day. The scissors in the drawer, the tools back on their designated nails, all arranged meticulously on the shed wall.

She had been so wrapped up in her grief, she realised,

that she had not opened her eyes to observe how Rosemount had truly looked on the day she arrived.

How many teacups had been on the table? Only one. Definitely only one. Her mind's eye searched the house. Slippers, coat, teacup, notes, diary. Teapot. The heaped leaves in the strainer. By her judgement, Tamsyn could tell her grandmother had used five teaspoons of loose leaves. She always used two scoops of her own tea leaves per person, and one for the pot. Someone had been with her. In the dresser, there were three teacups with the blue forget-me-nots. Where was the fourth? Had she seen it since she had been back? No, it definitely wasn't in the cupboard any longer.

Had Sylvia—or someone else—put the locket here? Tamsyn's head swam as she snatched up the scissors, pocketed the locket, and ran back towards the glowing lights of Rosemount.

5
IN WITH THE OLD

It surprised Celia to see that several members of the council were already in their seats. She was always the first one in, arranging the tables and chairs the way they liked them. She hurried over to the head of the table. Putting her bag down, she rummaged around for the minutes folder, unable to find her pen in the folds of the fabric.

'Sorry. Am I late?' she asked with a little irritation. Celia was not comfortable with change.

'No. We were told we should get here early this week.' Daisy Cartwright didn't look up from her knitting. The bright pink hat bobbed up and down on the needles, in preparation for the arrival of Daisy's eleventh grandchild.

'Oh, yes? Who told you that? I wasn't informed.'

More council members began to file in. Celia handed out the minutes, noticing as she did so that the other members were doing everything they could not to meet her eye.

'Gosh. It's very sombre in here today,' she said gamely,

trying her best to lighten the mood. 'And Gavin hasn't even arrived yet!' she joked.

Roy shuffled through the door, looking drawn out and exhausted as usual. Gavin followed shortly after, his chest and chin puffed out, doing his best to suppress a grin. Celia waited for them to be seated.

'Okay, I think that's everyone,' Celia said briskly. 'I haven't had any apologies come through yet, but let's begin. First on the agenda: next year's flowers for the Ostara Festival. Joan, how are you getting on with sourcing the bulbs?'

She turned to Joan and noticed with alarm that she looked distressed; tears glistened in the corners of her eyes.

'Ye—s,' Joan replied. 'Bulbs are all in hand. They'll be ready to go to ground in three weeks or so.' Her bird-like voice quivered, but then, it always did sound like it was about to crack.

'Fantastic,' said Celia, ignoring the growing feeling of unease. 'We always look forward to your excellent tulips. Next…' Celia looked over her half-moon glasses as Peter Bradshaw raised his hand. 'Yes, Mr Bradshaw?'

'Well, there's nothing on here about my sheep,' said Bradshaw.

'I know as much as you, Peter. As PC Thompson informed us, they have no fresh leads. As soon as they do, I can assure you that you will be the first to know about it.' Celia smiled at him.

'But shouldn't we be discussing it?' He poked the paper with a calloused finger.

'There is nothing new to discuss, Peter. I'm sorry, but we

can't keep raking over the same ground.' Celia fought hard to mask the irritation she could feel rising.

'Oh, there's plenty more to discuss!' piped up Dr Palgrave. 'Like the fact that it can't be a coincidence that, as soon as Tamsyn Pride returned to Much Wenlock, the poor things were carved up like mutton on a deli counter.'

Ah. There it was. Several members of the committee nodded their heads, murmuring in agreement.

Celia's countenance shifted as she bristled at the accusation. 'Dr Palgrave, I truly thought we had got past this nonsense. The incident with the sheep happened a few months after Miss Pride arrived in Much Wenlock. Accusing outsiders and even other witches is a thing of the past. We don't do that to each other any more, and I will not tolerate it in this chamber. My duty here was to put an end to the continuation of the persecution of witches, let alone by other witches! I'm sure none of you wish to see us return to where we were thirty years ago? We are no longer living in the sixteenth century, but the way we vilify people in this community, you would never know it!' She looked at each of them in turn as they stared back angrily.

There was a long silence as Roy slowly jotted down the minutes. When he had finished, Gavin stood to address the council.

'If you are referring to my tenure as chairman, Celia, I'd like the minutes to show that I only upheld what was common practice at the time. I had to make very difficult decisions to protect our community from deviant witches and druids. I did not take the matter of memory erasure or excommunication lightly. Under my tutelage, such measures were carried out only in extreme circumstances. I had the full support of the archbishop, and each case was personally signed off by the head of our church.' Gavin looked at the others for approval.

Roy bought the agenda up to his face. 'The second item—'

'If you don't mind, Roy,' Gavin interrupted, still standing, 'we have something we'd like to raise.' He swept his hand to indicate the rest of the room.

'Can it not wait until any other business, Gavin?' Celia said irritably.

'I'm afraid it can't. It pains me to say this, Celia—'

'Then don't say it.' She smiled in faux politeness.

'The council has asked me to represent them in this matter. We have come to the very unpleasant decision to hold a vote of no confidence in the current chairwoman.' He straightened his back, doing his best not to look too pleased with himself.

Celia stared for a moment. 'Did they ask you, Gavin? Or did you take it upon yourself to turn them against me as soon as my back was turned?' Her eyes glistened as she tried her best to stay composed.

'It's nothing personal, you understand,' Gavin said in his most reassuring voice. 'There is a feeling that there's not enough being done about the issues that really matter. Too much poncing about with the flower show—no offence Joan—or the Shrewsbury Arts Trail, and not enough tackling the crimes that are being committed within our community.'

Celia looked around the room, wide-eyed. 'One crime. It

was *one crime*. And you all feel this way?' she asked. The others looked down at their hands.

'I lost twenty ewes this summer. We still haven't found out who did it,' Peter Bradshaw piped up.

'Exactly, Pete. It's not even on the minutes, Celia,' said Gavin.

'There's nothing to report!' Celia banged her fist on the table. 'The police have no leads. As soon as I hear something, you'll all bloody know about it!'

'Please, Celia, do try to calm down,' Gavin said smoothly; he was visibly pleased. 'I don't think there's anything to be gained by these little outbursts.'

'Don't take it personally, Celia dear,' said Daisy. 'We're all very ruffled by all this... change. We don't like the threat of Tamsyn Pride being here, and the dead sheep. What if...' Daisy trailed off before dropping her voice to a whisper. 'What if... the others return?'

Frantic whispering ensued within the committee.

Gavin seized his moment. 'We need someone who will take definitive action. Someone who will keep our community safe. I'm sure you understand? We are very vulnerable.'

'*Vulnerable?* Don't make me laugh!' Celia said bitterly.

'I say we move to vote,' commanded Gavin. 'All those in favour of Celia stepping down from position as chairwoman, raise your hands.' He immediately stuck his hand into the air.

There was silence as, one by one, five more members of the council raised their hands.

Celia stared at Gavin, unabated fury rising as heat at the back of her neck.

'That's six. You know you need at least seven of the thirteen,' she said through gritted teeth.

There was a commotion outside the door and suddenly it swung open with a sound of metal scraping along the old oak doorframe.

A hunched figure in a wheelchair was manoeuvred through, a spattered rain bonnet covering their face. Colin, the owner of The Snooty Fox, breathless and drenched, pushed the chair from behind.

'Bridie!' Gavin said nervously. 'I wasn't sure if you were coming.'

Celia breathed a sigh of relief.

'You didn't wait for me, I take it?' Bridie cried, raising her bonnet and looking at the members' sombre faces. 'Well, the woman of the hour's here now. What are we talkin' about?'

Colin helped her out of her bonnet and wheeled her chair into a vacant space at the table. Despite not being a member, he hung at the back of the room, eager to hear the discussion.

'The council were discussing my resignation, Bridie,' Celia said, then turned to Gavin. 'I'm assuming it's so that you can resume your long-held position as chairman, Mr Hardcastle?'

'The vote must be held democratically, Celia. I am only acting on the interests of the chamber and the dissatisfaction that has been expressed to me by several council members,' Gavin replied. 'Your vote would push us over halfway to seven votes, Bridie.'

'Hang on a minute! This is malpractice! All thirteen members must be present for the vote,' Celia reminded him.

'Actually, they don't. Section 114a states that if members

of the council are incapacitated in any way, then as long as there is a majority in the remaining members, it holds. And, technically speaking, Celia, the chairwoman should not be present in the room when the vote takes place.'

'Ho! You can forget that,' she snapped. 'I want to see who sticks the knife in. Funny how my closest friends on the council are, as you put it, *incapacitated*?' she said, narrowing her eyes at Gavin.

'It wouldn't matter if they were here. I only need seven votes. What do you say, Bridie?' Gavin said, ignoring her. 'Can we count on you to do the right thing?' he asked nervously.

Bridie sat motionless, considering. She was completely unhurried and unphased by a room full of eyes upon her. 'Six of you have voted to remove Celia?' she said at last.

'That's right. Half of the council,' said Gavin.

'Hmm.' Bridie thought for a moment, before shrugging her shoulders. She slowly turned to look at Celia.

'I'm very sorry, Celia,' Bridie said, shaking her head solemnly. 'We need a united council. I go whichever way the wind blows.'

Colin let out a sharp breath from the corner of the room, putting his hand over his mouth in mock surprise. Celia turned white.

'Bridie! You cannot be serious!' she exclaimed in disbelief.

Gavin smiled.

'You got at them, didn't you?' Celia screamed at him. 'Whispering poison into their ears! And *you*, Bridie. Never did like to stick your head above the parapet, even when you're being consumed by rats!' Celia rose to her feet, pointing at Bridie with a shaking hand.

'See that Celia gets safely to her car, would you, Colin?' said Gavin calmly.

Celia's eyes opened wide. 'You snakes! Damn the lot of you to hell! I've given my all to this shitty, small-minded little council!' she raged as Colin strong-armed her to the door. 'Roy, Roy! Do something! Tell the others what's happened!'

The heavy door slammed behind them. The council members sat in silence as Celia's voice faded away down the echoing corridor and out into the car park.

'Now that's out of the way, I would like to put myself forward to return as the chairman of the council. Unless anyone has any objections?' said Gavin.

The council members looked at each other. Bridie answered for them.

'It's not a burden the rest of us would be willing to take on, I'm sure.' The others nodded nervously.

'Excellent!' Gavin replied, as if Bridie had told him he was the only man fit for the job. 'First on the new agenda, I would like to raise the issue of Rosemount. Where are we with the sale of the cottage and the presence of the young Pride girl?' He turned to Bridie.

'Haven't heard anything. Something tells me she might be in touch with me soon. After all, I was her grandmother's best friend,' said Bridie, matter-of-factly.

'Well, can you hurry things along and meet with her? Find out what her plans are and when she is leaving?'

Bridie huffed. She absolutely hated being told what to do.

'What if she doesn't leave? We could all be in terrible danger!' Daisy said to Gavin.

'We won't tolerate *that girl* in the village!' said Leila Ahmadi. 'She is from bad stock. I will never recover from the damage her mother did to my properties. This... Tamsyn, is it? She hasn't been a part of this community for a decade, and the last time she was here, there was that terrible accident with the bus. And God knows what else!'

'Precisely, Leila,' said Gavin. 'When Annalise Pride flooded our town and disappeared, we all suffered. When her daughter started following in her mother's footsteps... doing unnatural things... Well, it was clear what had to be done. The magic used to suppress her memory will begin to fade if she stays longer. She must go, and if she won't... Well, measures will need to be taken.' He looked at Bridie.

'Do you have a pen?' asked Bridie.

'A pen? Whatever for?' he asked irritably.

'My memory isn't what it was. I really need to write this down, and Roy's pen has run out.' She nudged him to stop writing. 'Hasn't it, Roy?'

'N—Yes.'

Gavin took a shiny gold pen out of his top pocket and held it towards her from the other side of the room.

'Could you bring it over, dear?' Bridie said sweetly. 'My legs get a bit stiff with all the sitting.'

Roy looked as bemused as ever. Gavin reluctantly rose from his seat and made his way over to Bridie. He held the pen out again, unwilling to get too near.

'Oh, do come closer, Gavin. I don't bite.' She smiled and

reached for the pen. When she touched it, she felt a connection. Briefly, almost imperceptibly, her eyes widened.

'Thank you, dear,' she said, a little shakily. 'Now, you must do whatever you see fit, Chairman,' she replied.

'Aren't you going to make a note?'

Bridie thrust the pen at Roy. 'You jot it down, Roy. Go on. *The Pride girl must go, or else.*'

Bridie smiled sheepishly at Gavin. She looked at her watch. 'Goodness! Is that the time? I must be getting off. My show starts in half an hour. Lovely to see you all! Come, Colin.' Bridie beckoned for Colin to wheel her out.

Roy quickly slipped Gavin's pen in his top pocket as everyone watched Bridie leave.

6

BRIDIE

'Hello?' After the fourteenth ring, Tamsyn made it to the kitchen phone, breathless.

'Hallo, that you, Tamsyn?' said a crackling voice on the other end of the line. Tamsyn recognised it immediately as Sylvia's best friend, Bridie Dawson.

'Hello, Bridie! How are you?' said Tamsyn warmly.

'Why haven't you been round yet? I've bin waitin'!'

'Oh. I'm sorry… Time just got away from me. When are you free?'

'Today. You can treat me to coffee and cake. Twelve o'clock at The Snooty Fox,' Bridie said. Tamsyn smiled; her grandmother's friend never did like to beat around the bush. There was grumbling and cursing down the line as Bridie dropped something.

'You'll 'ave to pick me up, though. I won't walk to the village. I'll be dead by the end of me street!'

'I'll come and get you, don't worry. Ten to twelve okay?'

More grumbling ensued.

'Ten to twelve. Okay. Okay. All right. Ta-rah. Bye—bye —bye.' There was more muttering and fumbling at the other end of the line as Bridie hung up clumsily.

Tamsyn was relieved she wouldn't have to go to Bridie's house; it had always given her the creeps. She felt guilty for that, but Bridie's house had always smelled of damp, and the biscuits were stale. Besides, it would be nice to go to The Snooty Fox again. It had been Bridie and her grandmother's favourite café to people-watch and collect the latest village gossip.

It would also be a useful venue to ask Bridie some questions about the village and to tell her about finding her grandmother's locket amidst the monkshood...

Tamsyn blinked. She was still sitting at the kitchen table, staring at the back door. She wasn't sure how long she had been there, staring. She focused on the door, remembering her grandmother, the top latch open as she leaned against the countertop.

She saw her there now, with her other hand resting on her sore back, reaching over to the counter to retrieve one of several brown paper bags, each labelled with a name. The contents of these parcels had to be packed and double checked by Tamsyn. She saw her own small hands carefully placing small vials in the bags, the labels scrawled with shakily written instructions. 'Sleeping draught. Add one tsp to warm milk. Never take after 11 p.m.' Other popular concoctions were usually restorative in nature, or basic herbal remedies to ease coughs and colds.

Tamsyn remembered for the first time in years how Sylvia would greet her clients as she opened the top latch. They would chat about their ailments or share little titbits of gossip, like how George and Daisy Cartwright were having another grandchild (when would poor old George realise that none of their children were his?). Everyone who came seemed to like her grandmother, and they certainly respected her. If only they had realised that she didn't really like any of them. The only person who really knew Sylvia was her best friend, Bridie, and the only people they truly liked and trusted were each other. Sylvia and Bridie would talk on the phone for hours, and sometimes Tamsyn couldn't help feeling a little jealous. What she would have given to have a relationship like that with Sylvia.

She walked to the dresser. Taking down a teacup, she tipped it upside down over her cupped hand to catch the locket she had placed inside for safekeeping.

Swinging open the door to the garage, Tamsyn looked unhappily at her pale green Nissan Figaro, which sat forlorn after months of neglect. Squeezing herself between the car and the wall, she pulled the silver handle, just managing to edge sideways into the driver's seat.

'Hey, Fig.' Tamsyn patted the wheel with a conciliatory touch that she hoped told the car *I'm sorry I left you for so long.* Closing her eyes and gritting her teeth, she turned the key in the ignition. To her relief, the engine turned over, and with a little rev on the accelerator it spluttered to life.

She inched the car out of the tight garage, the wing mirrors barely missing the brickwork.

Once Fig had made it out unscathed, Tamsyn unlatched the roof, folding it down into the back of the car. The glove box held a vintage silk Hermès headscarf and a large pair of Chanel sunglasses. They were the only items she owned that had belonged to her mother—those and an assortment of mixed tapes and photographs she didn't quite understand.

Tamsyn reflected upon the day she'd found the scarf, the glasses, the photos and tapes in a dusty shoebox at the back of her wardrobe. Pasted on the box were cut-outs of Prince and Kate Bush, with the words *Property of Annalise Pride* scrawled in biro.

Exhilarated at the discovery of this lost treasure, she'd hurried down to show the box to Sylvia. The box and its contents felt like they belonged to a mythical creature, a hazy figure that she constantly dreamed about. Opening the box excitedly and taking out the items one by one, she had asked Sylvia if she could keep them. Sylvia merely glanced at the box in disgust and said curtly that she could keep them, if owning stolen goods was her thing. But if Tamsyn knew what was good for her, she would burn the box well away from the house, with everything inside.

Tamsyn had nodded, allowing her grandmother to think she would do just that. Instead, she took the box back upstairs and tucked it away at the back of the wardrobe, right where she had found it.

On particularly lonely days, she would dig out the box as soon as she heard the front door slam. Endlessly studying the glossy photographs that had been discarded haphazardly inside, she thought that if she stared at the men and women in the pictures long enough, somehow she could figure out who they were. Or, at the very least, she might commit their faces to memory.

In one of them, her mother, Annalise, lithe, sharp-faced and beautiful, sat on a dark-haired man's lap, her head tipped back mid-laughter. In another, her dark hair blew wildly as she linked arms with a blond man with an athletic frame. They smiled like childhood sweethearts as they stood on a pier, looking out to sea. Of course, if she saw any of the men in these pictures today, they would be unrecognizable. But what if she happened to pass one of them in the street one day? What if they could tell her something, anything, about Annalise?

Tamsyn presumed from the differing handwriting on the cassettes that the mixed tapes had been made for her mother by various admirers. Tamsyn couldn't be sure what was Annalise's taste and what was theirs. However, she enjoyed imagining her mother listening to them in her bedroom full blast, while Sylvia beat the handle of the broom against the ceiling downstairs. She wondered if any of these tapes had been made by her father. Picking one out at random, she read the inscription on the white-lined card, written in permanent marker: 'My girl. Forever mine.' The last two words were underlined three times.

This had become one of her favourite tapes, and she kept it in the car with her. Sliding it into the car's player now, Tamsyn tweaked the volume up. Chris Rea's 'The Road to Hell' began to play.

When Tamsyn had left university and moved to London for work, she'd saved doggedly to buy the Figaro. Each time she visited Much Wenlock, she wore the headscarf and glasses in the car—until she reached the signpost for the village, at which point she'd take them off and stuff them into the glove compartment. Now, almost defiantly, she wrapped the silk scarf around her head and slid on the glasses. As Fig crawled down the driveway, Tamsyn still felt like Sylvia might be watching her from the window above, eyes narrowing at the sight of her wearing them.

The crisp November light filtered through the huge ash trees, their branches refusing to let go of their golden leaves. There was a chilling bite in the air. Perhaps winter was threatening to come early this year.

Tamsyn breathed deeply. She felt a tremendous relief being outside the cottage. The farther she was from Rosemount, the more she felt the heavy weight of grief alleviating. With a start, she realised that driving Fig, the only constant that had remained in her life for the past ten years, was the only time she felt free.

Passing through the country lane towards the village, Tamsyn felt the confusion and shame of the last few months begin to shift into sharper focus. Why had she allowed herself to sit idle in the cottage for three months, barely looking after herself, when she could have been out here, doing so much more with her life? Somewhere low inside her stomach, the black dog that never left her rolled over, threatening to wake. She turned her mind to the matter at hand, quelling the emotion before it took over.

As she drove through Much Wenlock, passers-by turned to admire Fig. She *was* rather noticeable, Tamsyn mused. It was probably not the best choice of car for someone who so hated drawing attention to themselves. Perhaps some of them remembered her mother and thought that she had returned.

Since Prudence Pride and her sisters had built Rosemount, the Pride women had become the big fishes in this particular pond. Everyone knew them. That was probably why Sylvia had so loved it so much here. However, Tamsyn had never felt like she belonged. She was the quiet, strange girl who never said much and always had her head in a book. *You can't do anything with her*, Tamsyn had heard Sylvia say more than once, all the while shaking her head. Tamsyn usually just scowled at her from behind the pages.

She stopped outside a row of terraced houses and pulled Fig up to the kerb. Bridie's house sat firmly in the middle of the row, its white render greyer than the others, the front garden kept neatly mown and free of weeds by her kindly neighbours. She saw the greying net curtains twitch, and as she made to get out of the car, Bridie was already out of her front door. Despite her stooped gait, she was surprisingly sprightly.

'I'm a-comin,' buddy bud! Don't get out!' Bridie crowed, seizing the car door before Tamsyn could help her. She flung the door open, Tamsyn wincing as the twenty-five-year-old hinges were stretched violently to their full capacity. Clinging on the top of the door frame, Bridie unceremoniously swung herself inside the car, which lurched as Bridie's weight fell into the passenger seat. She sat breathlessly for a moment before straining her arm towards the car door.

'Let me get that.' Tamsyn hastily got out of the car, ran round to the passenger side and closed the door gently after Bridie. It made her smile how alike Bridie and Sylvia were:

both stubbornly refused any and all forms of help. Bridie fumbled with her seatbelt. Her clothes smelled very faintly of mothballs and mildew, while her skin and hair smelled of floral-scented soap and Anaïs Anaïs. As Tamsyn restarted the engine, the tape blared its next song, Carly Simon's 'You're So Vain'. Bridie jumped, and Tamsyn quickly cranked down the volume.

'Sorry about that. One of my mother's exes obviously didn't like her very much,' Tamsyn joked. Bridie gave away nothing other than a thin-lipped smile.

'Nice scarf,' Bridie said, in a way that made Tamsyn self-conscious. Her eyes slid down to the locket around her neck, but she didn't say anything. They made small talk as they drove the short distance to the café, pointing at pedestrians and recounting to Tamsyn the terrible troubles everyone was having behind closed doors. As she directed Tamsyn to park directly outside The Snooty Fox, she told Tamsyn that the owner was expecting them. Sure enough, the man who Tamsyn assumed was the owner jumped up from behind the counter when he saw them coming.

'Bridie, my love!' he called. 'Come, let me help you. I've got your usual table ready, just like you asked. How are you?' He took her arm as he helped her up the stairs.

'I haven't been too good, Colin,' Bridie told him as they went. 'Not too good at all. My feet have been playing me up terrible.' Bridie stood breathlessly inside the café, surveying her domain.

'Come right this way, please.' The man smiled and gestured to the table in the bay window, stepping aside to let the two women precede him.

'That was our table,' Bridie said, looking up at Tamsyn. Her eyes were a faded grey-blue; the skin on her eyelids was tinged with purple, and the right lid hung half-closed. 'We liked to see who was passing by,' she continued. 'Very important to know what's happening, and to see who's out and about.'

Another couple sat in the corner. The mousy-haired woman was glowering at them over her menu. Tamsyn tried not to laugh: she and her husband had obviously been seated at the bay window table, and had been unceremoniously turfed out by the returning queen bee.

The owner seated Bridie and then Tamsyn, then frantically touched the plates, realigning them precisely, and polished the cutlery on his stained apron.

'Colin, you remember Tamsyn, Sylvie's granddaughter?' Bridie asked.

'Ah, yes,' he replied, feigning that he had only just realised who she was. 'We spoke briefly at Sylvia's funeral. She was such a marvellous woman. Very much missed. It really won't be the same without her. Now then, can I interest you in scrambled eggs? Sausage? The full works?' He grinned, revealing two rows of impressively white teeth.

'Our usual, please, Colin,' Bridie said, handing him the menus without a glance. Tamsyn hoped that whatever their usual was, it was the lemon drizzle cake she had spied on the counter, but she very much doubted it.

'Please may I have a black coffee?' Tamsyn asked. She had run out of coffee two days ago, and was dying for one. Her headaches had begun to subside, however, so perhaps it was a sign she should give up caffeine.

Colin nodded and scurried away. Tamsyn was faintly amused by the level of respect, or fear, her grandmother and Bridie must have inspired to warrant such service. Once he had retreated far enough away, Bridie leaned in with her shaking hands palms-down on the table.

'Now, let's get straight to it. I don't do idle chit-chat,' she said.

'Great. Neither do I,' said Tamsyn.

'People here want to know how long you plan to stay,' Bridie said bluntly.

Tamsyn was taken aback. 'Um. Well, I had planned on selling the cottage. But once I got here, I just couldn't bring myself to do it. Why? Is my being here a problem?'

Bridie sucked her lips back. 'For some people, yes. People here, they… they don't like outsiders.'

'But I lived here for eighteen years!' Tamsyn half-laughed at the absurdity of it.

'Yes. But you have been gone a long time. I—I don't think this is a good place for girls your age. There's nothing to do, for a start. Few eligible men knockin' about. You wanna get yerself somewhere lively.'

Bridie was watching her, her eyes suddenly alight. She reached out and grabbed Tamsyn's hand. Her skin was wrinkled yet felt completely smooth, and cold to the touch. Bridie squeezed her hand tighter as her eyes held hers, unwavering. Her face was like stone; her intense stare made Tamsyn want to look away. She tried to pull away, but Bridie was deceptively strong. After a moment she let go and turned to see where their order was.

'Well, well, well,' she said, turning back to Tamsyn. 'I

thought you'd have remembered more by now, being back this long.'

'Remembered what?'

Bridie paused and looked out of the window, considering what she should say next. 'Bet you've been like a bear with a sore head lately,' she said at length. 'Had many headaches?'

Tamsyn stared at her in puzzlement. 'Yes, actually. How did you know?'

Bridie's lips were pursed, as if she was fighting something. 'Gods!' she exclaimed in frustration. She thought for a moment. 'Here—d'ya know the film *Fight Club*?'

'*Fight Club*?' Tamsyn couldn't help but laugh.

'Don't laugh at me. I don't like being laughed at,' Bridie said indignantly. 'I might be old, but that don't mean I ain't seen films. Anyway, y'know how in the film, they can't talk about Fight Club?'

'Yeah—' said Tamsyn, still confused.

'Well, it's like that, see. No one here can—talk about…' She fought, struggling with her words. '…arggh! Fight Club!' Bridie's cheeks flushed. Tamsyn couldn't tell if it was through effort or embarrassment.

'Okay…' Tamsyn was starting to question whether she should start to worry about Bridie's sanity.

Bridie straightened up awkwardly when she saw Colin coming over with the cream tea and a plate of very dry-looking scones. He placed a cup of hot water in front of Tamsyn, with a sachet of instant coffee perched on the saucer. Tamsyn shot a look at the blackboard: £2.50 for a sachet of instant was pretty steep by anyone's standards.

As he busily laid everything out on the table, Tamsyn

watched Bridie closely. The old woman seemed lost in thought, her brow furrowed and her eyes darting furtively. After Colin left, Tamsyn tore open the sachet and began stirring the granules into her cup.

Suddenly the old woman seemed to come to life again. 'Quick!' Bridie picked up a teaspoon and thrust it towards Tamsyn. 'The bubbles in yer coffee—get 'em on the spoon before they pop! It's good luck.' She nodded her head towards the cup in earnest.

Tamsyn carefully lowered the spoon into the black water and caught the bubbles. Bridie nodded eagerly and encouraged her to slurp the bubbles off the spoon. She did as she was told, and the two women sat for a few minutes, eating and drinking in companionable silence.

Bridie's eccentric behaviour had Tamsyn wondering whether she should tell her about the locket at all. But then, if she didn't tell Bridie, who could she tell?

Tamsyn unclasped the locket from around her neck and slid it across the table to Bridie. Bridie looked at her for a moment, before taking it in her gnarled fingers.

Tamsyn lowered her voice. 'I found Grandma's locket. At the bottom of a patch of monkshood in the Poison Garden,' she whispered.

Bridie was staring at something in the middle distance, her hand closed almost protectively over the locket as it lay on the table.

'When I arrived at Rosemount,' Tamsyn continued, 'her teacup... you know, the one she always drank from? Well, it was still on the table. I didn't think much of it at the time. But you know my grandmother. She would never leave anything around without cleaning it and putting it away in the exact same spot. I found her scissors in the garden, too, next to the locket. And when I washed up the cup and teapot, I realised there were enough leaves in the strainer and teapot for two people.'

Bridie frowned, still staring off into the middle distance. Tamsyn wondered if she was even listening.

'Last night I checked her diary,' she went on doggedly. 'The page for the week she died has no visitors penned in for that day. Did she say anything to you?' Tamsyn leaned in.

At that moment Colin returned, asking if everything was all right with the food. Tamsyn told him it was wonderful, while Bridie said nothing, looking even paler than before. Her hand trembled over the locket underneath. Her eyes were dim, watering pinkly at the edges. Her expression remained blank, until at last she noticed Colin and shifted in her chair. She gave him a smile and a nod.

As soon as he had disappeared again, Bridie slid the locket hastily back to Tamsyn.

'By God, I thought he'd never leave. He nearly saw my breakfast!' Bridie said, her lips quivering.

'Oh dear, are you feeling okay?' Tamsyn asked worriedly. She couldn't stand vomit. To her surprise, tears welled in Bridie's eyes, before spilling over down her cheeks.

'Bridie! What's the matter?' asked Tamsyn, shocked.

'I knew something wasn't right. Absolutely nothing wrong with her heart! Someone was with her that day. Someone with a vendetta. And I bet I know who,' she cried, looking warily at the locket in Tamsyn's hand.

'You think someone hurt my grandmother? Why on earth would someone do that?' Tamsyn bristled.

'Pah! Why does anyone do anything?' Bridie crumpled a serviette and wiped her tears. 'I thought you lived in London. Surely you're not as wet behind the ears as all that?'

'Well, the people I know may have had professional or personal rivalries, but as far as I know they weren't willing to off someone over it.' Tamsyn stared uneasily at the old woman, unsure whether she should be entertaining these sorts of speculations. Her grandmother had died of a heart attack. It was tragic, but she was eighty-seven. She almost laughed nervously at the sheer lunacy of it all.

But Bridie was not to be diverted. 'Last night he... I saw... *ach!*' Bridie clapped her hands together angrily, causing people to turn and stare. Tears welled in her eyes again. Bridie looked around worriedly, waiting for the din of conversation to resume. She leaned forward conspiratorially. 'Listen... I can't tell you anything,' she whispered loudly. 'You need to find someone else, outside of here.' Bridie shook her head angrily, almost fearfully, and resumed looking out of the window.

Tamsyn sighed, suddenly feeling deflated and tired. She took a bite of the dry scone, which even the clotted cream and jam couldn't salvage.

'You look tired,' remarked Bridie, turning back to Tamsyn. 'You know what you need? A nice warm bath. Sylvie always had those nice salts in the bathroom. And those special candles she used to hand pour. She always said to me there's nothing that couldn't be solved after a good stew in the bath. She would open the curtains and windows. Let the moonlight in. She swore by it, you know,' Bridie said, trying not to cry again by stuffing her mouth full of scone. Tamsyn smiled, remembering how her grandmother had indeed loved a bath every night before bed.

'I wish she was here, Bridie,' Tamsyn said sadly.

'You and me both,' Bridie replied bitterly.

7
BY THE LIGHT OF THE MOON

Tamsyn began to fill the roll-top bathtub and gathered the things she had seen Sylvia use hundreds of times before. As the water gushed, she scattered powdered sulphur and then salts, bergamot, crushed corn poppies, peppermint oil and lavender in an attempt to hide the intense eggy aroma. They swirled around in the water, creating beautiful eddies and whirlpools. She found four violet candles in the cellar, hand-poured by Sylvia, the wicks already neatly trimmed, and placed them beside the tub in the holders that were covered in cascading waterfalls of dried wax from the numerous candles that had melted over the years.

Even though she felt a little silly, she drew the curtains back and opened the windows wide, just like Bridie had said. As she lowered herself into the hot water, she exhaled deeply and lay back, marvelling at the sight of the large full moon and the deep purple sky decorated with the early evening stars.

The salts and sulphur swirled and bubbled up in plumes underneath her. Holding her breath, she submerged herself entirely under the water. Tiny bubbles escaped from her mouth and nostrils and wriggled up to the surface. She closed her eyes, enjoying the feeling of being in another world, escaping her reality for a moment. Listening to the salts tingling as they dissolved around her ears, and her steady heartbeat pumping in her chest—

Tamsyn!

The voice was far away, muffled by the water. She sat up in the bath, looking around the room. The candles guttered in the dark, the large sombre moon still looking down on her from the window.

Willing herself to relax again, she slid back down into the water. She lay there for a while, letting the leaves and poppies brush delicately over her skin. She had no idea how long she stayed there, but she lay until the candles burned low and the water grew tepid. When she finally dragged her weary limbs out of the bath, outside the window, the moon had disappeared.

That night, Tamsyn tossed and turned in disturbed sleep. Images appeared, visions and snapshots shifted before her, disappearing again if she tried to look too closely.

Cloaked figures encircled her. She could not see their faces. They chanted together, and one of them came forward, holding a chalice. The next moment, she stood outside in the grey dawn. Long stems of monkshood swayed. Blackened roots reached down into a stagnant pool, its surface crusted over with flies. Brown, muddy water swirled with broken leaves. Tamsyn tried to back away from the water's edge. Something gripped her, her bare feet sinking into the mud as she willed her body to run.

Suddenly, she found herself on the landing, light falling over the floorboards from the crack in a doorway. Tamsyn looked through the keyhole and could see Sylvia standing on top of a ladder, straining to reach the wall sconce. Then the image melted away and she was standing next to Sylvia's bed; her grandmother was just a small figure lying in between the pillows. Her eyes and mouth gaped open, a grim, shocking spectre of a face that stared back at her, unrelenting.

Tamsyn sat upright. The wind shook the windows as the rain lashed against them.

She lay back in the bed, willing her heart to stop pounding. There would be no more sleep for her tonight, she knew. Lying awake, she stared at the ceiling until the light of dawn fell in lavender hues over the garden and fields beyond.

Tears fell down the side of her face and into her hair. The coil that had wound itself tightly around her brain had begun to let go. Fragmented memories returned. The mixtures she had helped her grandmother prepare—they were not mere herbal remedies. They were potions. Potions that could cure people.

She buried her face in her hands and sobbed. Dreamlike visions flitted in the periphery of her mind, visions that felt very real. They were memories of magic.

～

As dawn fought to break through the clouds, Tamsyn padded across the dark corridor to Sylvia's room. She paused at the door, her hand hovering over the doorknob. She had ventured into the room only once since arriving, to close the curtains and cover her grandmother's furniture with dust sheets. She closed her hand around the cool cast iron; the doorknob felt stiff and unwilling to turn. At last, with a significant amount of force, the old latch popped, leaving the door to swing open on creaking hinges.

She tried the light switch nearest the door. The overhead light was harsh against the early morning. Even now, Tamsyn felt she was trespassing. Sylvia's room was firmly her domain.

The pale sheets lay draped as she had left them. The temperature was always cooler in here. The windows faced the north; Sylvia had found it the optimal place for sleep, and the northern exposure had the added benefit of shielding her books from fading in the sunlight.

The silence felt heavy. The room was tidy, with its shining mahogany floor, French four-poster bed, single chest of drawers, simple washstand, and the neatly arranged shelves of books. The bed looked ominous, tented over with sheets as if it could house an intruder. Tamsyn began pulling them off, sending plumes of dust swirling into the air.

Rosemount's layout had remained the same for hundreds of years. The only changes Sylvia had made were to add some newer plants to the garden to cater for changing tastes, and to move the majority of the library from downstairs to her own bedroom. Now Tamsyn realised that she had moved them here to keep the magic away from her own granddaughter.

All of Rosemount's important books were kept here. After

Tamsyn had left for university, Sylvia had commissioned huge carved mahogany shelves, each encased behind wooden doors that covered every available wall space. The bespoke sections housed the vast collection, which were of course ordered and labelled meticulously, and a rolling library ladder gave access to the upper shelves.

Tamsyn unlatched the sash window, heaving it up with a groan as years of flaking paint yielded. The biting November air breathed new life into the room as Tamsyn dragged the dusty drop-sheets out onto the landing. The pale morning light shone through the diamond leaded windows, and Tamsyn returned to the bedroom window and gazed out. Sylvia's room overlooked Rosemount's driveway and had the perfect vantage point through the golden ash trees. No one entering from the front could escape Sylvia's withering gaze.

Tamsyn turned away and, gathering her courage, opened the sliding doors to the closest bookcase. She took a sharp intake of breath as she read the spines of each book in turn. The bulk of the collection consisted of endless tomes on herbology, centuries-old apothecary handbooks and every guide to advanced hedge-witchery known to humanity. She remembered poring over them as a little girl before Sylvia had taken them away. Tamsyn slid the ladder over on its brass rails, climbing the well-worn rungs to survey the books at the top. A mesh panel guarded them—from no one but Tamsyn, now. She pulled at the doors, and to her dismay found that they were locked.

She jumped when she heard a noise and turned to see Winnie sitting at the foot of the ladder. She let out a curt mewl to show her displeasure at Tamsyn's invasion of privacy. Either that or she was demanding breakfast.

'Yes, thank you, Winnie. I know I'm not supposed to be in here,' Tamsyn said, and carefully descended the ladder. 'Just one minute more, all right?' The cat stared at her pointedly.

Once she had located the healing remedies section, Tamsyn pulled out any books she thought might be helpful. Purifying spells, spell reversals, healing hexes and extracting poison. She had no idea what had been done to her to induce the fog she'd felt over the last few months; clearly, something had. But if a bath of purifying salts had helped her regain some memory, she was willing to try anything. Perhaps more baths, stronger salt baths, would help her remember more?

Making her way downstairs with the heavy pile of books, Tamsyn plunked them onto the table, fed Winnie and poured herself a huge bowl of cereal. Winnie gobbled her meal and then hopped up and sat on the kitchen table; a judgemental air exuded from her as she watched Tamsyn idly spooning in the cereal with the books sprawled open around her.

The familiarity of the pages flooded her with relief and horror all at once. Muscle memory seemed to return to her, for, without even turning to the shelves, she found she knew exactly where each ingredient listed on the pages sat in the pantry. For now, she decided, she would have to raid her grandmother's existing stores and start replacing and labelling everything meticulously. Many of the jars and bottles around the kitchen were starting to look less than desirable, but she hoped they would still hold enough potency to be effective.

Tamsyn looked through the books for hours. As her eyes

were beginning to feel strained, she stumbled upon a reference for *Memory Loss* in the appendices of a tattered, plainly bound book. She turned to the page eagerly. To her dismay, the entry contained one short line:

> *In extreme cases of forgetfulness or complete loss of memory, the subject has most certainly been the victim of Black Magick.*

Tamsyn had no one to turn to. No one but Bridie. And she didn't know if she could trust her, even if she was Sylvia's best friend of nearly seventy years. If she had had her memory wiped, then that meant her grandmother had known about it. Unless she had had her memory wiped, too? Tamsyn massaged her scalp to appease the growing pressure inside her head.

She looked at Winnie, who was dozing after finishing off her elevenses.

'Sod it,' she said to the cat. She picked up the phone. On its card, Sylvia had Tippexed 'BRIDIE' next to the number 1.

'Who is it?' came Bridie's cracking voice after several rings.

'Hi, Bridie. It's me… I think I've started to remember.' She paused to wait for a reaction.

A heavy sigh came from the other end. Bridie did not sound relieved. In fact, she sounded quite the opposite. Nevertheless, her reaction confirmed to Tamsyn that Bridie knew exactly what she was talking about.

'The bath worked. Sort of, anyway. There are a few bits

I'm still hazy on. Like, why couldn't I remember that my grandmother and I practised magic in the first place?'

There was a long silence on the other end of the line. 'I— I told you. No one here can help you,' Bridie said sadly.

'What do you mean? I have no one else to turn to! And I want to know why I can't remember. Were we... are we...?' Tamsyn fought the feeling of being silly and forced out the word in a whisper. 'Witches?'

More silence. Was Bridie figuring out what to say next? Tamsyn refused to say any more until Bridie eventually cut through the tension down the line.

'Did your grandmother ever tell you about the story of Sabrina?' Bridie said quietly.

'The goddess of the River Severn?'

'That's the one. It was one of her favourite... stories. I think she probably still has it.'

Tamsyn knew for certain now that whatever had happened to her, Bridie was unable to talk about it. She sighed. She felt so very tired.

'Thanks, Bridie. I'll see if I can find it.' Tamsyn hung up the phone. She was angry at her. Angry at Sylvia. Angry at Much Wenlock and everyone who lived there. But she also knew that if she was going to find out anything about what had happened to her, the answer would be in Sylvia's locked bookcases.

8

THE SNOOTY FOX

Colin was just sliding a luxurious blackberry, fig and chocolate gateau into the fridge when he saw Bridie Dawson hobbling to the front door. She must have walked from her house, he reasoned, as she looked like she was about to drop dead.

'Bridie, Bridie, Bridie, my love! Why didn't you call me to come and pick you up?' Colin rushed over, putting his arm around her. Her wheezing had always creeped him out, but even more so now; it did not sound good. Thankfully, there were no other customers. She tried to speak, but couldn't catch her breath.

'Come and sit down here and I'll get you a hot toddy.'

'B-brandy,' Bridie managed.

Colin poured hot water into a double of Rémy Martin and scurried back to her. He held the glass to her lips. With a shaking hand, she reached into her breast pocket and retrieved a vial. She uncorked it, tipped it back, and placed a drop of the amber liquid under her tongue. They sat in silence as they waited for her breathing to slow.

'Sylvie made me this. For me heart.' She held up the small glass tube. 'This is the last of it,' she said sadly. 'I'll have to use that bloody spray the doctors give you. Makes your head feel like it's gonna explode.'

Colin gave her a sympathetic look.

'She—she remembers,' Bridie said eventually.

Colin's eyes widened, his mind running through all the possible ramifications.

'I—I don't know what to do. I can't tell her anything. I tried, and the Seal... my tongue was on fire! The Seal won't let us tell her a damn word. But remembering she is a witch puts her in grave danger. I promised Sylvie I would never let anything happen to her.'

'Slow down,' Colin said soothingly. 'Don't stress yourself. Deep breaths, now.' He waited while she took several deep breaths in and out. 'Listen, we don't know for sure yet that she knows. We shouldn't jump to conclusions.'

'We *do* know! If the council finds out she will wind up dead. A "natural accident". That's always the way.' Bridie shook her head bitterly. 'You promise me, Colin. You promise me you won't tell a soul. Since Sylvie left, I don't know who I trust in this place. But you have always been a good friend to us both.'

'Of course, my darling. The secrets I hear in this place, you wouldn't believe.' Colin mimed a zip closing up his lips.

9
HUBBLE BUBBLE

Tamsyn paced to the far side of Sylvia's bed. She flicked the wall light switch three times. Nothing. She pulled the ladder along on its rails, as close as she could get it to the light, then climbed up the rungs and leaned across, just as she had seen Sylvia doing as she peered through the keyhole in her dream the night before.

Carefully lifting its translucent dome she peered inside the light. There was no bulb inside. She leaned farther, precariously balancing the glass dome in her left hand as her right hand felt around the brass fitting. Tamsyn sincerely hoped that the circuitry was disconnected as she lightly prodded her finger around the empty bulb socket. There was a loose scraping sound as something skittered around at the bottom. She grasped her fingers around it, fearing an electric shock.

It was a small brass key.

Shoving her prize in her pocket, she replaced the glass dome over the light socket, scrambled back down the ladder, and then moved it over to the forbidden library shelves. She went back up the ladder and tried the key in the nearest lock. After a few moments of fumbling with it this way and that, it clicked open. She withdrew the key and tried it in the next compartment. Another satisfying click. She breathed a sigh of relief; it seemed to open all the upper compartments in Sylvia's library. Tamsyn marvelled how, at eighty-seven, Sylvia had regularly climbed that ladder and retrieved the key.

She set to work looking over the books. Most of the locked compartments housed volumes on the subject of dark magic: necromancy, mind control, forbidden rituals, and any practice Sylvia deemed outside the realm of hedge-witchery. There were books about mythical creatures, gods, demons, spirits of all kinds. She scanned the spines until her finger fell upon *Water Sprites, River Nymphs and Goddesses of the Severn*.

Judging by the accumulated dust, the books had sat undisturbed since Sylvia had moved them to their new home. She plucked the book off the shelf, tucked it under one arm and continued looking. To her right were forty or so black leather-bound books, with Roman numerals on the spine in gold foil.

Tamsyn picked out the latest, XLII. She remembered her grandmother drilling into her the importance of keeping full journals documenting all aspects of life at Rosemount: outgoing and incoming expenditure, records of the weather, accounts of how much the garden had produced that year, plus a full itemised breakdown of the produce stored in the pantry. Tucking the ledger under her arm with *Water Sprites*, she headed downstairs. In the kitchen, Tamsyn heaved the heavy books onto the table, fed the ever-ravenous Winnie some lunch, brewed tea and built a fire in the hearth.

Seating herself at the table, she began flicking through the journal. Tamsyn was surprised to discover that in between lists and columns of numbers, Sylvia had also written short diary entries. She skipped to the end to see the last entries.

28th April 2015

The winter vegetables in the greenhouse refuse to grow. I gathered what I could out of the cellar, and presented them in offering to Hecate. I asked for her strength and guidance, and called upon my sisters. The shadow continues to draw near, but never ventures beyond the mount's protection stones. As the wind blows east, a foul stench infiltrates the house, souring any fresh food and wilting the cut flowers.

Hecate. Tamsyn glanced at the carving of three Greek goddesses on the mantlepiece, each with her back to the others. It represented the three forms of Hecate, of whom the Pride women had been devout followers as far back as their records began. She was the goddess of witchcraft, protector of the household, and the guardian of crossroads. The figure facing left held her arms out wide, a snake coiling itself around them. The one facing outwards held torches, while the third held out a dagger. Dried bunches of lavender and wild garlic stood around the base of the carving as an offering, untouched now for over ten months. The Pride women may have worshipped Hecate, but she had done little to help Tamsyn or Sylvia, she thought bitterly.

30th April 2015

As dusk drew near I thought I saw something moving between the ash trees. I feel safe in the knowledge that my defences around the cottage are impassable. Perhaps my mind has fallen prey to some dark apparition? Nevertheless, I will fortify the protective spells and check on the stone circles surrounding the cottage. The stench permeates everything in the house. Sometimes I think I can smell it upon my clothes and hair; other times, I think it is coming up through the sink and bath plug. I have blocked every entry, large and small, to the cottage. I will deliver offerings to Hecate, and entreat her to fortify the protection around our beloved Rosemount.

That was the last entry. Sylvia had been found four days later, when Bridie had raised the alarm after Sylvia had failed to make their usual appointment at The Snooty Fox. Bridie had immediately summoned Sylvia's doctor, Anita Palgrave, and, armed with Bridie's spare key, they were able to gain entry into Rosemount.

Tamsyn felt a chill run down her spine. Something or someone had been trying to get in, and it looks like they had succeeded.

Tamsyn picked up *Water Sprites, River Nymphs and Goddesses of the Severn*. As she sat down in front of the fire, she realised that for the first time in months the dull ache at the back of her skull had disappeared. The fire snapped and crackled, and she looked nervously over at it. The wood she had collected must have been slightly damp, for its bark spat and spluttered behind the guard, threatening to burst over onto the rug beyond.

Looking around the room, it was as if she was seeing Rosemount in a new light. The monstrous fireplace was of intricately carved walnut. Its wooden columns depicted coiling grapevines, serpents and berries. The mantlepiece featured expertly chiselled flowers, interlocked with vines and surrounding three moons; to the left and right were a waxing and waning crescent, cradling a full moon at the centre.

To the right of the statue of Hecate, a silver frame housed an image of Sylvia sitting on a beach with a young Tamsyn on her lap. Sylvia was wearing sunglasses rimmed in white and was looking lovingly down at Tamsyn, who sat smiling, wrapped in a beach towel and wearing a straw sun hat. Tamsyn must have been three or four in the photograph, not long after her mother, Annalise, had left. Sylvia always lamented, *You were so precious as a little girl…* but she always stopped short of finishing the sentence. Tamsyn knew she wanted to say, *What happened?*

Tamsyn sighed and turned her attention to the book in her lap. She flicked through and stopped. The chapter on Sabrina had a bookmark nestled between the pages.

…After a fierce battle with the Huns, King Locrin of England fell in love with the captured princess, Estrildis. However, Locrin had already agreed to a diplomatic marriage to Gwendolen, the daughter of Corineus, ruler of Cornwall. Under threat of violence, Locrin acquiesced to marrying Gwendolen, and together they bore a son, Madan.

Although Locrin had agreed to matrimony, he refused to

give up Estrildis. He hid her in an underground cave, and together they bore a daughter, Sabre, known in Latin as Sabrina. Upon learning of the death of Corineus, Locrin immediately divorced Gwendolen, placing Estrildis on the throne as queen, and naming Sabrina the princess of England.

Enraged, Gwendolen readied the Cornish army to battle against Locrin. He was killed, and Gwendolen took the throne on behalf of their son, Madan. Estrildis and Sabrina were drowned in the river, immortalising the young maiden as the River Severn.

Tamsyn yawned widely and rubbed her eyes, which were suddenly heavy. She had been up since dawn. Letting the book fall to the floor, Tamsyn pulled the soft blanket over her and decided to succumb to the temptation of an afternoon nap.

10

TOIL AND TROUBLE

Tamsyn took a stroll through Rosemount's garden to clear her head. The old windmill marked the Rosemount's boundary, which was bordered on one side by Farmer Bradshaw's land and on the other by a thicket of woods. It was already approaching dusk as Tamsyn came to the tree line. Huge red leaves from the horse chestnuts littered the ground. Among them, a scattering of spiked green seeds peered out from their leafy beds, their brown eyes shining through the split green skin.

As Tamsyn picked her way over the mossy ground, the trees grew sparse, the leaves on the ground dissipating as she neared a clearing. Tamsyn wrinkled her nose in disgust as the pungent smell of sewage and rotten vegetation hit her. Buzzing flies skimmed past her ears. The trunks of the trees grew darker here, and as she stepped into the circle of trees, she noted that the branches were already stripped of their leaves, almost as if something had disturbed them.

A dark lake lay in the clearing, its surface completely still.

An ancient alder tree leaned over into the water, its gnarled branches dipping in and back out again, piercing the carpet of duckweed. It would soon be winter, but still clouds of black flies danced around her, buzzing and swirling in irritation and hunger. The smell of decay and open sewer caught at the back of Tamsyn's throat. She held her hand over her nose and watering mouth as she retched.

The pool was just like the one she had seen in her dream. Had Sylvia been here? Could there be another piece to the puzzle, like the locket or the key in the light, near here? Tentatively, she neared the pool. She picked up a loose stick. Swishing aside the covering of duckweed, she could just about see down through the water, where thick ribbons of pondweed swayed as if caught in a current.

Tamsyn breathed deeply, trying to steady her rapidly beating heart. Despite the salt bath, it would take time for her memories to find their way back to her. Like a fog lifting, she saw snippets of herself, her teenage hands working as she practised magic. But just as if it were a dream, she couldn't yet grasp the full picture. She couldn't quite remember the last time she had performed a spell. She did however recall an incantation Sylvia had always used when she had lost something around the house. This one was simple, tiny. Even better, there was no one around to see. She swirled the duckweed in a figure eight and closed her eyes, whispering.

'What is lost, become found,
Return to me, safe and sound.'

Tamsyn sat on her haunches to get a closer view of the

surface. Between the curtains of weeds, she could see the long tendrils swaying. They danced this way and that, as if trying to make pictures. She sat transfixed as the ribbons parted, like mermaid hair.

She waited. Eventually she sat down, beginning to feel weary as the rush of adrenaline she'd felt when performing the small spell began to subside. There was a terrible sorrow to this place, she thought. Picking up the stick again, she threw it into the water and watched the small ripples. And then, to her horror, she saw two pale yellow eyes just above the carpet of duckweed. A woman's face emerged, rising slightly above the surface, drawing closer. Her eyes focused on Tamsyn, wavering for a moment.

The woman began to rise out of the water. Her head of raven-black hair fell in strings, clinging to the water-bloated skin. Tamsyn gave a strangled scream and struggled to her feet. A plume of sickly-sweet stench followed, as if a bandage had been lifted off an infected wound. The deathly figure blinked the water away, droplets falling from her dark eyelashes and hair, streaking down her face. Patches of moss clung to her decaying skin, and Tamsyn fought the urge to retch again. The corpse did not speak; it simply hung there, staring back at Tamsyn, waiting.

Tamsyn stood frozen in fear. She tried to run, but found she was rooted to the spot. 'Who... who are you?' she croaked.

The apparition seemed faintly amused by this; a ghastly smile appeared at the corners of her rotted lips. Perhaps she sensed Tamsyn's fear and realised she wasn't a threat.

'I have heard you seek revenge... for your grandmother's

death?' Her voice creaked, with a sound like the branches of the alder tree above them swaying in the wind.

'No! I—I am not here to hurt you. I'm just out walking. Please, let me go.'

'You do not seek justice?' The woman's voice was a breathy gurgle, like water on the lungs. She gave a wet laugh.

Tamsyn's stomach tightened as she realised the awful truth: this woman, the dark figure, the stench Sylvia had written about in her journal—it was her.

'Was it you? Did you... kill her?'

The lifeless eyes did not move; they held Tamsyn's gaze, unblinking.

'Tell me! Who are you? What happened to my grandmother the day she died?' Tamsyn tried desperately to stop her voice from faltering.

'Who am I?' The figure gave another mirthless smile. 'I am the forgotten. I am no one.' She started to sink below the surface once more.

'Wait! I need to know! Did you kill my grandmother?'

The woman stopped in mid-descent, her thin smile broadening to reveal sharp and broken green teeth. Tamsyn stared at her, remembering the old folkloric tale Sylvia used to tell her to keep her away from deep water... What was the woman's name? She racked her brains. Wicked Jenny?

'I did not kill her,' the woman intoned. 'She did it to herself. It was quite pitiful. Monkshood can be... rather painful.' Her head tilted towards the far bank, where dead sticks of black monkshood rose from the water. Tamsyn followed her gaze, her mind racing. Her grandmother's death had been a suicide? That made no sense at all. Unless she laced the wrong tea in her panic.

'She obviously intended to kill you. Why were you there, scaring an old woman out of her wits? What did you want with her?' asked Tamsyn. Although she was more defenceless than a trapped rabbit, she couldn't hide her anger.

The apparition shook her head. 'Now I have given you two answers. Where is your offering for me in return? The law states, to summon a water spirit with nothing to offer must mean you wish to die.' The water retracted from the bank imperceptibly as the woman leaned forward. 'I shall unburden you from your stupidity and kill you here and now.'

'I did not summon you!' Tamsyn cried hastily, trying to back away. 'I just repeated a spell to find something, a clue about how my grandmother died. You were summoned—you must be the clue. But I didn't know what I was doing— please!' said Tamsyn, struggling again to move. She stared, mesmerised, into the dead woman's eyes, not daring to look away. 'There must be something more you can tell me,' she pleaded. 'I just want to know—if you didn't kill her, why were you there? Why did she put monkshood into the tea? Who *are* you?' Despite herself, the questions tumbled out all at once.

The cadaverous woman gave Tamsyn a look of disdain. 'So many questions,' she answered, before slipping silently beneath the surface.

Shaking with fear, Tamsyn found she could move her legs once more. She backed away from the bank, wondering if her ordeal was over.

'Where are you going, little dormouse?'

Tamsyn scanned the water suddenly feeling extremely exposed, but the woman was nowhere to be seen.

'If I dragged you under, who would come looking for you?'

No, the voice was no longer coming from the water. Instinctively, Tamsyn looked up. The dead woman was in the branches of the alder tree, eyes dull and wide, her mouth twisted into a smile.

'I am owed a great debt,' she intoned. 'The death of every last Pride won't pay it, but it's a start.'

Her black form writhed down the trunk until she reached the ground, where she stood in her wet, shredded rags. Underneath them, her rotted skin clung to exposed bone. She advanced on Tamsyn, one hand reaching out, her long, splintered nails grasping.

'Stop! Maybe I could help you?' said Tamsyn. She stepped back, holding her hands up in supplication.

'You are a helpless rodent. I will drown you,' the woman spat. Without effort, she flew forward several paces and suddenly her bony fingers were around Tamsyn's neck.

Tamsyn saw black tendrils creeping around the corners of her vision. She thrust her head upwards, towards the sky, gasping for air.

In a moment she was lying somewhere else, in the mud by the side of the river. Crows cawed overhead, circling. One swooped down to her side. It approached her, unblinking, cocking its head and peering at her arm. It pulled back sharply, a tendon in its beak stretching taut. Another crow landed on her chest, its surprising heavy body shifting from one clawed foot to the other. It plunged its head downward and she could feel its beak inside her, plucking and scraping between her rib bones.

The clouds writhed, and day quickly turned to dusk. The rain showered her paralysed body until the river rose, lifting her on its muddy swells. Her lifeless body drifted with the current, her unblinking eyes staring at the grey sky as droplets of water plummeted from above, directly into her eyes, which she was powerless to close. The river carried her for a while until she sank beneath the surface. The current was strong, and her body slammed against the rocks and debris littering the river bed.

As the river began to slow, she meandered lifelessly until the water became deep and still. Dense swathes of reeds surrounded her on all sides, and small fish sucked on her loose flesh.

Then she saw it: the head of a lily floating past, perfectly white and ghostly. It brushed against her hand. As it did, her hand took on a life of its own and grabbed it.

Tamsyn opened her eyes. Opaque green water filled them. She was deep underwater, weeds tugging at her arms and legs, dragging her towards the bottom of the deep, dark pool. Her heart was hammering in her chest; she closed her eyes, ears ringing. Bubbles of air escaped from her lungs as she struggled.

Behind her closed eyes, there was a searing flash of white light. The ribbons of weeds that touched her skin were disintegrating to ash, only to be replaced by new ones rising up from the deep. Tamsyn thrashed her arms and legs, ripping at the whip-like ropes with her hands and kicking her feet. She saw a pallid face in the depths, wearing a look of anger and surprise. It was the woman from the riverbank, but she looked different now: beautiful, enshrouded with dark, flowing hair that extended out until she and the weeds were one. Hundreds of snaking vines reached for Tamsyn, but the face was receding.

She had no idea how long she had been underwater, but the increasing need to inhale told her she had run out of time. Tamsyn panicked. She had no idea which way was up. She looked around for the beautiful, enraged face. Her lungs screamed for oxygen. She opened her mouth in desperation, expelling the last bubbles of air from her chest. With a mighty heave, Tamsyn kicked towards where she thought the surface would be, her nostrils and mouth filling with water.

11

SOMETHING WICKED

Tamsyn limped back to Rosemount in the dark like a stinking stray cat that had been in a fight and lost. Desperate though she was for a hot bath, there was no time: she grabbed her grandmother's journals from the shelves to see if there was anything that could help her. What if that thing came to the house again? Tamsyn had no doubt that if she did, she would succeed in killing her.

After feverishly flipping through the journals, she came to one labelled *Protective Runes and Spells*. She stopped dead as a spark ignited inside her mind. A memory came back to her, so vivid she felt she could reach out and touch it. Her grandmother stood, hunched as she pointed to the runes on the brickwork of the old crumbling walls, showing her again and again the importance of blocking every place through which either a purely physical or a magical being might get in.

Tamsyn pored over her grandmother's elegant handwriting, committing the incantations to memory before heading out to Rosemount's perimeter. Whoever that woman in the woods had been, she had managed to evade even Sylvia's defences. Tamsyn scoured the outside walls again, reciting the spells over and over again, until carved runes glowed, orange and fierce. Despite her fear of the woman coming upon her at any moment, pure elation fizzed through her veins when she saw the glowing embers of the runes. She could still do it. She could still perform magic!

At dawn, she stumbled into the cottage, made herself tea, and took it back out to the veranda, where she collapsed onto the peeling wooden chair. Winnie leapt up onto her lap, scowling at her with irritation at having been left. She sniffed Tamsyn's clothes and promptly bounded back onto the floor.

Tamsyn leaned against the back of the chair, fighting a wave of nausea and exhaustion. She sipped the piping-hot tea and momentarily closed her eyes, listening to the sweet sound of the dawn chorus and fighting back tears. She knew she would be unable to sleep. She would not be safe until she discovered how and why that woman had got to Sylvia. Still, the birdsong threatened to pull her into slumber; that and the soft trickle of water from the stone statue in the garden, cascading, carrying her mind away.

She sat upright. *The statue.* If that woman in the river was some sort of water spirit, she could potentially use water as a means of getting into the house. Sylvia had written in her journal that the drains had smelled rotten. Perhaps she'd got into the house through the pipes? Or the fountain in the garden? But its water was sacred, Tamsyn knew: if she stopped it from flowing, the entire garden might die. She set down her teacup and ran through the garden to the foot of the statue, where she examined the green and black moss streaking down the marble face and breasts, like a road mapped out, and ending at her feet before it disappeared into the ground.

Salt. She heard the voice in her head ring clearly. Of course. Tamsyn hurried to the pantry to collect a large jar. She opened the huge bag of Morton's Iodized Salt and scooped up a generous load. *Never use sea salt for protection*: she heard Sylvia's voice and saw her wagging a finger; *it attracts sea dwelling creatures.* Tamsyn stood holding the jar of salt, relieved that her memories were starting to return, whilst the grief of losing her grandmother hit her anew.

She gathered herself and headed back outside. She poured out a ring of salt around the statue, but feared that it would not be enough. The water flowed into the ground, into the roots of every plant and tree that grew in Rosemount, which meant that the woman could appear from anywhere. Her mind raced, thinking of all the natural routes in and out of Rosemount. And what was to stop her from using the water pipes themselves?

She turned to see Winnie watching her. Scooping her up, she headed inside, where she took the quickest bath she could. As she scrubbed away the river grime and the dirt from the garden, grim flashes of the green-toothed woman's deathly face and rotting flesh tormented her. The copper pipes groaned inside the walls. Tamsyn watched a drip from the tap. She could not tell if it was a trick of the light, but the teardrop looked like it was turning black before her eyes.

She got out of the bath as quickly as she could. Still in her towel, she went to the basement and turned off the water to the house. Upstairs again, she put on warm, dry clothes and then restlessly paced back and forth, trying to calm herself. She ran through her options. Calling Dominic was out of the question. There was Bridie, but how did she know she could trust her? What if Bridie had had something to do with her grandmother's death, or knew more than she was letting on, and her next step was to get Tamsyn out of the way? The only other person she knew for sure she could trust was her old work friend Sarah. Perhaps she could stay with her in London while she figured things out.

Fetching pitta bread and taramasalata from the fridge, she laid them out on the kitchen worktop and then grabbed her mobile phone. Fingers shaking, she pulled up Sarah's number, but the service bars on the device remained non-existent. With a groan of frustration, she set the mobile aside and called the number from her grandmother's house phone. Heart racing, she waited while it rang out. Staring out of the window at the yews swaying in the breeze, she absentmindedly dabbed a chunk of bread into the pot of taramasalata. She was about to give up when Sarah picked up.

'Hello? Sarah speaking.' She sounded annoyed. Tamsyn could imagine her digging around at the bottom of her bag, trying to find the phone, only to see a number she didn't recognise.

'Hi, Sarah, it's Tamsyn. How are you?' Tamsyn could hear the rumble of a bustling restaurant. The old familiar sound set off a pang of longing inside her.

'Tam! So lovely to hear from you. I am well, thank you. So, how's everything been since the last time we spoke?' Sarah sounded genuinely happy and surprised to hear from her. They had been inseparable at work, and Tamsyn realised now how strange it had been not catching up every lunchtime over sushi and a Diet Coke.

'I'm still here, at my grandmother's. It's… okay. Are you busy? I hope you don't mind me calling?'

'No, please! Tell me everything! I want to hear it all,' Sarah replied eagerly.

Everything. Tamsyn wanted to laugh and cry. How on earth could she tell her any of this?

'It's a little weird being back here, if I'm honest,' she said wearily. 'I'm sorry I haven't been in contact much. It's been tougher than I thought it would be, going through my grandmother's things.' Tamsyn looked around the kitchen, feeling her unease about being in Rosemount begin to fade now that she was speaking to another person.

'I'm just having lunch with Emily,' said Sarah over the restaurant din. 'Sorry, it's so loud in here, but I can just about hear you! Sorry you're having a rough time of it. It's so hard, isn't it? I felt the exact same when I had to go to my grandmother's house after she died. It was so strange seeing all her things.' Tamsyn could hear Sarah talking to someone, Emily she assumed, asking her to order the spring rolls and matcha coffee. 'Sorry about that, Tam. Anyway, I didn't recognise your number when you called. Do you have a new phone?'

'No, I'm on the house phone. The signal is bad here. That's the other reason I've been so bad at keeping in touch. How is work?'

'Blimey, you must really be in the middle of nowhere!' Sarah laughed. 'Work is work, same as ever. Not the same since you left, of course. Your replacement seems pretty dull. Which means the boss loves her, naturally!'

Tamsyn's leg shook up and down restlessly. She was already stressed beyond belief, and this conversation wasn't helping. Even though Tamsyn had grown to realise that she was not cut out for the world of advertising, the idea of her successor being adored stung her in a way she did not think possible.

'And what about you?' Tamsyn asked, steering Sarah away from the topic.

Sarah paused. 'Um. Well, I'm up for a promotion,' she said hesitantly.

'Ah, Sarah, that's brilliant! Congratulations—you really deserve it!' Tamsyn said, and she meant it.

'Thank you. And, well, I don't care about the money. It's the title, isn't it? They're making me Director of Marketing, reporting in to the exec. I'll get a team and a company car. Maybe I could finally come and see you!'

Tamsyn knew there was no chance of Sarah wasting her weekend driving any further north than St Albans. 'That would be lovely,' she said.

'So, have you sorted the house? You've been gone ages! When are you coming back?'

'No, I—I'm not really sure what I want to do yet,' Tamsyn said, holding the phone with her shoulder while dabbing another piece of bread at the pink paste.

'Oh, you absolutely *have* to sell! Now is the best time! So many of my uni friends are moving north. You'll make a packet. People are really going for those cutesy old-world villages too.'

'I know. I will. It's just harder than I thought it would be, you know? Saying goodbye to my childhood home. There's so much history here. I can't help but think about what my grandmother would say.'

'Not to sound insensitive, but it's not about what she would have wanted, Tamsyn. She's not here any more. You have to do what's best for you. I'm sure that's what your grandmother would have wanted for you, too.'

'I don't know about that.' Tamsyn half-laughed, even though she wasn't making a joke. Suddenly she felt exhausted all over again. She was not sure where she had intended the conversation to go. Had she thought she could confide in Sarah, tell her she thought her grandmother had been killed? That she herself had just nearly been killed? She felt the cracks between her and her old friend widen even further. There was no way she could ask to go and stay with Sarah. Tamsyn watched as a large bee batted itself against the kitchen window, driven by the arrival of cooler air to seek a place to overwinter. Tamsyn felt a sudden urge to follow the bee, to get away from this house. She was jolted back to the present by Sarah's voice.

'You know,' said Sarah breezily, 'if you need money, I'm sure I could find some freelance work for you. Have you set yourself up on the portal as freelance? Just email me your details.'

'No—no. That's okay. I've got lots of work on,' Tamsyn said quickly. 'Thank you so much, though.' There was nothing she could think of that she wanted to do less. Even more so when it was work sent out of pity—even though she could have done with the funds. She had been living off the money she had saved for a deposit. Although she had been careful, she couldn't imagine she could survive on it for much more than a year.

'Well, if you change your mind…' Sarah trailed off, distracted, as the clink of cutlery on china and the rolling and swelling of conversations continued in the background.

'Can I ask you something?' Tamsyn said nervously. 'Have you heard from Dominic at all? Is he… okay?' She had no idea why the words came out of her mouth. The words of his voicemail flashed into Tamsyn's mind: *Sarah told me you've handed in your notice.*

'God no.' There was a brief pause before the recollection hit her. 'Although, I did see him one night, shortly after you left.'

'I see,' Tamsyn said. 'Did he seem okay?'

'To be honest, Tam, I always thought he was such a nice guy, but there he was, all over some girl at the bar. I think he's dealing with it just fine,' said Sarah.

Tamsyn took the phone into her other hand, leaning back against the counter. A little surprised, but still faintly relieved. Maybe that's why the texts had stopped, which for her could only be a good thing. 'That's good. I want him to be happy.'

'Yeah. But I still think you're best to forget him. He spoke to me about you. He was worried… We were *all* worried, the way you took off like that. He said he thought you might need some, you know, *help*.' Sarah paused. 'You know you can call me any time—really, Tamsyn. Any time, day or night.' Tamsyn knew Sarah was trying to be nice, but they both knew it was just words.

'Yeah, I know. Thanks. I'm absolutely fine. Erm… Did

Dominic look… hurt?' Tamsyn twisted the phone cord. There was a long pause on the other end of the line.

'Hurt? What do you mean? As I said… he looked fine to me.'

'No, I mean… physically hurt?'

'No, no. He was right as rain.'

'Did he say anything about the night I left?'

'Hmm. Yes, he did, actually. He told me he thought he would lose the deposit because the window was smashed. He said some thugs outside must have thrown a brick in. But he couldn't find anything. He said you cut your hands trying to clean up.'

Tamsyn breathed a sigh of relief.

'Anyway, Tam, my food has just arrived. Please keep in touch, won't you? And come visit us—we all miss you!'

'I will. Bye, Sarah. Say hi to everyone for me—' But she was already gone. Tamsyn's ears felt hot as she replaced the phone back into its cradle. She felt foolish for thinking she might have been able to ask to go and stay with Sarah. Although Tamsyn had gotten used to being entirely alone, it still stung to be reminded that she had no one to turn to when she needed help. *Perhaps I've done this to myself,* she thought. *Maybe I have pushed everyone away.*

But, she told herself, if she had pushed them away, it had been necessary. There was no way she had been able to share the reality of where she had come from, and what she had been through, with her old friends.

$$\sim$$

97

Rosemount had always been home to unearthly sounds, but now the banging of the pipes made her jump. She put the television on and curled up in a blanket with Winnie in an attempt to distract herself. Even with the fire lit, a chill lingered in the house, permeating her bones. The wooden frame of the cottage groaned as it shifted. Winnie arched her back, fur standing on edge, leaping off her and scuttling away upstairs.

On the coffee table lay *Water Sprites, River Nymphs and Goddesses of the Severn*, still open at the page she had been reading the night before. Flicking to the last page in the book, Tamsyn found the black-and-white portrait of the author, with a short biography:

> *Ellis Rowlands is one of the last practising Druids on the Isle of Anglesey, and the last surviving member of the Rowlands dynasty who have served the Anglesey community for thousands of years. As well as a lecturer, philanthropist and motivational speaker, Rowlands is a celebrated mountaineer, climbing all but two of the world's fourteen highest peaks.*

Ellis Rowlands. She recognised his name. And Anglesey. Sylvia and Tamsyn had enjoyed holidays there when she was a teenager, and Sylvia had always attended the annual Order of Witches and Druids conference. He had been there, she remembered now. He was slightly older than Tamsyn, but she remembered him being a prominent member of the Druidic Order. She heard Bridie's voice: *You need someone else, someone else outside of here*. Meaning Much Wenlock. Rowlands was part of the magical community, but not part of *this* community.

Tamsyn leaned forward and scrutinised the photo. His smiling eyes and perfect teeth didn't give much away. He had fine lines around his eyes but looked to be no older than his early forties.

She headed upstairs to find something warmer to wear. As she pulled her jumper over her head, she thought she saw something in the mirror. A flash of something dark. She turned abruptly. It was nothing, but goosebumps pricked Tamsyn's cold skin. That was the last straw, she told herself. She could not stand waiting around, jumping at the sight of her own shadow, in this cold, creaking place. She needed to get out of Rosemount as quickly as possible.

Throwing some clothes and her toothbrush into an overnight bag, Tamsyn dashed down the stairs. Grabbing her grandmother's latest journal, along with *Water Sprites, River Nymphs and Goddesses of the Severn* off the table, she shoved them into the bag. Heading into the kitchen, she picked up the phone and dialled 1 for Bridie.

'Ach, *Jesus*, who'th this now?' the old woman croaked down the mouthpiece after the ninth ring.

'Hi, Bridie, it's Tamsyn. Sorry to disturb you.'

'Whath's the matter then? Has something happened?' Her voice sounded muffled, and she was lisping her words.

'Yes, something's happened. I have to go somewhere for a few days. Would you be able to look after Winnie if I bring her over?'

There was a pause. 'She'll have to sthay upstairs. I havth

cats come to the back door. I don't want her getting out and fighting!'

'I'm sure she'll be fine with that.' Tamsyn looked around for Winnie, but she was lying low somewhere. 'I'll be round in fifteen.'

'Fiftheen! I haven't even got me teefth in!' Bridie protested.

'Thanks so much, Bridie. See you shortly!' Tamsyn put down the phone before Bridie could change her mind.

After twenty minutes spent finding and catching Winnie, Tamsyn waited at Bridie's front door. As she held the cat carrier, she could see Winnie's paws darting out of the holes in the grill, claws bared, positively apoplectic that she was being treated with such indignity.

Bridie answered the door in a kaftan. Thankfully her teeth were in, but she hadn't yet got round to brushing and taming her wild hair, which stood on end, defying gravity. She looked utterly peeved to be caught off guard.

'Thanks so much for doing this. It will only be for a couple of days.' Tamsyn handed over the box of cat food and placed Winnie's carrier down just inside the door. 'I've put her favourite blanket in there. She'll probably just sleep in there if you leave the door open. She can have one wet pouch per day, and as much dried food as she likes.' Tamsyn bent down and looked at Winnie through the door of the carrier. Her eyes were wide and scared.

'I love you, Winnie,' she said soothingly. 'I promise I won't be long.'

Bridie looked at Tamsyn with concern. 'Where are you going? What has happened?'

'I'm doing what you said. Finding someone outside of here. I need answers about all of this. Oh, and please don't go to Rosemount. It's not safe.'

'Not safe? Did you find something? About Sylvia's killer?'

'Yes, I saw her.' Bridie's jaw gaped and her teeth nearly fell out. Tamsyn pressed on. 'Don't take this the wrong way, Bridie, but... I can't tell you anything more than that. I really don't know who I can trust in Much Wenlock...'

Bridie looked gravely offended.

'I will call you when I've figured things out. One wet pouch a day and as much dried food as she wants,' Tamsyn repeated. She bent towards the cat carrier again. 'Please make sure you eat your dry food, okay, Winnie? I'll see you soon.' She stood up and took hold of the door handle. 'Thanks again, Bridie. I really appreciate this.'

Before Bridie could object, Tamsyn turned and bolted from the house as though she were on fire. She had no idea what information she could and couldn't trust Bridie with, and she'd rather her whereabouts weren't broadcast. Besides, any conversation she had with Bridie would cost her another hour at the very least.

PART TWO

I like spring, but it is too young. I like summer, but it is too proud. So, I like best of all autumn, because its leaves are a little yellow, its tone mellower, its colours richer, and it is tinged a little with sorrow and a premonition of death. Its golden richness speaks not of the innocence of spring, nor of the power of summer, but of the mellowness and kindly wisdom of approaching age. It knows the limitations of life and is content. From a knowledge of those limitations and its richness of experience emerges a symphony of colours, richer than all, its green speaking of life and strength, its orange speaking of golden content and its purple of resignation and death.

—Lin Yutang

12

THE SIREN

Earlier that year before the old crone's death, a grain of inspiration seeded itself inside Gavin, irritating him, like the early inception of a pearl. It led him to the library, where he trawled the archives looking for the right candidate. He had cross-referenced articles from local papers, dating back forty years, detailing local sightings. A strange woman seen in the River Severn... The tail of a monster spotted by a drunk walking along Shrewsbury's Quarry Park... He eventually narrowed down the area of the sightings and correlated them with a handful of bodies found in the same area along Shrewsbury's riverbank. They were mostly suicides and accidental drownings, and two murders. One of them was a perfect hit.

No one in the magical community had ever reported seeing the Siren. And if they *had* seen her, it certainly wouldn't have been reported in the local papers. Gavin held a tight ship. The local constabulary fed anything remotely untoward directly to him, and he made sure such information was disposed of with immediate effect. He had nothing in his ledger regarding this *thing*.

This Siren, then, must have been a woman who had found herself at the unfortunate mercy of Lady Severn herself: Sabrina. Nothing was known of the goddess or the spirits that dwelled in Sabrina's domain, but legend stated that Sabrina would take pity on drowned women, giving them renewed life as spirits of the river. Some were Sirens; some were half woman, half snake; others were water demons or nymphs. There were also spirits and Selkies and God knows what else down there.

It was a blog post from 2009 that piqued his interest. It told of a photograph taken by a young girl of her mother eating an ice cream against the backdrop of the sparkling river. On the opposite bank was a black figure. A woman standing, staring. Dripping black hair covered her face, and she was entirely cloaked in black. The image had gone semi-viral when it was posted on social media, and had sparked many conspiracy theories surrounding the identity of the chilling figure.

Gavin knew, as soon as he saw the fuzzy image, that the woman clothed in black must have been a soul with a hatchet to bury. He also suspected that in a former life she had been a witch. Civilians don't wander around in black cloaks. There was one individual, at the University of Bangor, who had hypothesized that these drowned witches became Sirens. These half-humans, half sea-serpents became the handmaidens of Sabrina, goddess of the River Severn, patrolling the murky depths and doing their mistress's bidding. It would certainly explain the various sightings of 'a large serpent tale in the water', always seen near or around the Quarry Park at dusk.

Since the Dark Ages, it had been explicitly outlawed for mortals, witches or druids to make contact with these immortal beings. It never ended well. Especially with Sirens, who were the most dangerous, devious and manipulative creatures of all. Gavin had read with intense fascination and disgust how their mere beauty could leave the strongest men whimpering in the dirt. Their songs could turn a man against his family, his country and all he held dear with a mere whisper. If he was going to seek out this supposed Siren, he would have to send someone with nothing to lose.

Gavin left the library on that clear March morning, nodding and smiling warmly at the people he passed in Shrewsbury town. Most nodded back at him in recognition of his years of faithful service on the council. Some, he noted, appeared to have no idea who he was, despite the library being named in his honour. He remembered thinking to himself that the town was going to rack and ruin. That's when he'd flicked through his phone and called the contact he had saved as 'the Apprentice'.

13
DRUIDS' ISLE

The road to Anglesey snaked along the coastline, the sea glittering in the cool November morning as Tamsyn's car raced by. The dense greenery of the surrounding hilltops was slowly becoming peppered with yellow, orange and red.

Tamsyn had not been to Anglesey since she was fifteen years old. Known as the Island of Druids, it was where the Order held an annual fair for its executive members. Witches were chosen as representatives of their coven from up and down the country, and Tamsyn's grandmother had always made the cut.

Tamsyn's knuckles turned white from gripping the steering wheel so tightly. She thought about the last time she had been in Anglesey. Sylvia had always dragged Tamsyn to Llanddwyn Beach to meet with her friends before the conference began the following day. When Tamsyn was younger, she would sit next to her grandmother, building sandcastles or eating ice cream, while Sylvia caught up with witches and druids belonging to Anglesey's Occult Council. But by the time she neared sixteen, she found she could no longer mask her boredom and impatience with it all. Thankfully, for the first time, Sylvia hadn't insisted that she remain with them, listening to their conversation and taking it all in. She'd waved Tamsyn off with dismissive irritation, allowing her to explore the beach on her own.

Relieved and excited to be alone, Tamsyn made her way to the edge of the white dunes, towards the wind-stripped Corsican pine trees lining the beach, and set off along a path that led into the trees. Further inland, the forest became dense and black. Tamsyn looked back at the group, sat huddled in a circle against the wind. She could just make out their hunched figures, sipping tea from the lids of thermos flasks. Sylvia's white hair billowed wildly in the strong wind, her sunglasses masking her expression.

Climbing a steep path that led through the trees and out to a cove on the other side of the bay, she was relieved to see that she had the beach to herself. Picking her way amongst the seaweed and slick rocks, she bent down to examine a crab stranded in a rockpool.

She sat for a while, listening to the crashing waves, keeping the crab company while it waited for the sea to return. She jumped when she heard a familiar voice behind her.

'What have you got there?'

Tamsyn stood up in surprise. Turning, she recognised a man from the conference. He was always a keynote speaker, and every year his tedious lectures on Anglo-Saxon magic overran, until the audience squirmed in their seats. His name was Gavin Hardcastle, an executive member of the Druid Grove. Sylvia had always made sure Tamsyn memorised everyone's name, so as not to appear rude.

He appeared to be no more than his late fifties, with dyed brown hair combed neatly backwards and a polo shirt stretched tight across a large pot belly hanging over his belted chinos.

'Sorry, did I startle you?' He grinned at her, a large smile that didn't quite reach his eyes. Tamsyn quickly shook her head. Unsure of what to say or do, she folded her arms and looked out to sea.

'You really shouldn't wander off on your own, you know. There are things out there that could lure you in.' He, too, looked out at the wild waves, attempting his best benign and wistful expression.

'Will you be joining us at the guild party tonight?' He turned back to her, shoving his hands in his pockets against the wind.

'Err. Y-yes. I think so.' Tamsyn, still on the cusp of being a young adult, was still not sure how to navigate speaking to adults, particularly older men.

'Come, sit with me.' He gestured to an outcrop of large, jagged rocks. Unsure of how to say no without seeming rude, she followed him. He pulled up the legs of his trousers as he sat down on the edge of a smooth boulder, worn by the onslaught of the rain and sea. Tamsyn remained standing, feeling like the crab trapped in the pool, or, more accurately, like a small fish trapped alongside it.

'Don't be shy.' He tapped the rock next to him. 'I won't bite.' He flashed the same grin.

Gingerly perching on the edge of a sharp rock, Tamsyn sat and twisted her fingers together in her lap. She desperately wanted to make her excuses and leave. She hated herself in that moment, loathed her crippling shyness and inability to speak up.

'The last time I saw you, you were this big,' he said jovially, holding his hand flat three feet from the ground.

Tamsyn half-laughed nervously. *What is he talking about?* she thought with repulsion. He saw her here and in Much Wenlock all the time.

'It's great to see young witches such as yourself attending these events. We are really low on the ground in terms of youth volunteers. You know, I have set up a great training programme, working with disadvantaged kids across North Wales. We really need young people like you. These kids don't want to see those geriatrics telling them what to do.' He nodded back in the direction of the group.

Tamsyn smiled politely and looked away. 'I would have to ask my grandma,' she replied, looking out to sea.

'I have a holiday home here, you know. Very beautiful place. You would be welcome to stay any time to do some work experience. I can talk to Sylvia for you, if you like? It would look really impressive on your CV,' he said.

Tamsyn could feel him staring at her. The blood rushed to her cheeks.

'You've grown into a beautiful young witch.' He moved closer, brushing her hair off her face and behind her ear. She froze. He shifted closer, putting his arm around her shoulder. Tamsyn stiffened, her mind racing. She was in danger. His hand moved down, lightly brushing against her t-shirt with his fingertips, gripping harder as he cupped her left breast. In one quick movement he pulled her to him. She turned her head away and he kissed her on the cheek.

Tamsyn stood up abruptly.

'I think my grandmother is calling me.' Petrified, she couldn't even look at him. She turned and ran, her heartbeat thundering in her head.

Later that afternoon, when Sylvia and Tamsyn returned to their holiday let, Tamsyn thought she was going to explode. Red-faced, angry and ashamed, she had relayed to Sylvia what had happened on the beach. Sylvia sat motionless, thinking.

After a time, she stood up, keeping her back to Tamsyn and looking out of the glass doors at the incoming tide.

Tamsyn watched, waiting. Her pulse hadn't slowed since the encounter.

'Well? Aren't you going to say something?' she asked angrily, unable to contain herself any longer.

'I told you not to go wandering off where I can't see you!' Sylvia replied. Her voice was hard and hot, reflecting the anger in Tamsyn's own voice back at her.

'Oh, so it's my fault? How dare I walk by myself? I was *asking* for it?' Tamsyn couldn't believe what she was hearing. She waited for Sylvia to say something.

Instead, the older woman sighed irritably, walked over to the armchair, sat down and picked up her knitting. 'Well, there's nothing to be done,' she concluded.

Tamsyn stared at her in disbelief. 'We should tell the council!' she shouted.

Sylvia tutted. 'The council won't be able to do anything.

Gavin Hardcastle is an executive, soon to be chairman of the Much Wenlock Council. We will just create more trouble for ourselves.' She continued working on her pattern, the needles clicking rhythmically.

Tamsyn stood motionless, the growing sense of dread tying her stomach in knots.

'Y-you *have* to tell them! Can't you speak to someone? If you tell them, they might stop him from being chairman!'

'Don't be so naïve, Tamsyn,' Sylvia snapped. 'That is not the way the world works. Boys will be boys. It happens to all of us at some point. You just have to know how to handle yourself, and to know what situations to avoid. Take this as a learning opportunity.' Sylvia did not look at her. Tamsyn had the sudden feeling that maybe this *was* all her fault.

'He shouldn't be able to get away with this.' Hot tears pricked the corners of her eyes, before spilling down her cheeks, hot and salty, and running over her top lip.

'These things happen, Tamsyn. You cannot avoid it. I know, it's not nice. What matters is how you learn to handle yourself. It's hard to understand now, but trust me, it is character building.' Sylvia's tone was more soothing now, her half-moon glasses perched on her nose as her needles clicked together, veined hands working.

Tamsyn's stomach trembled as she clenched her fists into a ball.

'I will not accept it. Ever. I will ruin him,' she said through gritted teeth. The sound of glass smashing made their heads jerk towards the coffee table. The vase housing the pink lilies had fallen to the floor.

Sylvia's needles halted. She gave Tamsyn an angry, piercing stare.

'Enough,' she warned. 'You don't want to do anything… *silly*. We've had enough of that lately.' Then she laughed as though vaguely amused. 'Just forget about it now. I'll clear this up. Start getting ready for tonight.'

'I'm not going to the stupid party!' Tamsyn stormed out of the room, slamming the door as the vase water spread steadily over the floor.

Tamsyn recalled that she had sat in her room for the rest of the night, fearing punishment from Sylvia for refusing to go to the guild party, and terrified that Gavin Hardcastle would come to the place they were staying if he found out she was there alone.

Now, as an almost thirty-year-old, she raged. Raged for her fifteen-year-old self who had no one to turn to and that the advice from the only guiding force in her life was to 'keep calm and carry on'. She vowed that if she were ever to have a son or daughter, she would never dismiss them. She would protect and honour them with every fibre of her being.

But what had Sylvia meant by *You don't want to do anything silly?* That there *had been enough of that lately?* Tamsyn thought that most of her memories would be back by now, but there were still unanswered questions. Like, why had she been made to forget she was a witch in the first place?

Tamsyn glanced at the speedometer as the steering wheel juddered in protest. The needle was hovering at eighty miles an hour. She slowly eased her foot off the accelerator. As the car rounded a corner, the trees cleared to reveal the magnificent Menai Bridge. As Fig rolled over the huge suspension bridge and headed towards the town, Tamsyn noted that the tide was still out.

When she reached Menai, Tamsyn pulled up outside a small coffee shop. Grabbing the book from her bag, she headed inside. A quick internet search had revealed that Ellis Rowlands lived somewhere near here, and held regular lectures at the School of Ocean Sciences at Bangor University.

Tamsyn ordered a coffee from the man at the counter. He didn't speak to her, but seemed polite enough, giving her a curt nod. He had huge shoulders, a thick dark beard and black bushy eyebrows. As he made the coffee, Tamsyn marvelled at his intricate tattoos. White and blue foaming waves crashed and swirled around his forearms, but the sleeves of his shirt hid the crest of the wave.

She read another chapter of *Water Sprites, River Nymphs and Goddesses of the Severn*, or pretended to, as she racked her brains about what she was going to say to Professor Rowlands.

She finished her coffee and approached the young man at the counter.

'Hi there. I have tickets to attend a lecture at the School of Ocean Sciences,' she fibbed. 'Is it possible to walk from here?'

The barista glanced down at the book in Tamsyn's arm, then pointed out the door. 'Up that way and turn left.' He turned back to cleaning the spout of the milk steamer.

'Thank you.' She turned to leave.

'If you want my advice, you don't want to waste your time with any of that nonsense.'

Tamsyn turned back to answer him, but he had his back to her, stacking cups onto the shelves.

14

THE CROW'S NEST

G avin walked down a narrow alleyway, paved with uneven stone and surrounded by crumbling brick walls. Ahead lay a set of steel gates, wrought with twining leaves that acted as spikes to stop intruders from climbing them. The sensors whirred as they swung open on to a cobbled stone courtyard littered with pots that over-flowed with ivy and hellebores.

After his mother's death, Gavin had renamed the house the Crow's Nest, and had a bespoke sign made. Between holly trees, the house loomed, narrow and tall. The frontage wasn't too impressive, but the real beauty lay at the back of the house.

Climbing the steps, he glanced upward, scanning the sky. The air was changing, turning with a sharpness, signalling the threat of winter. Turning the key in the vast blue door, he stepped into the foyer, placed his briefcase on the tiled floor, hung his hat and coat on the pegs, and placed his shoes in their designated cubby. Gavin could never tire of returning home to his Victorian townhouse. The stained-glass gothic windows overlooked the Dingle, the Quarry Park and the River Severn that ran through the heart of the town.

Taking out a large bunch of keys from the drawer of the bureau, he made his way inside. Padding over to the corner of the sitting room, he lifted up the edge of the plush carpet and unlocked the small door that he had built into the floorboards, then lowered his arm inside. After a moment of fishing around, he pulled up the wad of paper reports that had come from the archbishop.

Gavin made tea and settled into his La-Z-Boy. Inside the report there was a sheaf of black-and-white photographs. He pulled out one showing a 1991 Nissan Figaro heading up the A55. This put a serious spanner in the works, he thought, as he sipped on his piping-hot tea. The clock on the wall ticked laboriously, the gold pendulum swinging in what seemed like slow motion. Gavin surveyed the room. It seemed lifeless. If his mother were here, she'd know exactly what to do.

The doorbell rang, causing him to spill the still-scalding tea onto his hand. He swore as he made his way to the front door, wiping his wet, stinging fingers on his trouser leg.

Roy stood on the front step, looking as happy and bewildered as ever. What must it be like, Gavin wondered, to be so blissfully unaware, so utterly thick, that anything that happens to you in life rolls off like water from wax?

'Royston. What can I do you for?'

'Hullo Gavin. Bridie thought you might like some stew.' Roy held out a red cast-iron pot, streaked down the sides with years of burned gravy.

'How kind. She really shouldn't have.' Gavin moved aside. 'Do come in.'

He took the pot and carried it through to the kitchen. He would absolutely not be eating the muck sent by some old spinster, probably to poison him. Or worse.

Roy made his own way to the sitting room. He walked to the window and admired the view. 'Never gets old, I bet! If my Gladys saw this view, she'd absolutely die!'

'Then you should bring her over,' Gavin joked. Roy looked offended, but Gavin knew Roy had been secretly poisoning his poor pathetic wife for years. Not that she didn't deserve it; from what Gavin remembered of her she was a real harpy.

Roy plonked himself down onto the sofa and looked expectantly at Gavin.

'I don't suppose I could trouble you for a drop of sherry? I have a little tickle in me throat.' He patted underneath his chin to illustrate.

'Yes, of course,' Gavin replied, expertly hiding any irritation he felt. He went to the sideboard, took out the bottle of cheap sherry he kept for such guests, and poured some into a glass.

Handing it to Roy, he waited for him to elaborate about what this intrusion was in aid of. He watched Roy slowly raise the glass to his lips. He sucked the sherry through his teeth, before loudly smacking his tongue and sighing in appreciation.

'I do love sherry. Though I must say, I would love to try that Versos 1891 you keep in the cellar.' Roy's blue eyes twinkled as he shot Gavin a wink.

The sheer audacity of the man, to think he would ever deserve a glass from an £8,000 bottle of sherry. 'Maybe next time. How can I help you, Roy?'

'Oh, err... yes. Bridie told me to give you this. She thought it might be useful.' He fished around in the inside pocket of his moth-eaten tweed jacket and handed Gavin a filthy-looking envelope. It was sealed with dark green wax, but to his surprise it had been stamped with a generic seal instead of her usual swirling initials, B.D. That reminded him: he must look into getting one of those seals made.

Roy held up his hands. 'Bridie said it was very important that you open it alone. Doesn't want me seeing, I suppose. Like I'm going to tell anyone!' He laughed and didn't seem at all offended by Bridie's insinuation that he couldn't be trusted with seeing what was inside. His eyes roamed the room, and he let out a faint whistle in appreciation of the grand surroundings.

'Thank you, Roy. Is there anything else?'

'Oh—oh, yes. These are from me.' He produced a brown paper envelope. 'More pictures—of the Pride girl.'

'Great work,' said Gavin, taking them from him. 'Thanks, Roy. That everything?' He got to his feet. 'Sorry to rush you. Lots on, you know?'

Roy looked shocked. 'No, no. That's all, I think. I was hoping to sit and enjoy your lovely view here.' He gestured towards the window.

'I really do have a lot to do I'm afraid. Maybe some other time.'

'Ah... um. Okay.' Roy downed his sherry as Gavin waited impatiently by the door.

'Oh, one more thing,' Roy said as he hobbled to the entrance.

'What's that Roy?'

'Bridie needs her pot back by tomorrow.'

'Will do Roy,' Gavin said as he slammed the front door behind him and scurried back to his chair.

Putting on his reading glasses, he tore open the envelope. The letter within was written in spidery, shaking handwriting.

Thought this might come in handy. Tamsyn gone to Anglesey. Not sure when back.

Gavin studied the pencil marks underneath. They were instructions on how to heat the stew.

'Silly old bat.' He screwed up the paper. She hadn't told him a damn thing he didn't already know. He was wholly undecided as to whether to trust her. On the one hand, she had offered up the information, but at the end of the day she would always be Sylvia Pride's best friend.

Tamsyn had gotten away, and he was running out of time and funds.

Gavin waited until the dead of night before making his way down to the river. He already felt out of his depth. He *detested* getting his hands dirty.

Every year in March, during the vernal equinox, the town held a memorial ceremony for the drowned witches. Wreaths of spring flowers and floating candles were placed into the river, along with dried fish, salted meats and poached fruits. This year, he had left a message inside one of the urns… and to his surprise, it had worked. Two months later, Sylvia Pride was dead. Now he could finally buy Rosemount as soon as it came to market. But then, that runt Tamsyn had come back, and, worse, was making no signs of selling up.

That's when he had had the idea to send that fool Colin, whom he called 'the Apprentice,' to mark those sheep. Making Colin think he would teach him a bit of magic and allow him on to the council was all the carrot he'd needed to dangle. Gavin had been sure that the idiots on the council would easily swallow the notion that Tamsyn, the newly returned outcast, was responsible.

But alas, they hadn't taken the bait. So when that hadn't got rid of her, he'd sent Colin directly to the Siren. It just went to show, he told himself, if you want something done, you've got to do it yourself.

Searching in his back pocket now, he found the incantation he had copied out earlier, along with the pencilled diagrams that needed to be set alight at the exact time he said the incantation. This summoning spell was ancient witch magic, not something he was accustomed to using. But desperate times called for desperate measures.

It was customary to bring an offering to a river spirit, especially if you wanted something in return. But for what he wanted to achieve, enraging the creature was a necessary evil. Although Gavin happily enforced the rules against using summoning spells and other outlawed magical practices, he enjoyed playing fast and loose with the rules himself. What the council didn't know wouldn't hurt them, and he was willing to do what he had to for power.

Nevertheless, the idea of using this kind of magic repelled

him. He had been raised in a strict household, where the lore of Science, Philosophy and Politics were his mother's religion. However, Gavin had learned a lot since dear Mummy's departure; not least among the lessons was that letting your integrity reign led to nothing but closed doors. He reread the words several times, committing the spell to memory.

Finally, he stood, holding the paper over the water.

From the river that flows east to west,
I summon a servant of Sabrina,
Hear my plea, and aid me in my quest.

Gavin took out a box of matches. Trying to hold the paper over the water and strike a match at the same time was clearly not something he'd thought through. After he struck the first one, it ignited for a moment before guttering and extinguishing in the wind. He swore, fumbling to get another. He struck it, this time nearly losing his grip on the paper. He grasped at the falling paper, dropping the match into the water.

Gavin felt a surge of anger swelling in his stomach. This was the Apprentice's fault for not making sure the Siren had killed Tamsyn when it had had the chance.

He crouched down, striking another match and holding it in his cupped hand. He recited the incantation again, quickly and nervously.

From the river that flows east to west,
I summon a servant of Sabrina,
Hear my plea, and aid me in my quest.

He held the match to the paper; the flame took a moment to catch, the edges smouldering with a tinge of orange before turning black. He watched as the flame spread, down, up and across the pencil lines, before reducing the paper to a smudge of charred remains. Gavin said the incantation for the third time before finally dropping what was left of the paper into the water.

He watched and waited. After a few minutes, he decided to sit and wait on the muddy riverbank. The night was silent and black. The mud felt cold and wet beneath him. He looked up and down the river, taking in its slow-moving churn. That was when it was at its most dangerous, he thought. You could see the power beneath the surface. If you were to step into it, it would pull you under that calm surface and never let you go.

The mist began to thicken. He felt certain the spell hadn't worked. Magic was a lengthy process, one that took years of practice and study. The witches sometimes got lucky, but mostly they took coincidences as verification that they had supernatural abilities. He sighed in disappointment. Ah well. He would go back to the Crow's Nest and adhere to his logical approaches in order to find an answer.

Gavin stood to leave. He looked out one last time and saw that the mist hanging over the water was being disturbed somehow. He squinted into the darkness and saw something moving through the water. Swirling white mist curled around the surface as it drew closer. The water glowed with an eery purple haze; he could barely make out a sound as it drew nearer to the edge of the bank.

Gavin's heart pounded as the water churned, and

suddenly the Siren broke the surface of the water. He could see her clearly now. She was the most striking woman he had ever seen.

She did not speak. She stared implacably back at him with large hazel eyes, glinting like a cat's eyes in headlights. Her wet hair hung in long, dark waves on her olive skin. She rose from the water until her waist was above the surface. Around her, he could see the water lapping against something large, monstrously large, just under the surface. *A tail.* It writhed in the water around her, twitching with muscular strength, as if a huge snake were moving in to consume her.

He had never seen anything like her. He had clearly underestimated the situation, and despite himself, he felt paralysed with fear.

Holding his hands up in supplication, Gavin turned his eyes away from her face.

'My apologies,' he called out. 'I did not mean to disturb you.'

The trembling water parted, and the end of her tail whipped the surface.

She was staring at him, waiting. At last she spoke.

'This is the third time I have been summoned by a human. We do not do your bidding.'

Gavin felt his head turning, betraying him. He tried desperately to look away, but he could not prise his eyes away from her extraordinary beauty. He felt his feet take a step towards the water's edge.

'Please. I mean you no harm. I merely seek your help.' Gavin willed his arms to move; he tried to bring his hands towards his eyes. They hung uselessly at his sides. His limbs felt like stone. Her pull was irresistible. If he could not look away, she would lure him into the water and he would never come out again.

Gavin used every ounce of strength to close his eyes. Even then, he saw her face, burned into his retinas. She was smiling, an angry, hateful smile. She despised him. She thought he was pathetic. He thought of the Crow's Nest. What would become of it? What would happen to his mother's things? Would they erect a statue of him in the town centre?

Her magnetic pull bore down on him. Something grazed against his leg and he opened his eyes momentarily, making sure to keep his head down. The gigantic, scaled tail had encircled him on the bank. Part of him wanted her to take him. He longed for her. She was beautiful. Her power was intoxicating. Maybe she would make him her plaything, he thought. For how long, though, before she devoured the flesh from his bones? To his horror, he was becoming aroused.

'Don't touch me, vile snake!' he spat. His breathing was ragged with fear. He turned his body, willing it to move with everything he could muster. He let out a guttural scream as he shouted at himself, telling his legs to run up the bank. Still, they did not move, as if they had already accepted that running was futile.

'You seek my help, yet you bring no offering. You have come to your death.'

Gavin was distracted as the tail tightened around his legs; his hand brushed against his pocket. He felt the outline of his keys, attached to his pocket knife. *Come on, fight, damn you*, he pleaded with himself. His hand clasped the familiar shape, flicking out the blade.

'Together, we could change everything,' he cried. 'If you help me, we can achieve something extraordinary!' He willed his fist to clasp the handle tighter.

'We do not do the bidding of mortals,' the Siren repeated. There was anticipation in her voice: she would soon satisfy her hunger.

Do it, Hardcastle. Do it now, you pathetic worm! Too scared to open his eyes, Gavin stabbed wildly at the tail encircling him. One of the jabs must have done damage, because a deafening screech rang inside his head. He felt the massive muscled appendage constrict further, and then a searing pain lashed the back of his head. She coiled around him, gripping tighter and tighter. As he cried out in agony, she used the opportunity to get a better purchase around his chest. The spiral of the tail wrung him tightly as she pulled him towards the river.

The air in his lungs had been expelled by her crushing strength. Gavin went loose. He stopped fighting and allowed himself to languish in her exquisite power.

His eyes were half-closed, but he could almost taste the sickly-sweet scent of her. As she drew him closer, he felt her hot breath on his neck. Her lips were open and expectant, drooling in anticipation. He fought the visceral, stirring realisation that he *wanted* her to devour him. What if he succumbed? Let her take him, rip him apart, so he could be part of her…

No. He had vowed, long ago, that a woman would never control him. His mother had done so for far too long. He would make this thing pay—he would make them all his servants. Bridie, Tamsyn, this water-worm. Gavin used the last of his strength to inhale sharply. He fought the fugue she was using to suppress his will. Grasping his pocket knife, he slashed her open. She screamed and Gavin felt her muscles slacken. Her high-pitched wail echoed across the river, reverberating along the sides of the riverbank. He dared to open his eyes now. Making a slash across the palm of his hand, he buried it into the wound he had made in her scales and intoned the final part of the spell.

Sangues meus sanguine tuo;
Dominus ad Servum,
Vitam nos tram vi i obligo!

Gavin felt his head hit the ground, and then the world went dark.

15
ELLIS

The auditorium was nearing full capacity as Tamsyn found a seat near the back. The lights dimmed, causing the chatter from the audience to die down. A dark-haired man walked into the spotlight and over to the lectern. His brown eyes surveyed the audience before he cleared his throat.

'Good afternoon. As most of you know, my name is Professor Ellis Rowlands. It seems we have a full house today. I'm glad to see Ocean Sciences is so popular.' Several members of the audience tittered, although he didn't seem to be making a joke. Tamsyn noticed that the entire two front rows were all women, staring adoringly up at him.

Rowlands pointed a small remote at the projector screen behind him. It showed an image of a snaking river, its various tributaries bleeding away and into it, like veins and ventricles criss-crossing a forearm. The title read 'The Lost Village of Llanwddyn, by Professor Ellis Rowlands, BSc, MSc, PhD'.

'The River Severn or, in Welsh, Hafren, is our longest

river here in Britain.' He clicked to the next slide, revealing a detailed map.

'As you can see here, the source of the Severn begins on the slopes of Plynlimon, and flows for one hundred and eighty miles in a semi-circular route and out into the Bristol Channel.' He clicked to the next slide, a picture of a beautiful gothic tower in the middle of a still lake, surrounded by autumn trees.

'You will no doubt recognise the picturesque Lake Vyrnwy. The lake was created in 1889, when the village of Llanwddyn was completely submerged underwater to create a dam to provide drinking water for the city of Liverpool. However, the citizens of Llanwddyn were not consulted, and despite petitions being raised against it, the Liverpool Corporation Waterworks forged ahead with the reservoir.'

The next image showed the reservoir today, the low water level revealing the tops of buildings and the bell tower of an old church. Tamsyn gasped quietly: a ghostly underwater village.

The next slide showed a sketch of a small church.

'This is St John's Church in 1874, originally built in the thirteenth century by the Knights Hospitallers. The Llanwddyn community were given very little time to save anything they could from their beloved historic landmark. The community's forsaken church was rebuilt within a few days, with little to no regard to maintaining the original features. The villagers had to exhume the dead from the churchyard and bury them in the new St Wyddn's Church, provided by the Liverpool Corporation, as quickly as possible. On 22nd November 1989, the village was gone forever.'

Some members of the audience scribbled in notebooks, while others tapped on laptops.

Professor Rowlands clicked the remote again. 'The next slide shows a black-and-white photograph of the original church before it was flooded. Outside the building, to the right, is the only existing image of the Davies sisters.

'I'm sure many of you have heard of the Davies sisters, Gwendolen and Margaret. They were the granddaughters and heiresses of one of Britain's greatest industrialists, David Davies. Although much is known about the world's richest spinsters, little is known about the third figure in this picture. It is rumoured to be their sister, Maud Davies.

'Now, although Maud has been written out of history entirely, recently discovered papers show that an M. Davies purchased the Vrynwy Hotel.'

Tamsyn opened Rowlands' book, which was sitting in her lap, and scribbled *Vrynwy Hotel* in the back in case she ever got the chance to visit one day.

Ellis Rowlands continued with his lecture to an enraptured audience, detailing a brief history of the Severn to date and how Vyrnwy's reservoir flowed into the Severn and through Shropshire. As he concluded and the lights came up, Tamsyn remained in her seat as everyone around her stood to leave. She watched Rowlands gathering his papers from the lectern, as several female students gathered around to speak to him.

Tamsyn concluded that it would be a while before they had finished twirling their hair and blushing as they asked their questions.

'Excuse me?' A gawky male student who had been sitting next to her had doubled back. 'Can I ask, what book is that?'

'Oh, this?' Tamsyn held it up with the cover facing him.

'Yes. Can I ask where did you buy it from? I have all of Dr Rowlands' books, but I have never seen that one.'

'I found it... in the library.'

'Ah, okay.' He peered round at the spine of the book. 'Can I ask what the reference number is?'

Tamsyn paused and then turned the spine towards him so he could read the numbers her grandmother had printed on it, knowing that the book would forever remain a mystery to him.

'Great. Thanks.' He noted down the title and numbers in his notebook. 'A weird title... I look forward to reading it.' The young man headed out of the auditorium with the crowd.

Tamsyn watched him go and then hastily stowed the book under her arm, worried that she had made a mistake in bringing it. Making her way to the bar that overlooked the foyer, she made herself comfortable in a leather bucket armchair and opened it, this time keeping the title hidden from prying eyes. The next chapter caught her attention: it was entitled 'The Legend of Ginny Greenteeth.' Her eyebrows rose as she read the short introduction.

A river hag, known throughout Liverpool, Lancashire and Staffordshire as Jenny or Jinny Greenteeth, her other names include Ginny Greenteeth, or Wicked Jenny in Shropshire and Cheshire. Thought to be a common folkloric tale dating from the 19th century to warn children away from water, particu-

larly water that appears solid due to the abundance of duckweed.

Could it really be a coincidence that the creature that had nearly killed her had had those horrible green teeth? Could Ginny Greenteeth and that half-rotten woman be one and the same?

Before she could gather her thoughts, she spotted Professor Rowlands exiting through the swivel doors. He walked quickly, as if hurriedly trying to avoid any more questions from eager female students. She closed the book with a snap, leapt to her feet and hurried after him. She almost had to jog, just catching up with him at the end of the car park.

'Excuse me, Mr Rowlands?'

His shoulders rose in visible tension before he turned round, managing to meet her with a smile that expertly masked any annoyance he must have felt. A cool wind had picked up, and it was starting to drizzle.

'I'm so sorry to bother you,' Tamsyn said, panting slightly. 'You probably don't remember me; my name is Tamsyn Pride. I used to attend the... the conference here in Anglesey. With my grandmother, Sylvia?'

His eyes widened momentarily before he glanced around.

'Um, yes, of course. I remember Sylvia well. I remember you too—head always in a book.' He smiled politely and put out his hand.

She shook it, scrutinising his face. His eyes gave away nothing. He caught sight of *Water Sprites, River Nymphs and Goddesses of the Severn* under her arm. She continued, 'I attended your lecture. I read your book too. I was wondering whether I could ask you some questions?'

'Did you bring that in there?' he asked worriedly.

'Yes. I'm sorry,' she said. She could see he was confused but mostly annoyed. She definitely had made a mistake, then.

'My apologies, but I'm afraid I really can't stop. I'm about to walk home.' He glanced at his watch with concern. 'It's getting rather close to the bone. The tide will be in soon.'

'I have a car,' she offered.

Rowlands looked extremely uncomfortable.

'Please. I really need to speak with you. Today.'

'I'm sorry, really. Can you send me an email?' He started walking away. 'If I don't get back in twenty minutes the path will be under and I will be stranded on the island for the night.'

'My car is just here. I wouldn't normally be so bold, but I think I'm in danger and I would really appreciate your help.'

Ellis looked around the car park again.

'Okay, but quickly, please. I won't make it on foot now anyway.'

Tamsyn led the way to the little Nissan. Professor Rowlands continued looking around anxiously to see if anyone was there to see him getting into her car.

Tamsyn turned on the wipers as the rain began to batter the windshield. Rowlands directed Tamsyn as they followed small, winding streets.

'You really shouldn't get into your car with a stranger, you know,' he told her. 'And you definitely shouldn't go to their house alone.' He quickly glanced at her as she squinted though the heavy rain beating down on the glass. His voice had no discernible accent, other than it was perhaps very faintly Welsh.

'I know. At least you're not a complete stranger. Don't worry; people know I'm here and that I have come to see you.' That was a lie. She had, however, left a sticky-note next to the phone with his name on it and the date she'd left. Just on the off chance that he did murder her, at least the police would know exactly who had done it.

The road turned right down a narrow alleyway before descending into a gravel track. Parts of it had seen better days; in places, the sea had eroded the stones and tarmac, which appeared to have been re-laid over and over again. Ellis hadn't been exaggerating; the tide was coming in quickly. Fig's tyres were sending up a spray from four inches of sea water that now covered the track.

They were headed towards a tiny island, enshrouded on all sides by trees. As they neared it, the path sloped upwards.

'Don't you keep a boat in case you get stranded?' Tamsyn asked.

'I did,' he replied. 'Until it broke free from its moorings in the last storm. I haven't got around to replacing it,' he said distractedly.

The road wound through dense trees already bereft of their leaves, black, gnarled and ancient. Finally, they rounded a corner and saw a low, squat building, with severe modernist angles, sitting nestled in the trees. The face of the house looked out to sea. It was completely clad in pine, with huge dark-framed windows; it was nothing like any of the buildings she had seen in the area. The mailbox at the entrance read *Ravenscourt*, in delicate forged letters.

Tamsyn followed Professor Rowlands out of the car. Covering their heads, they ran towards the entrance through the driving rain, while trying to avoid the huge puddles that had accumulated at the doorway. As Rowlands swiped a key-card to open the front door, Tamsyn looked up at the trees behind them. The wind caused them to sway wildly, and in their branches dozens of cawing ravens flapped and shifted in their nests.

The heavy steel and pine door swung open to reveal a large foyer. A looming carving stood opposite the door, a huge slab of stone etched with runes that had almost disappeared inside itself. As soon as the heavy-duty door closed behind them, the atmosphere was one of intense silence, but also of complete tranquillity.

'Can I take your coat?' the professor asked, holding out his hand.

'Thank you,' she said. Beads of water dripped from the coat as she handed it to him, marring the highly polished floor.

'Can I get you a hot drink? I don't have anything with caffeine in the house, I'm afraid. I'm not used to having guests. I have an assortment of green tea, matcha, herbal teas, chai?' Although he was clearly uncomfortable with having an unexpected guest, Tamsyn appreciated him trying to make her feel at ease.

'A chai tea would be perfect, thank you.'

'Please, make your way into the lounge. The only thing I ask is that you leave your shoes by the door.' Ellis gestured towards a sunken, open-plan living area, and Tamsyn made her way over to it, craning her neck to look around. The outside of the house had appeared deceptively small; inside, the ceilings were lofty. Every wall was painted a crisp white. He clearly didn't have children, for there wasn't a mark to be seen and there was a distinct lack of furniture or clutter of any kind. A slouching but sleek off-white corner sofa sat on a tatami mat, facing a floor-to-ceiling window.

Tamsyn perched on the end of the sofa as she marvelled at the scenery. The side of the building facing the sea had no walls, so that the entirety of the view could be appreciated through the floor-to-ceiling windows. Navy, grey and black clouds hung over the slate-coloured sea as seagulls whirled to find cover against the oncoming storm.

'Wow. It's so beautiful. It looks just like a painting!' she called back to him. In that moment she felt like a child, but the view took her breath away.

'You can lose hours looking out there. I sometimes sit until nightfall just watching the tide come in,' the professor said, coming into the room with her tea. He handed her a glass mug; a spicy aroma rose from the steaming and spiralling foam. He took a seat at the other end of the sofa. Now that she sat opposite him, she noticed his salt-and-pepper hair, his stubble and his deep brown eyes. She could see why his students fawned over him. She began to feel awkward under his gaze, and immediately chided herself for wanting to cover her stringy wet hair and tired face.

'This place is beautiful. How long have you lived here?' she asked.

'Four years. The longest I've lived anywhere. I have to travel a lot, so I'm not here as much as I'd like to be.'

'It's very unusual. I imagine you don't see many buildings like this in Anglesey?'

'No. I built it myself. In my twenties I spent a lot of time in Norway and Japan. I wanted to bring a piece of those places back with me.' He smiled at her, but his eyes regarded her with a certain coldness. 'So, you said earlier that you believe you might be in danger?' He looked at her gravely; the time for pleasantries was over.

'Yes. To cut a very long story short, I believe my grandmother may have been murdered by some sort of water spirit or demon, and now I think it may try to murder me.' She sipped the scalding-hot tea and studied his face for a reaction.

He stared at her. 'Sylvia's dead? Oh dear. I'm so sorry to hear that. And you think she was murdered? Is there a police investigation?'

'No, no. Nothing like that. It all looked very straightforward. Dead in her bed, no signs of struggle. Her autopsy ruled it was a heart attack. However, as time went on I began to notice things. Things seemed out of place.'

'Interesting. For example?'

'Well, she hadn't cleared away the teapot and cup. I know that sounds so silly, but believe me—hell would freeze over before she ever left anything out.' Tamsyn spoke quickly, impatient to get to the point.

'Perhaps she was unwell?'

'Yes, that's what I had assumed. It wasn't until later, when I was digging up the garden, that I found her locket near the base of some wolfsbane—'

'Wolfsbane?' He leaned towards her, his interest clearly piqued.

'Yes. So anyway, I noticed that she'd left her garden scissors where they fell, but her garden gloves were put away neatly in the tool shed. I know… I sound insane. But to say she was fastidious would be an understatement. I also realised, when I washed up the teapot and strainer, that there were enough loose leaves for two people. By the time I washed them up, they were a dried black mound. I didn't notice anything awry at the time. But I wasn't looking. I believe she may have laced the tea leaves with wolfsbane in order to kill her guest. I don't know whether she drank the wrong tea by mistake. Or handled it with no gloves—'

'But wolfsbane would look like heart failure or a heart attack on an autopsy.'

'Exactly.'

'A very desperate attempt indeed, using wolfsbane.' The professor was frowning; he sounded unconvinced.

'There's more. When I returned to Rosemount, I suffered from headaches. I started seeing visions, visions of things I couldn't quite remember. So, I went to my grandmother's best friend Bridie for answers. She couldn't tell me anything, but she did advise me to take a purifying salt bath. My memories began to return… and they were all to do with magic. For over ten years I was living in London, believing my grandmother was simply an eccentric who sold herbal remedies and dabbled in Paganism. And that I… was just normal.'

Rowlands breathed out, taking it all in. His face was set in stone, completely unreadable.

Tamsyn hesitated for a moment, and then plunged on. 'But then the oddest thing happened. I was out walking one day on my grandmother's property. Past the boundary of Rosemount there is a small lake in the forest. I was... attacked, by a woman clothed in black who came up out of the water. She looked... dead. Decomposing. There was a smell of blocked drains and rotten flesh.' Tamsyn rifled through her pack and pulled out her grandmother's journal. She pointed to the last entries.

His eyes scanned the words, his brow furrowed. 'This is unprecedented. Absolutely remarkable.'

'*Remarkable?* I was nearly killed!'

'Yes, of course. There's a lot to unpick here.' He stared out to sea.

Tamsyn suppressed the annoyance that welled inside her at the idea of Sylvia's death being some fascinating case study.

'I read the chapter in your book about the legend of Ginny Greenteeth in Shropshire. The description you wrote seemed to fit the bill. Do you think she could be the one who killed my grandmother?'

'It's possible, I suppose. However, by all accounts Ginny Greenteeth's victims are totally random. I doubt she would ever leave the water to come to someone's house. Unless there was some sort of link between her and your grandmother?'

Tamsyn thought for a moment. 'It seems unlikely. Sylvia was very careful that she only stuck to hedge-witchery. The idea of becoming entangled with a water demon would be an aberration to her.'

'The Severn has a long and gruesome history when it comes to drowned witches. I will do some research, see what I can find. There is one thing I do know...' Rowlands got up and sat down again opposite her, looking like he was about to break bad news.

'Go on.'

'Much Wenlock is... a very strict, closed community. We have people from there living in Anglesey. Some left because of the stringent, almost archaic rules that are imposed upon them and the rules around practising magic. Others fled because, well... if you show signs of power that they do not understand, or they are scared of, they subject you to a ritual. I have only heard about it through whispers. It involves them binding the person's memories of magic so that all traces of it are wiped, and subsequently the person is unable to use it— or even to remember that they have the ability at all. The individual is then sent away from the community to live a normal life. Over the years it seems they have improved the spell, so that a person retains their memory of family and friends. Rumour has it that when it was first performed, some people lost their memory entirely. Went mad. Lived on the streets.'

Tamsyn felt sick to her stomach. Tears welled in her eyes. 'Did my grandmother hate me so much that she would do that to me?'

'Sylvia would have had little choice. When she was a girl, they used to throw women in the river instead. In her eyes, this would have been the safest way to protect you.'

'To protect herself from whatever my "ability" might be is probably more accurate.'

'You still don't know what your power is?' he asked.

'No... no, I don't.'

16

DRIP, DRIP, DROP

Tamsyn opened her eyes and sat bolt upright. She must have fallen asleep on Professor Rowlands' sofa. The morning light was violet-grey, casting a pallid hue through the large window into the room. The tide had finally receded, revealing the muddy sea floor and scattered rowboats like broken bones. Pools of water remained; in them, sandpipers and seagulls searched for prey that had made the unfortunate decision to stay behind.

Tamsyn checked her watch: 9:30 a.m. She glanced around, seeing no sign of the professor. They had stayed up late into the night talking. He had put a blanket over her and left a glass of water on the coffee table with a yellow Post-it underneath: *Will be back before tide comes in. Breakfast in the fridge.*

Tamsyn had no idea what the tide times were. She walked over to the small, sleek kitchen, just off the living area. He had left a bowl of Bircher muesli, covered in blueberries and strawberries, and a glass of green juice. Tamsyn made a face;

healthy eating wasn't particularly high on her agenda. She looked around for a suitable place to eat.

Carrying her bowl and glass, she wandered back through to the entryway. Three lofty hallways spread from the centre. Down one were three closed doors, which she assumed must be the bedrooms and bathroom. The next hallway led to a huge room, much like the living room but housing a huge, solid wood dining table. The gargantuan windows looked out on to a mass of tangled trees. The room was sparse, and from the lack of furniture or anything functional, she guessed that it was hardly ever used, even by Professor Rowlands. Clearly it had originally been designed for entertaining, but Tamsyn couldn't imagine the professor opened up his sanctuary often, if ever.

Something moved in the trees. Tamsyn stared out, still and hardly breathing. She watched and waited for another sign of movement. In the silence, she heard the rustling and flapping of wings beyond the window pane. It must have been a raven returning to its nest. Tamsyn was suddenly acutely aware of her vulnerability. The tide was out; she was alone, and anyone could be watching her through the trees. She didn't feel scared, but she hastened her eating and drank her juice quickly. If anything, it got the taste of blended grass over with quickly.

Standing to leave, she noticed a lone photo in a frame on the wall. A youthful Ellis Rowlands, standing in front of a snow-capped mountain, holding a rosy-faced baby. He smiled at the camera, happily clutching the small child who was bundled up in a snowsuit. Tamsyn stared for a moment, wondering if the child was his, or a niece or nephew. She hurried back to the kitchen, already feeling guilty for venturing around the house.

After washing her bowl and glass, she headed to the bathroom to freshen up. Glancing at her watch, she saw it was already 10 a.m. Having no idea how much time she had to kill, she decided to do what she always did when she was bored as a child. Running a bath and wallowing the time away would kill at least forty-five minutes and allow her to finish reading Professor Rowlands' book.

Feeling discomfort at the idea of searching through a stranger's bathroom cupboards, Tamsyn ran a bath without adding any of the usual things she would have liked. Her grandmother wouldn't step foot into a bath without salts and candles at the very least. There was not a candle in sight. The bathroom befitted the rest of the house: a slightly masculine, minimalist design. The bath was raised and clad in expensive wood. There were no material possessions: no ring of toothpaste from an electric toothbrush, no stray water stains on the matte tiles.

Tamsyn sat on the edge of the bath, watching the steam rise from the water as it cascaded into the tub. It was the first time since arriving in Anglesey that she had had a moment of reflection. Now, the weight of everything that had happened seemed to be closing in on her. Breathing deeply, she made an effort to relax her shoulders. She reached one hand back and tried to knead the knot between her shoulder blades.

The image of Sylvia's face in death, thin and wide-eyed, came unbidden.

Shuddering, she got to her feet and shook her head, willing it away. In its place came the image of the half-rotted woman she had seen at the stagnant pool. A sick uneasiness came over her and again she shook her head, trying to chase the pictures away.

She shucked off her clothes and slid into the scalding-hot water, the heat almost searing her thighs, the blood rushing to her cheeks. At Rosemount, she knew the exact amount to turn the taps to draw the perfect bath. She breathed through the pain as her body adjusted to the temperature.

Lying back, the heat enveloping her shoulders, she thought of Sylvia on their last holiday together. She could see her grandmother's white hair blowing in the wind as she had turned to Tamsyn and then back to the water, her tanned, veined hands clinging to the railings as the two of them had looked out to sea at Benllech Beach. But the more Tamsyn tried to picture how her grandmother had looked on that day, the stronger grew the image of the last time she had looked upon her face, as still as if it were carved in stone, eyes wide, mouth slightly open.

Tamsyn began reading the chapter on the Three Sisters of Plynlimon. She felt the bath growing cold. Leaning forward, she twisted the hot tap. She continued to read, enraptured by the tale of Ystwyth, Wye and Severn. Leaning back again, she breathed deeply, enjoying the feeling of the hot water encircling her toes.

She read on, trying to focus on finishing the last chapter. As her eyes grew heavy and her mind began to wander, she read the same sentence three times before she gave up and put the book on the side. She sniffed the air. A putrid scent filled her nose, sulphuric overtones followed by a sharp, rotten decay. Suddenly alert again, she peered around the bathroom. The water from the tap was spluttering now. Gaseous bursts of black water poured into the bath.

Tamsyn leapt out of the tub, dripping pools of water all over the tiles as she tried desperately to turn off the tap. Behind her, the groan of metal was followed by the loud hissing of water being forced through the pipes into the sink. She turned to see black-green mulch sputtering out onto the white porcelain, droplets flying onto the worktop and the floor beyond.

Tamsyn tried to stop the flow from the taps, but no matter which way she turned them, raw sewage pumped out. In her panic, she used a towel against the tap in the sink. She saw her panicked face in the mirror and then went rigid with fear as, over her shoulder, she saw a black hooded figure standing in the corner of the room. A pale hand stretched out, two eyes blazing in the blackness surrounding them.

Fear pulsed through her body. She tried to scream. She tried to turn to face it. Her body trembled as she attempted to force air from her lungs out through her mouth.

She heard a splash. Her arms shot out either side of her, grasping on to something hard. She awoke from the dream, still in the bath, naked and alone. She looked around the room, heart hammering in her chest. The tiles were peppered with large droplets of water, but all was as it should be.

Tamsyn sat on the sofa watching the clock tick as her mind reeled. After what felt like an eternity, she heard the clunk of the heavy front door.

'Hello-o?' Professor Rowlands called from the hallway.

'Hi. I'm in the sitting room, Professor Rowlands', Tamsyn called back. She wondered if he'd hoped he would return to an empty house. Professor Rowlands entered the room. He was dressed smartly, but his eyes betrayed how little sleep he'd had.

'Good afternoon. Did you find the breakfast I left?' he asked. 'And please—call me Ellis.'

'Yes. It was delicious, thank you.'

'How are you feeling today?' His tone was clinical, like a doctor with a clipboard at the side of a hospital bed.

'I'm fine, thanks. Although I had a nightmare... about the woman in black. But thankfully it was just a dream. Thank you for covering me with a blanket last night.'

Ellis smiled and waved a dismissive hand before making his way to the kitchen.

'Would you like some lunch?' he called. 'I can't think straight when I'm hungry. Is halloumi salad okay?'

'That would be lovely,' she answered, trying her best to sound convincing. She could really do with a big fat cheeseburger after the nightmare she'd just had.

Ellis set to work chopping a red onion for the salad.

'How was your morning?' she asked, following him into the kitchen.

'Pretty dull. Answering emails, admin. The usual.'

In the light of day, Tamsyn felt awkward at being in a near-stranger's house again. 'Are there any good B&Bs you could recommend? I don't want to put you out for another night.'

'Not at all. There may be a problem with that, though.'

'Are they all booked up this time of year?' It seemed unlikely, in November. But then this was Anglesey.

'No, it's not that.' He handed her a bowl of salad as she followed him through to the dining room, where he pulled out a seat at the table for Tamsyn and took a chair opposite her. The trees were swaying vigorously in the strong wind. Skewering her fork into a chunk of halloumi, she was pleasantly surprised at how delicious it was.

'Before you came to the lecture, you stopped at a café?' he asked, digging into his salad.

'Yes… Shouldn't I have?'

'The barista—nice guy. Miserable, but nice. Well, he's from Much Wenlock. When I went in this morning to get a coffee, he seemed shaken. He said that there was a young woman who stopped by the day before, in an old-fashioned car. And that when you drove away, there was a man photographing you. He was shaken because he recognised the man. He couldn't remember his name, just said that he was incredibly old and wore a green anorak over a knitted tank top. Do you know that man?'

'Err… I can't say I do. There are lots of old people in Much Wenlock.' Tamsyn was still processing the information.

'It's not safe for you to stay in a B&B. I don't know if they know you're with me, but let's assume they do. At least I can protect you here, for now.'

Tamsyn sat, saying nothing.

'We must not return to Much Wenlock until you are armed with the answers,' said Ellis.

'We? You will come with me?' she asked.

'Of course. If you are in any danger, I cannot with good conscience send you back there. I know what they're like. What *it's* like. And after what you've been through, you need a friend.'

Tamsyn didn't know how to respond. She had not anticipated such kindness from someone she barely knew.

'Thank you,' she said.

'From everything you have told me, it strikes me that the thread running through the heart of all this is your grandmother.'

Of course it is, Tamsyn thought with an anger that shocked her. Everything was always about her.

'You need to speak to her.'

'I'm sorry?'

'You need to ask her what happened on the day she died.'

'Do you mean... a séance?'

Ellis furrowed his brow.

'God, no!' He laughed. 'Have you heard of Journeying?'

'Remind me,' said Tamsyn.

'Journeying takes place in the mind. But it is as real as you want it to be. It has been practised by humans for millennia. It can be accomplished in many ways, but it entails going into a deep meditative state. Once there, you can access the Otherworld.

'You may have heard of the Otherworld, in which there are three realms. The first is the Middle World. This appears familiar to us all, as it is a mirror image of our own. Next is the Underworld. This is where all of our ancestors dwell. It is a place of knowledge and natural power—this is where you will find your grandmother.'

'And the third?'

Ellis smiled. 'The third takes years of practice to reach. The Upper World is a place of enlightenment. It allows the individual clarity, the beauty of vision. It contains all that was, is and will be.'

'Wow. And you've been there?' she asked.

'Sadly, no. Like I said, it requires years of practice. You must thoroughly explore the first two realms and learn all there is to know about yourself. Some say the gateways to these worlds can only be found at the tops of the tallest trees and mountains. Others say that it is only possible to access the Upper World shortly before your death.'

'Is that why you climb mountains?'

'How did you know I climb?'

'It's in your bio, at the back of your book.'

'Ah, yes. It's one of the many reasons, yes. I briefly meditated on the tops of Everest and K2, in the death zone, yet still the gateways have eluded me. Which merely tells me that I have much more to understand about myself.'

'So, in the Underworld, I will be able to speak to my grandmother? How will I find her?' she asked.

'I have a book on the subject that tells you all you need to know. You will need to read it—*thoroughly*. However, if your grandmother does not wish to be found, you will never find her. If she does not wish to speak, you must be prepared to find other ways to seek the truth. Always remember, the dead owe us nothing.' He wiped his mouth on a napkin and stood up.

'So, what do we do next?' Tamsyn asked.

'I have a busy week, I'm afraid. However, there is much for you to learn. I will give you the literature you require. You can use this space to brush up on your skills. I have a workbench in my library, with every book you can think of regarding herbology, spiritualism, hedge-witchery, druid law. Read as much as you can. Since I don't have much time to teach you, you can practise getting into the meditative state. This should make things a lot quicker when we come to make the first journey,' said Ellis.

Tamsyn stared at her plate, dismayed. A week of reading and practising meditation sounded like torture to her. 'And when we finally journey? What will happen?' she asked, feeling impatience rearing its ugly head.

'Once you find yourself in the Mirror World, you must find a gateway. Gateways to the Underworld are usually holes in the ground: wells, tunnels, caves, that sort of thing. Please give some thought to where it might be and what it might look like during this next week; it will save us valuable time. Many of my students have reported the gateway being located in a vivid memory from their childhood.'

Tamsyn thought for a moment. She had no idea where or what it might be; she could think of dozens of possibilities right off the bat.

'Once you're through the gateway,' Ellis continued, 'first things first. You must find your spirit guide. You will not be able to navigate the realms without them. They can take any form, but it will be something recognisable to you. Something or someone who has always been there—an animal, a person, or even an aquatic lifeform. There will be a path of some sort. Everyone has a unique path and a unique guide, so unfortunately I cannot give you directions.'

'Do you have a spirit animal?'

'Of course. You may have already seen him.' Ellis stood up and collected their plates, ready to head back to the kitchen.

'Seen him? You brought him back to this world?'

Ellis smiled. 'Yes. Oh, and there is but one imperative,' he said, changing the subject.

'Only one?' Tamsyn joked.

'If nothing else, you must not leave the path. Under any circumstances.'

'I won't,' Tamsyn said, still wondering what his spirit animal could be.

'Promise me. Do not stray from the path.'

'I won't. Promise.' Tamsyn looked through the window and into the trees.

'Before you begin studying, I must ask, are you able to clearly visualise objects and places in your mind?'

'Yes, of course. You mean some people don't do that?' Tamsyn asked, genuinely surprised.

'Some people don't. It makes it almost impossible to journey. My father couldn't.'

Ellis paused and seemed to ponder something. 'Okay. Stand up and face me.'

Tamsyn folded her napkin onto the table and slid her chair back, then, wondering what he was going to do, she stood squarely in front of him.

'Please, close your eyes for a moment. If I ask you to imagine a red apple on my dinner table, would you be able to do so?'

Tamsyn closed her eyes. She pictured a red apple on the table they had just been sitting at, its skin pinpointed with light from the reflection of the window. She reached out her hand, her fingers encircling it. It felt light in her palm, its skin slightly waxy. She drew it to her mouth, sinking her teeth into its flesh. The apple was tart, with a sweet aftertaste. She observed the bite mark, the ridges her teeth had made in its off-white insides. She placed it back onto the table and opened her eyes.

'Yes, I can,' she said. Suddenly she thought of the man following her, aiming his camera at her car. Her insides fizzed with adrenaline.

'Good. Great.' Ellis looked exhausted. 'We shall reconvene after dinner. Apologies, but I have a lot of work to get through in the meantime.'

As Tamsyn and Ellis left the dining room, a raven stood outside, watching them from a gnarled branch, his beady black eyes trained on the window. He cawed and tilted his head. On the table stood an apple, already starting to rot in the winter sunlight.

17
A NEW NAME

The Siren saw flashes of the moon whirling before her eyes as her head jolted around. The cool, dark night gave way to blinding light and an intensely uncomfortable heat. Her body burned; her head felt like it was going to explode. She remembered vomiting violently. As she tried to open her eyes, the room spun wildly around her. She could make out a lamp, a low table. The effort made her nauseous again. Someone held a cool glass to her lips. She drank thirstily; whatever it was, its aftertaste was both sweet and bitter. She closed her eyes and fell back into a sleep plagued with nightmares.

Hours later, she awoke to the smell of fried bacon and eggs. Groggily, she attempted to rise. She found she was lying on a mattress on a floor. Looking around, her eyes slowly focussing, she saw that the room was small, with a low, slanted ceiling. Near the head of the mattress, a low round window looked down on to the street below. This must be the attic room, she thought, in too much pain to give heed to her fear. As she rose to her feet, every muscle screamed. She held her hands to her head, swaying dangerously.

Staggering to the door, she tried the handle to no avail. Looking down at her body, it took her a moment to realise there was no tail, just scrawny, weak legs. She stood barefoot on a dirty beige carpet, in a floral nightgown so large she wondered if it had once been curtains.

Besides the mattress on the floor, the room had been stripped of its belongings. An old school desk sat in the corner, with a chintzy bedside lamp atop it.

The desk had various carvings etched into its surface. *Shrewsbury F.C.... Old Arthurians... Gavin 4 Kate...* She looked inside. It was empty, save for blotches of spilled ink and more graffiti.

She let go of the desk lid as a knock at the door startled her. It banged loudly, and her heart raced in her chest as her breathing quickened. A key turned in the lock. She stood, frozen.

'Are you decent?' called a voice as the door swung open. Her eyes widened in fear. A man with a balding head and a pot belly stood in the doorway holding a silver tray.

'Ah, glad to see you're up and about. I've made you bacon and eggs. Are you feeling a bit better?'

The man from the river. Like a nightmare upon waking... Her memory felt like shattered glass. Frantically, she tried to grasp at thoughts that skittered by. *Who am I?* Her voice was frantic inside her head. *You are a handmaiden of Sabrina. A Siren of the River Severn... What is my name?*

'Would you like to eat downstairs? With me? It's far more comfortable down there.' He turned to leave. To her abject horror, she felt a tug in her chest. A tether between them, pulling at her insides as he walked down the hallway. Like a thread twisting in between her ribs, it loosened again as she started to move. Her legs followed him, disobeying the screaming voice inside her head.

'No!' she managed to say. She felt like she had been drugged.

Still, she followed him like a lost puppy, down the twisting staircase. The harder she fought, the more a fog descended upon her. He led her to a grand front room, the early morning light streaming through the windows. Outside was the most magnificent view of the town skyline, and beneath it, her home. The river meandered by, dark and grey. She let out a whimper.

'I have thought of the perfect name for you,' he said chirpily. 'How about… Vivien? Like the Lady of the Lake? It's clever, and I think it suits you rather well.' He paused and gave a self-deprecating smile. 'Gawd blimey, where are my manners? My name is Gavin. Pleased to meet you.'

With every fibre, she focused on controlling his mind. She could make people do whatever she wanted them to. She held up her shaking hand, trying to infiltrate his thoughts. She told him to jump out of the window. That twisting knot in her ribs tightened so sharply she grabbed at her side and cried out in pain.

'That won't work, my sweet thing,' he said evenly. 'Our blood is one.' He laced his fingers together. 'You belong to me now. Would you like some bacon, Vivien?'

'That's not my name,' she hissed through gritted teeth.

Even trying to remember her own name caused the thread that bound her to twist.

'Try again.' He wagged his finger. 'Eggs?' He gestured to the table laid with silverware. She breathed through the pain, collapsing into a chair.

'Look, it will be far easier for you to go with the flow. Ha, ha—get it? Because you were a fish—No? The only magic you will perform is what you are instructed to do on my behalf.' He poured tea from an ornate silver teapot.

'Sabrina will come for me,' she croaked. 'She will show you no mercy.'

'I'm very much hoping she won't find you. And if she does, I will explain that I had to use blood magic in self-defence, because you were going to kill me. That will put her in a very awkward position. I will offer you back, call it even. How do you take your tea?' The sunlight glinted through the golden-brown liquid as he poured her a cup.

'But until that day comes, my dear, sweet Vivien, we have work to do.'

18

A SAFE HAVEN

Tamsyn had spent five days reading, pacing the silent hallways and experimenting with various exotic plants, each meticulously labelled, in Ellis's library workroom. She read book after book, absorbing them with a ferocity that both surprised and scared her. Some magic she remembered, but most of the things she read were entirely new to her. She wondered if Sylvia had known any of it, or whether it had been kept from her too, along with every Pride woman before her.

The first three days had been difficult. Unable to relax, she had found her mind wandering as she read. She watched the clock, counting down the hours until Ellis returned home. But by the fourth day, she found that there were not enough hours. By the time the door swung open, and his familiar 'hel-lo' reached her in the library, she was shocked by how quickly the hours had passed.

Over dinner, she talked about everything she had learned that day, barely stopping to draw breath. Ellis nodded, tired but pleased that she was throwing herself into it so enthusiastically. She asked him if he thought it would be okay to go into the village the next day to pick up a few essentials and to get fresh air. He seemed reticent but agreed.

The next morning Tamsyn stood at the front door, ready to leave but feeling anxious. What if there was someone lurking, ready to take her picture? At his suggestion, she scraped her hair into one of Ellis's caps and donned one of his hoodies. She thought about the past four months, and how, until now, she had barely left Rosemount yet alone seen or spoken to many people. And then there was the business with the woman in the water, the people in Much Wenlock… the friends and partner she had left behind in London. Tamsyn couldn't shake the feeling of displacement.

Walking into Menai Bridge, she noted how much it had changed since she was a teenager. There were vegan restaurants, trendy plant shops and high-end art galleries. Unsure where to go, she found herself heading back to the coffee shop with the surly barista.

As the bell above the door signalled her entrance, he looked up expectantly. Upon seeing it was her, he looked disappointed. Tamsyn made her way over to the counter, quickly scanning the contents of the display cabinet.

'Hi,' she said. 'Please may I have a black coffee and an almond croissant?' Immediately she regretted it. She didn't even want the almond croissant, she wanted a panini, but for some reason, she had panicked.

'I'll bring it over.' He sounded gruff and sullen, even more so than the first time she'd encountered him.

Tamsyn chose the leather armchair next to a small round

table at the window. Retrieving the latest read from Ellis's library, she sat for a moment, letting the sunlight soak into her face. She loved this time of year, when it was just turning cold and the sunlight pierced crystal clear. After a few moments, the steaming cup of black coffee was placed in front of her along with the most perfectly shaped golden croissant.

'Thank you so much,' she said. She attempted to catch his eye and smile at him, but a telephone began to ring from behind the counter and he rushed away.

Tamsyn sipped on the scalding-hot coffee, absentmindedly chewing pieces of croissant as she got back to the last chapter she was reading.

The bell above the door signalled the arrival of another customer. A young woman in baggy, ripped jeans and a cropped t-shirt made her way to the counter. Tamsyn reflected how, in her early twenties, she too had been able to get away with not wearing a coat in November. The barista came from the back of the shop, his eyes turning in an instant from wounded and sad to wide and alive.

'Hi. You want to come round the back?' he asked the newcomer, trying to keep his voice low. Tamsyn buried her face in the book, trying her best not to eavesdrop and concentrate on the words in front of her.

'No. I told you, Dylan. Stop phoning me. Please, leave me alone.' The young woman gripped tightly on to her bag, her blonde hair falling down her poker-straight back.

'Can we just talk? *In private?*' he pleaded.

Tamsyn peeped over the top the book. She could see the tension in the young girl's shoulders.

'There's nothing to say. I've met someone else. Delete my number. Stop calling me, okay?' She turned on her heel, her golden hair streaming behind her as she made her way to the door.

'Wait!' Dylan came out from behind the counter. In three strides he was upon her. He grabbed her wrist.

'God, Dylan, get off me!' She yanked her arm away and disappeared though the door, the bell ringing behind her.

Dylan stood, fists clenched so hard the skin turned pale. He swept one arm across the table next to him in explosive anger, the dirty cups shattering on the floor. Cursing, he stormed into the back.

Tamsyn's heart began to beat in her ears. She looked down, seeing Dominic's hands around her forearms. She was back in their kitchen. The weight of his body pushing her back against the counter. *Get off me*, she heard herself say, firm but wavering. *You're not leaving*, his voice echoed back. His large frame loomed in front of her, blocking the exit. *Let me go, now*, she warned. She tried to break free, but his hands only gripped tighter, hurting her. She closed her eyes tightly. Anger bloomed inside her gut. Her blood fizzed in her hands.

Inside her head, she heard herself screaming with rage. She shut her eyes even more tightly. She thought about lashing out at him. Could she knee him in the groin and run for the door? She was afraid of what he would do. He could certainly outrun her. She felt her arms stiffen as his grip burned into her skin, her bones feeling like they could snap at any moment.

Then, she heard cracking. She opened her eyes in time to see the window behind Dominic growing veins where the glass was splitting. Time seemed to stand still, until suddenly the window shattered inwards with alarming force. Dominic let go immediately; the two of them were sprayed with tiny shards, most of them peppering into his back.

She saw his eyes bulging with fear and confusion. He was hurt. She saw his pupils shrink, before the fear began to dissipate, replaced with renewed anger—

Tamsyn was breathing hard. She was alone once more in the coffee shop, staring at the half-empty cup in front of her. It was in two pieces, cut clean down the middle, its black contents pooling on the table and dripping off the edge.

Hastily, she grabbed some napkins and mopped it up. Retrieving the two halves of the cup, she rammed them inside her bag. She grabbed her things and headed for the door. Thankfully, Dylan was nowhere to be seen.

Tamsyn walked as quickly as she could back to Ellis's, her mind racing. Was there CCTV in the café? Probably. Would someone come after her if they saw her staring at a cup which then spontaneously split in two? She had no idea.

Then there was Ellis. If she told him, would he put back teaching her how to journey until she had herself under control? He was so careful, so considered, and Tamsyn couldn't waste weeks or perhaps months putting things off.

And then there was that other question, poised further back, nagging her... *Can you even trust Ellis?*

19
THE AMBER ROOM

It had been a week since the night at the river. Already, Gavin felt a profound shift. Each day, his egg yolks were perfectly golden, the whites spherical and glossy in the pan. Every traffic light turned green at his approach. The butcher handed him the largest slab of beef he had ever seen, the juicy crimson intricately laced with white. When Gavin handed it back irritably and told him there must be a mistake, that his order was the brisket, the man simply shook his head. 'This is for you, sir,' he said, with a strange look in his eye. When Gavin fished out a twenty-pound note, the butcher simply turned back to his chopping block. As he headed to the door, he saw her, standing, watching, her face sullen, gazing longingly at the piles of meat under the counter.

Two days ago, the proprietor of the Amber Room, the trendiest bar he could think of in these parts, had informed Gavin that all event bookings were blocked out until January and perhaps he should call back for a cancellation in the meantime. He had called again yesterday, and some prepubescent little git had told him the same.

Gavin had visited the Amber Room again earlier today, this time with his new friend in tow. He had informed the young man stacking glasses that he would like to speak to his manager.

'Tell him it's Councillor Hardcastle,' he said. 'Tell him we spoke on the phone,' he called after the boy as he disappeared through the arched brickwork and trudged up the stairs.

When a stocky, bald man emerged moments later, he looked as though he was ready to punch Gavin in the face. From the gold sovereigns on his fingers, Gavin surmised they had seen a lot of action.

'Didn't the kid tell you earlier, no reservations?' His voice was ragged from too many cigars.

'Yes. He did. But surely you could make an allowance this time? This meeting is exclusively for the elite of Shropshire's businessmen, MPs, and prominent landowners. All here, spending lots of money, in your bar,' replied Gavin.

'I don't give a f—' the manager began.

Gavin raised his hand to stop him. 'No profanities, please. Not in the presence of a lady. My assistant, Vivien, will handle the details.' He was so pleased with her new name. 'Gavin and Vivien' had a great ring to it.

The manager took one look at Vivien. 'Y'know, I think a space has just opened.' He clicked his fingers at the boy. 'Write it down, Oliver. Seven-thirty onwards, yeah?' He did not take his eyes off her.

∾

The two of them walked into the bustling bar later that evening. Pendant lights hung low from the arched brick ceilings, their orange orbs buzzing. Gavin felt a rush of exhilaration as all eyes turned to watch the beautiful young woman at his side with the long, dark hair and olive skin. Vivien's large brown eyes glinted in the golden light as they furtively scanned the room.

Terence Buchanan stood when he saw Gavin enter, his rosy red face already flushed from too many brandies. He held up his glass.

'Well, well, well, Hardcastle. And who might this be? I didn't think any women were invited?' He guffawed loudly, the other men joining him in his laughter, despite what he'd said not being remotely funny.

'This is Vivien.' Gavin pulled a chair out for her to sit. She kept her eyes averted from him as she took a seat.

'This the new girlfriend, then? Bit young and attractive for you, isn't she?' Terence nudged Gavin, looking round at the others to see if they were laughing. Indeed, they were. Behind their envious eyes, that was what they were all thinking.

'Vivien is my assistant. She's here to help me with the new plans.' Gavin caught the eye of the barman and mouthed *brandy* while making a tipping motion with his hand.

Gavin had made sure he was the last one to arrive. Some of the men started to migrate over to him, while others, in obvious disdain, kept their distance. No matter, he thought with a smile.

'Mr Hardcastle!' A hard thump landed on his back. He turned to see Charles Furth, a behemoth of a man at six foot seven, who owned hectares of land across Shropshire and Powys.

'What's the meaning of this meeting, then? I hope I haven't come all the way to sleepy Shrewsbury for nothing?' boomed Charles.

'All in good time, Charlie,' Gavin assured him. Furth looked taken aback at being shown such irreverence and skulked back to his seat.

Vivien sat with her hands in her lap and her head down, trying to keep herself as small as possible so as not to be noticed. But everyone had noticed. Gavin took a seat beside her and looked around the room; the men were still staring at her. One man nudged another, whispering in his ear. They laughed in unison, their gaping mouths wide open, revealing black fillings. Men are animals, he concluded. The time of the gentleman was clearly over.

Gavin's brandy arrived. For the first time, he felt nervous. He downed it, then stood and made his way to the small wooden stage nestled between two pillars.

He took a deep breath and cleared his throat.

'Excuse me. Hello. Good evening.' The mic screeched; the din in the room lingered before petering out. All eyes were on him, save for Vivien's. She continued to sit, shoulders hunched and head down.

'Welcome, gentlemen. This is what I hope will be the first meeting of many, in which the prominent men of Shropshire will work together to form a task force;' Gavin's eyes skimmed over the crowd, glistening with pinpoints of light. 'Where we are given a safe space,' he continued, 'to discuss pertinent issues without fear of judgement. Issues that are plaguing our towns and villages. I know many of you are concerned with the number of rough sleepers littering the doorways of your establishments, making our beautiful town look untidy. Has enough been done by the current establishment about the rise in crime that has been plaguing our farmers?'

He waited for an answer. Dozens of eyes stared back at him. Some were half-amused, in faces ruddy with the alcohol their owners had already consumed; some were bored, and others were angry. He wondered what they would say about him tonight as they lay in the dark next to their wives. Would he be reduced to a joke? Dismissed between two heads on pillows, as he had been his whole life?

'This brings me to the solution to it all,' he went on. 'The reason I asked you here today. There is untapped magic, flowing over our countryside, through our waterways. The ancient ley lines that cross our landscapes have been forgotten. We have forgotten ourselves. Our past. I am here to lead us into a new future.' He paused for dramatic effect. 'I believe I can reconnect these lines.' There was murmuring and some tittering from the crowd.

'Most of the old landmarks have been destroyed, Gavin. There's nothing left.' Charlie stood with his hands in his blue trouser suit. His grin thinly masked the disdain he felt for him.

Yes, you saw to that, Gavin thought to himself. Miles and miles of newbuilds, cutting straight through the middle of the sacred routes.

'There is still one.' Gavin stared down at him pointedly.

A few members of the crowd shifted awkwardly. No one

messed with Charlie Furth. But Gavin knew there wasn't a
local in the room who approved of the swathes of soulless
boxes, housing yuppies and their children from the big cities,
overpopulating the already stretched schools and doctors'
surgeries.

'You're wasting our time, Gavin. This is nonsense—'

'Just hear me out.' Gavin held his hand up. 'I have a plan.
I trust you will dig deep into your pockets, gentlemen. But
first, some light entertainment. I'd like to introduce you all to
Vivien. Vivien?' He beckoned her over.

She rose, slowly, keeping her head down and her shoulders slightly hunched. The room silently watched as she made
her way to the stage. She stood next to him, squinting against
the harsh light.

Every muscle in her body ached, as if it were trying to turn
itself inside out in order to escape. She kept her head bowed.
Her senses screamed with overwhelm. The burning lights.
The smell of diesel that clung to damp skin, of dried urine on
cotton. The salted food, dried to petrification, hanging in
plastic behind the bar. Someone had tried lazily to clean up
sick from one of the chairs, the artificial floral smell mingling
with that of vomit. Her eyes and mouth watered as she
fought the urge to throw up herself.

He had briefed her earlier that day as she sat, perched
awkwardly on a chaise longue in his stuffy front room, feeling
cumbersome, heavy, and weary to the marrow. She had stared
out of the window, looking down towards the river, her

home. The water sparkled in the sunlight, making its way southward. Without her. He handed her a piece of paper. She heard his voice, far away, asking if she knew Welsh.

'Unless, of course, you speak Brythonic?' He laughed, but waited in silence for her to answer.

'I speak many languages,' she replied flatly. That was as good an acquiescence as he would ever receive from her.

'I have very important work to do here,' he'd told her. 'I have invited all the men who I believe have the power and influence to… make life difficult for me. You will convince them otherwise.'

She had let her mind drift away again, working through thousands of scenarios in which she would make him pay. He had stolen any and all autonomy from her. She could not run, couldn't make him hold a knife to his throat and slit his own windpipe. But he couldn't stop her mind from looking for a way out, however minuscule the hole might be.

The only option she saw was to wait for some opportunity that might or might not ever arise. Would she even know it when it came? If she acted at the improper moment, he could lock her in his cellar instead of just the spare room. He might even kill her. *Was he capable?* she asked herself. Her mind answered yes. *Do not underestimate him*, she warned herself.

'Vivien?' Gavin repeated. She was back on stage, perspiring. 'Will you sing us a song?' he asked with a smile that didn't reach his eyes.

They all stared. He stared, waiting. Her puny legs swayed, almost causing her to lose her balance. She was not accustomed to being out of water for so long. The room rocked like a boat being tossed in the waves.

His question was a rhetorical one, for of course she had no choice.

'I know we have a lot of Welsh speakers here tonight.' He grinned at her, an expectant, boyishly naïve smile, then turned to the crowd. 'Take it away, Vivien!'

Some members of the audience looked at each other, smirking. One nudged another and laughed.

It didn't matter what she sang. All that mattered was the intention. She clenched her eyes shut to quell the rocking motion of the room. When she opened her mouth, the song came forth of its own accord.

Rwy'n ysu i dy deimlo unwaith eto
Nid oes derfyn ar dy haelioni.
A thrwy'r oll, yr rwyt yn llifo i'r môr
Ymlaen a 'mlaen, hebddof i.

Wyt ti'n fy nghlywed, Hafren?
Clyw gri fy llef
Cymer fi ymaith, gwna beth â fynni.
Pam wyt ti wedi troi dy gefn arna'i?

A wnes i golli'th ffafr?
Pob nos, ni allaf gysgu.
Ni allaf gysgu, na bwyta chwaith
Dwêd wrthyf sut, ac fe wnaf y cyfan yn iawn.

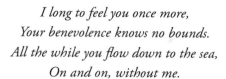

I long to feel you once more,
Your benevolence knows no bounds.
All the while you flow down to the sea,
On and on, without me.

Can you hear me, Hafren?
Hear my Siren's plea.
Take me away, do what you will,
Why hast thou forsaken me?

Have I fallen out of favour?
Sleep evades me every night,
I cannot sleep, I cannot eat,
Please tell me how and I will make it right.

A few yards away, in the cool, dark night, the sides of the river swelled. A night fisherman grabbed his can of beer as the water rushed to meet his feet. He watched in bemused silence as it rose higher, as if it were searching. Then, as quickly as it had risen, it fell back again.

In the Amber Room, Vivien opened her eyes. The men stood; some had their mouths slightly agape. Others sat motionless, tears in their eyes. She turned to look at Gavin. He grinned from ear to ear, the smile reaching his eyes now, his skin pale and clammy in the harsh stage lights.

20

INTO THE UNKNOWN

Entering the living room, Tamsyn could immediately see why Ellis had chosen to journey here. The lights were off, but the room was flooded with blue light from the moon. It hung over the sea, illuminating everything its silvery light touched below. The tide was in again, the water glassy and calm.

Ellis struck a match and began to light dozens of amber-coloured candles. He moved the coffee table aside and placed two large cushions on the floor. Beside one of the cushions lay a large drum, covered with a taut, stretched goatskin and nailed to an ochre base.

'Did you read all of the literature I gave you?' he asked. The light from the candle flames danced across his face. His eyes, however, remained in darkness.

'Yes, I read it all. Twice over to make sure I remember.'

He didn't answer. Even in the low light, she remarked that he shifted nervously.

Tamsyn had learned that the fundamental rule to being able to journey was to be open to it in the first place. The books she had read were so abstract, though, that they made it sound like guided meditation. She suspected that Ellis would not appreciate her interpretation.

The concept of allowing your spirit to journey to another realm was something that Sylvia absolutely would not condone. Tamsyn understood this now; her memories had been returning with alarming clarity. She recalled the time when she was seventeen and her grandmother had been dusting the shelves in her bedroom. A year prior, Sylvia had stopped letting Tamsyn borrow whatever books she wanted. She was worried, she said, about her misusing magic in the silly tiffs she had with girls at school. The second Sylvia left the room, Tamsyn had darted in, blindly snatching a book from the top of the pile.

She had pored over it for two days, devouring the incantations greedily. There was one spell, for astral projection, that made her blood fizz with awe and excitement. Imagine being able to appear wherever you pleased—so long as you returned to your body before any malignant spirits caught sight of you.

Inevitably, though, Sylvia had caught her reading it. She had confiscated the book and did not speak to Tamsyn for two weeks. It was after that incident that Sylvia had begun keeping the 'forbidden books' under lock and key.

She recalled the words Sylvia had said to her after the agonisingly awkward two-week silence: 'You should know this, Tamsyn. While your spirit is left to roam, you are most vulnerable to the devil! Do you want your soul to be ripped apart? To be dragged into the Underworld for eternity? Don't be a reckless fool like your mother.'

Stung, Tamsyn had blurted out, 'Being dragged to the Underworld would be a damn sight more interesting than being here with you!' Sylvia had slapped her, hard. It had been the start of something new between them. It was the first time Tamsyn had truly begun to resent her grandmother.

She had been going through one of the toughest times of her life. The kids at school shunned her. She had no mother or father. She wished she could visit herself in that moment and hold her seventeen-year-old self. But how could she explain to that young girl that she would learn to live with loneliness and even come to enjoy it? That she needed only herself, and that it was okay. She was enough. She didn't need anyone's validation.

'Everything okay?' Ellis was looking at her with concern as she wrapped her arms around herself.

'Yes. Yes, I'm fine. I'm ready.'

Tamsyn sat down on the cushion, watching Ellis light the remaining candles. As he sat opposite her, dark shadows played across his temples, dancing down onto his cheekbones. He looked grim in the candlelight. Even in the low light his eyes betrayed dark circles from an evening spent at his desk.

'We can do this another time, if you prefer?' she asked him with concern.

'Time is not something we have much of, I'm afraid. Besides, the moon is perfect tonight.'

Tamsyn looked up at it once more. She always thought

the moon's face looked benevolent, like a friend half surprised to see you. She wondered if tonight it looked at her with warning, that usual surprised 'O' turning to a call of alarm. Taking a deep breath, she steadied her breathing.

'This is your first journey,' Ellis began. 'You are not expecting answers. Your aim must be to familiarise yourself with the environment and to find your guide through the spirit world. When you find them, whatever form they choose to take, you will know them. Remember, stick to the path. The path is your lifeline, and if you stray from it, I won't be able to pull you out. Okay?'

Tamsyn nodded.

'When you are ready, we shall begin.' Ellis's voice had a deep, rich tone to it now.

Tamsyn closed her eyes. She drew a long, deep breath down into her lungs, then exhaled slowly.

A deep echo came from the taut skin of the drum as the wooden beater struck it.

'Focus on your breath. Take the air down, down, down into your lungs.' Ellis's voice sounded different, but Tamsyn couldn't think about that now.

The drum sounded twice, louder this time. The heat from the candle flames kissed her face and hair, the warmth growing in intensity. She felt the weight of the sea lying dormant beyond the glass. She heard a nesting bird shifting its wings. A dormouse stirring in the undergrowth. An owl swooping silently overhead.

'I want you to follow the sound of my voice until you reach the place of contact.' Ellis's voice remained with her, but the beating of the drum sounded farther away. She felt herself being gently pulled, as if by the tide. Slipping further out with each wave. Further away, into sleep, out to sea, into space.

She felt the urge to let go. Into the darkness and oblivion. To succumb entirely to it. To float away and never come back.

'Tamsyn? Are you there? Can you open your eyes?'

Her lids felt heavy. She wanted desperately to sleep, and to let the dream take her where it would. Fighting the overwhelming lethargy, she forced herself to open her eyes.

A sepia-toned light made her squint for a moment. She was standing on a familiar road. Shrewsbury's Milk Street was entirely deserted. The jutting, uneven cobbled street wasn't exactly the tarmac road she remembered. Some of the shops she recognised, while others were unfamiliar. A barber's shop stood as if recently vacated, its chairs dusty, long bereft of clientele. A yellowing wedding dress stood like a spectre in a boutique Tamsyn had often marvelled at as a young girl.

Tamsyn looked up to the windows above. They were black, empty holes, with no sign of life inside them. Some had curtains. If they had been coloured or patterned, they had long since faded to grey. The world stood silent, as if paused in time.

Rounding the corner, she saw Old Chad's church on its high grassy mound, its perimeter surrounded by a wall. What had been the ruins of a red sandstone church during her childhood now stood complete again. Tamsyn marvelled that the Lady's Chapel, the only section of the church left, was now joined on to a larger building. The arched stained-glass windows glinted despite the sunless sky. There was a glow emanating from within, the red, blue and green glass shining with an inviting warmth.

Following the road that led to a gap in the wall, Tamsyn made her way down the pathway to the church. There were many more tombstones here than she remembered, some so ancient they had been worn entirely smooth, while others stood sharp and clean, the earth in front of them newly churned.

The same flame-red tree Tamsyn had stood underneath months before at Sylvia's funeral stood to the north-east. Walking towards it, she stopped when she saw that the place where her grandmother should lie in rest was a gaping hole in the ground.

Tamsyn never had understood Sylvia's insistence on being buried in a long-forgotten churchyard, in front of a ruined chapel. Her grandmother had brought her to this spot many times, pointing to the ground beneath the tree. 'Here,' she would say. 'I paid in full for the plot long ago. The receipt is in the bureau in my bedroom. Right here.' Each time, she drew a rectangle in the air with her gnarled finger. 'In a bronze casket. I've been paying *Taylor & Sons* fourteen pounds a month since 'eighty-five.' Tamsyn had nodded each time, as if it was the first time Sylvia had told her. But it wasn't the sort of thing you forget easily.

Fighting hard, she tried to picture her grandmother's face as it had been in that moment, hoping it wouldn't contort into her final death mask. Had she looked sad? Proud? Grim?

Now that she was older, she could see things with a rather different and unsettling perspective. The way Sylvia had traipsed the same route her whole life: Rosemount to Much Wenlock, Much Wenlock to Shrewsbury. Almost as though she were eagerly anticipating the day she could be buried in the ground, while all the time secretly believing that day would never come.

She had wondered how long Sylvia had been paying the funeral directors and had worked out that the coffin must have set Sylvia back at least ten thousand pounds. An odd decision for a woman who cared little for fine things, enjoying thrifting wherever and whenever possible.

Despite Sylvia's small body, the casket, made of solid bronze, had been so heavy it could not be lifted by the pall-bearers. Instead, it was wheeled over from the hearse. The trolley had rattled over the uneven pathway, then had to be dragged over the grass to her final resting place. It was clear no one had experienced lifting a solid bronze casket and then lowering it into the ground. The six pallbearers strained, sweat beading on their foreheads as they looked to one another with panic when they realised they could not lift it.

After a moment, Gavin Hardcastle had stepped forward, beckoning to Peter Bradshaw and Roy Pegg. They were all in the winter of their years. Nine men, with gritted teeth and veins throbbing in their temples, hauled her onto the wooden struts. The wood creaked, groaning and threatening to splinter underneath the load.

The high priest, who had travelled from Surrey to conduct Sylvia's transition into the Underworld, looked worried. He made a curt nod to one of the pallbearers, making it clear he thought the wood was about to give way, and that they should lower the casket into the ground without waiting for him to conduct his eulogy.

The ropes were hastily laced through the handles. All nine men held the ends taut, digging their heels into the ground. As the wooden struts were removed, like a ship sinking beneath the waves, the weight of the coffin almost pulled them in with it.

Tamsyn had looked away, fighting the overwhelming urge to both cry and burst into laughter at the most inappropriate time. The more she considered the scandal it would cause, the more the laugh threatened to burst forth. She pushed it down, and the onlookers mistook her turning her face away from the grave as being overcome with emotion.

That had been the last time she had felt the urge to laugh. After that moment, the unbearable weight of what had happened began to hit her. The realisation that, without Sylvia, she was truly alone. Endlessly and without reprieve, colossal waves of grief had crashed over her, until she was so tired they kept her submerged entirely.

She was pulled from the memory when the previously still and silent air picked up, stirring the branches of the tree. Blood-red leaves swirled and tumbled down around her. She watched as a few stray leaves spiralled down into the empty grave.

Ellis's voice was no longer audible, and Tamsyn wondered if the drum was still sounding. She sat down on the edge of the hole on the crumbling earth. She peered down into the blackness beyond, her hands gripping the exposed roots of the tree. She felt the hard, woody roots give way in her grasp.

As she looked down, she saw that they had turned to mulch. She looked up to the branches. The leaves had already disappeared, leaving the tree bare.

Tamsyn inhaled deeply and pushed herself off the side, down into the darkness.

21

THE PRISONER

Two weeks had passed since the rendezvous in the Amber Room. Things had moved forward with pleasing speed. Gavin smiled to himself, content that, finally, things were coming up roses. He had already secured the land he needed from several estates across the county, as well as planning permission for numerous sites. He had reshuffled the council and alerted the new members to join him at the new headquarters, the Crow's Nest.

With Vivien's help, they had cleaned the house from top to bottom and prepped for the three-course dinner for the meeting that night. Gavin did not believe in hiring cleaners or catering. A ridiculous waste of money, his mother would say. She had taught him from an early age to cook, clean and launder the sheets to five-star-hotel standards. He was only too pleased to be able to pass this knowledge on to someone else.

Vivien kept her head low, so far seeming amenable to his directions. When he had shown her the correct way to shine silverware, how to carefully fold the napkins and set the table, she had done so without complaint. He was particularly pleased at her progress in cooking, and tonight's menu was certain to spark envy amongst the others. He glowed at the thought of their jealousy: a beautiful young woman on his arm, a dinner cooked to perfection, in the most coveted home, overlooking the town spires and the Severn itself.

When Gavin was out on important business, he made sure to bolt the door of her room as quietly as he could. They both knew she was a captive, but he did not want to shatter the bliss they had created together. He had one tiny complaint, however. Vivien rarely spoke, and had to be coaxed to make conversation over dinner. He had no desire to ask her about her life before she came here, however; he didn't want to reignite painful memories for her, or stoke the flames of rebellion that he had successfully quelled. After a few awkward nights of eating dinner in silence, he realised that it was probably natural that she would not have much to contribute. She had not, after all, had the benefit of an education. He chided himself that he had been so blind. This poor creature had been swimming around in the muck beneath the surface of the water, sheltered and kept ignorant by whatever wretched being she served there. But he was perfectly poised to give the gift of an education to this poor woman. This could be one of his greatest gifts, he realised.

His mother, Ivy, had also not been granted the benefit of a higher education. While her brothers had been sent to private schools, later going on to Oxford and Cambridge, she had been kept at home. She had been a veritable sponge, however, as she listened to the conversations her brothers had at the table, and had ultimately decided to take the task of her education upon herself.

Gavin smiled sadly as he looked over at her armchair, at the deep crevices, carved out over years of sitting, reading by candlelight if she had to. Eventually, Ivy had gone blind, and Gavin had been given the job of reading to her. Perhaps he could do that for Vivien, he mused. He imagined what their evenings could look like, with a swelling sense of charity and pride.

Gavin broached the idea with her over an early supper of roast chicken, new potatoes, vegetables and gravy. It was a one-pot affair, the garlic, oil and thyme infusing with the fat of the chicken to provide a simple and tasty dish. Although Vivien did not give much away, he watched her intently as she took her first bite. He waited until she looked up at him, and he grinned, nodding enthusiastically.

'Good, yes?' he asked. She gave a small nod of the head, and continued to eat. 'It's good to line the stomach before a big event. Now, Vivien. I have been ruminating over your position here,' he said, shovelling a mouthful of roasted pepper into his mouth. Vivien halted eating, looking up at him sharply.

'No need to worry. I'm not getting rid of you.' He chuckled. He thought he saw the corner of her mouth twitch. She bowed her head once more, continuing to push her food around the plate.

'I thought a reward system might be suitable. As you have no monetary requirements, I was thinking that upon completion of your chores, it might be nice if I were to read to you. I have a wealth of books here. It's a shame to see them sitting there getting dusty. I can start with some of my favourites. Only if, of course, that would be of interest to you?'

'What kind of books?' asked Vivien, looking at him for the first time with interest.

'Well, we could start with some very general ones. Books on maintaining an orderly household, cooking, sewing, etiquette, that sort of thing. I can read to you in the evenings, before you go to bed, if you like?'

She narrowed her eyes. 'You will read them to me?' she said.

'Of course! It's much better than watching TV before you go to sleep. Also, it will give us something to discuss over dinner.'

'I will learn faster if you give me the books to read,' she replied, seeming to quickly understand his motivation. Gavin's knife and fork paused, hovering over the plate.

'Oh. I apologise. I assumed… I assumed you could not read.'

'I can read,' she said flatly.

'Oh. I see. All right, then… well, in that case… I will find a book for you this evening.' Gavin slumped, feeling deflated. Reading to his mother was one of the things he missed most. He had been hoping it could have become something he could share with Vivien. Immediately he regretted offering her such a generous olive branch.

The rest of the meal was spent in awkward silence. At least they would be able to engage on the books she read, he thought dejectedly. He went into the library, carefully poring over his mother's well-thumbed books. He ran his fingers over their fraying spines, tears in his eyes as he remembered

Ivy reading them to him as a boy. He started with the essentials: *Robert's Rule of Order*, *Elements of the Table*, and of course Debrett's *Handbook*. He carried them downstairs to her and handed them over.

The next morning, Vivien carried all three books down to breakfast with her. Gavin was relieved that she appeared to be in a more amiable mood.

'Thank you for the books.' She placed them on the table next to his egg cup.

'You do not wish to read them?' he said, almost getting angry.

'I have finished. I enjoyed them very much.'

Using a teaspoon, he cracked open the top of the egg, peeling off the shell and decapitating the soft egg white inside.

'You've finished them already?' Gavin asked dubiously. Vivien nodded with the nonchalant air that infuriated him.

'I made you an egg.' He gestured for her to sit. Every morning he made Vivien a perfectly cooked soft-boiled egg with buttery toast soldiers, since he noticed it was the only thing she really seemed to finish eating. She sat, eagerly tapping the spoon on the shell.

'Where did you learn to read?' he asked tentatively, his curiosity getting the better of him.

She looked at him warily and shrugged uncertainly. She scooped out the golden egg yolk and popped it into her mouth.

~

On top of the man's heinous criminal acts, Vivien had to endure his over-cooked eggs each morning. It was the only thing he made that she could stomach. The only thing that his fingers couldn't touch—protected from him by the outer shell. If only the imbecile would take it out two minutes sooner, she seethed.

Every day, before Gavin left to run errands, he would stop by her room to deposit the latest reading material. Upon his departure, he would quietly bolt her door. Vivien had never been a particularly voracious reader in her former life; however, now she told herself that her life might just depend on it. She made sure not to let him know that she was already familiar with the majority of the texts he offered, but she reread them now, in a bid to find out as much about the pathetic creature as possible. If she could discover what made him tick, perhaps, in some way, it could lead to his destruction.

Vivien had begrudgingly come to accept that she would need to humour him in order to be granted more privileges. It would not be beneficial to her if she allowed herself to tell him that his bland, tasteless and greasy cooking was as disgusting and unpalatable as he was. Besides, that first week, when she had fought against the pull his blood magic exerted over her, she'd felt like she would die from exhaustion.

She devoured the books, asking for more each time they were together. She noticed that he was particularly careful about what he would allow her to read. As the week progressed, she forced herself to make small talk with him over dinner about what she had read that day. Eventually, he began bringing her fiction titles to supplement her reading.

He would not permit her to go inside the library. She also noted that he never gave her books to do with Druidism or anything containing even the mere mention of magic, as if she did not know it all anyway. Instead, he gave her books on political history, philosophy and art history.

Vivien read so quickly that eventually he grew irritable. It was impossible, he said, that she could have read five hundred and forty-four pages of *A World History of Political Thought* in three hours.

From his armchair, he had looked over the rim of his glasses, his yellow-blue eyes surveying the book she had placed beside him.

'I am ready for another,' she said. She would be damned if she was going to ask him like a pleading orphan.

'Another? Already?' he asked, the deep lines between his brows increased.

'Yes,' she said.

'You have read *every single page*?' He prodded the book three times as he reiterated each word.

'Yes,' she said again.

'Impossible!' His eyes betrayed a mocking disbelief. 'Okay then. Which three philosophers were responsible for shaping political thought around the Social Contract?'

Vivien controlled herself; the urge to roll her eyes at him was irresistible.

'Hobbes, Locke and Rousseau,' she said blandly.

'What is Kant's theory on morality?' He snapped his fingers, his face and neck growing pink.

'Kant believed that morality is set by rationality. Also known as the Categorical Imperative.'

Gavin drew air into his lungs. His chin jutted out; his eyes squinted slightly.

Vivien continued, 'Can I ask, do you think using blood magic on someone to control them and imprisoning them would fall into Kant's idea of the Categorical Imperative?' The words spewed out of her. She knew letting her emotions get the better of her was a mistake, but her hatred for him had formed like a peach stone, poisoning her from within.

Gavin gaped at her, eyes wide with disbelief. His lips formed into a snarl. 'Kant also said that autonomy was governed by the self, rather than heeding to a set of rules imposed by others. You were going to kill me. I had no choice. I put it to you: do you think it's right to control people's free will? That is what you have done for all of your sorry little life as a Siren, is it not?' The muscles in his jaw bulged.

She stared at him coldly. After a moment, she walked over to what she assumed to be his mother's armchair. The fabric was deep red, embroidered with gold fleurs-de-lis. The pit where she had rested her large backside was shining and threadbare. The back of the armchair was greasy from years of unwashed hair resting against it.

'Don't you dare—' he started.

It took Vivien every ounce of strength she had. Despite her revulsion, she promptly sat in the chair, panting from the strain of going against his command.

Gavin flew out of his chair. He grabbed her by the arm and pulled her up.

'How dare you touch my mother's chair!' he raged, spit

flying from his lips. No longer able to control his anger, he slapped her hard across the face.

Vivien felt heat as her lip split open; her left ear was ringing painfully.

'You think you're cleverer than me, don't you?'

There's no doubt about that, retorted the voice in her head. She just looked at him with contempt, flames burning in her eyes.

He let her go, his hands shaking.

'Look at you,' he said, face pale and trembling. 'I said we'd meet the Palgraves for drinks tonight. You should cover up that lip.'

She did not reply. She dabbed her lip with the back of her hand. Dark blood smeared against her olive skin. She would not need to conceal her arms or face. Her skin would heal itself within a matter of hours—but she wasn't going to tell him that.

He steadied himself against his mother's chair, unconsciously patting the headrest.

'We should not be fighting. I don't think we'll be having any more philosophical discussions.' He tried to laugh mildly. 'Best to go back to the sewing books, eh?' He attempted to sound breezy, trying to eradicate the fact he had dared to lay his sweaty palm on her. 'Speaking of which, did you make a start on your dress for the big event?'

'Yes. It will be finished in a few days,' she said coldly.

'Good. Make sure it is. We must make an impression. Now, do excuse me. I have dishes to attend to.' He smoothed down his yellow pinstripe shirt, brushing what was left of his grey hairs back. She watched him walking towards the kitchen.

'Sewing books are fine by me,' she said under her breath. And she meant it. She loved memorising the different stitches, imagining herself sewing up his mouth and eyes.

22

THE OTHERWORLD

The air smelled of petrichor as Tamsyn looked around the dense woodland. A glade of ferns carpeted the ground. Tamsyn walked between the feathered leaves, noting the springy moss that covered the earth. The literature she had read had described Journeying as travelling within the mind. Tamsyn always believed herself to have a good imagination, but this place was undoubtedly real.

Wind whipped through the canopy, disturbing the branches so violently the leaves made the sound of hard rain on a tin roof. Seeing no signs of life, she continued along the thin pathway through the trees. A faintly decipherable gap in the ferns traced through the greenery like a hairline fracture.

Her senses were on high alert. She scanned the gaps between the trees, squinting up into the sky. Would her guide be an animal hiding among the ferns? Would it be perched high up on the branches? Sudden movement caught her eye. A red squirrel clung to the bark of a nearby trunk. It paused, black eyes staring at her, before scurrying up to safer heights.

Tamsyn continued walking until the ferns petered out and the path begun to slope imperceptibly downwards. Birds flapped overhead, calling to one another, and the familiar and lazy coo of a wood pigeon made Tamsyn feel more at ease. She laughed, imagining revealing to Ellis that her spirit animal was a regal, portly wood pigeon. That would be about right, she thought.

After ten minutes of walking, with no sign of anything, the bank began to veer sharply down towards a stream. Could you eat and drink in this realm? she wondered. Surely Ellis would have expressly forbidden it if she couldn't. Tamsyn stopped for a moment, bending down towards the crystal-clear waters. She didn't feel hungry or thirsty, despite the fact that dinner had been hours ago. She extended her finger to touch the water. It was cold, parting around her finger. The air was warmer here. Much too warm for November.

Tamsyn took off her jacket and tied it around her waist. She cupped her hands and tasted the water; it was ice cold and refreshing. She dabbed a little on her forehead. A snapping twig broke the lull of the babbling brook. Her head jolted up towards the sound. Further upstream, a lone fawn was drinking from the river. She was perspiring now, her pulse pounding in her neck. Tamsyn rose as silently and as slowly as she could. Even so, the movement startled the fawn, and it its glossy brown eyes locked with hers. Every muscle in the animal's body was stayed by fear. It stared at her, unsure what to do. Tamsyn stood motionless.

If you are my guide, she thought, *don't run*. The deer stood in its statuesque form for a few moments longer. After careful consideration, it bent its neck back to the water, the delicate tongue lapping at the surface.

Flies buzzed around it, its ears twitching to flick them away as it moved to chew the tender stems by the water's edge. After a few moments, it turned its hindquarters to her and began walking slowly away, following the brook upstream. Tamsyn stood rooted to the spot. The bank in front of her created a high ridge on the other side of the stream that she was unable to see over, making it impossible to see whether the path continued. The water cut through the forest like an artery. The fawn was already making considerable progress. She feared that at any moment, it would be far enough away that she could lose sight of it.

Through the gap in the canopy, Tamsyn could feel that it had started to rain. She batted a buzzing fly away, before deciding to follow the fawn upstream. Unsure whether her movements would frighten it, she trod as lightly as she could, afraid that it would bolt at any moment. Tamsyn walked on, following its bobbing white tail, until the stream began to narrow. The trees that lined the water here were smaller in stature.

Eventually the trees petered out, and the terrain grew rocky and steep. The fawn stood on a grey outcrop of boulders, its ears twitching as it watched her scrambling up the rocks below. As she neared it, it disappeared into a tall, narrow crevice. The rain began to fall in earnest now, coming down in heavy sheets.

Tamsyn strained to pull herself up onto the ledge, her fingers slipping on the wet stone. Her foot found purchase on a rock below, and she heaved her body onto the outcrop. Brushing herself off, she stood, looking out over the forest. She could see for miles around, hundreds of miles of uninterrupted trees. She shielded her eyes from the large droplets that had begun to hammer down. She peered into the cave, but could no longer see the fawn. Perhaps it had gone deeper inside. There was no higher point than the ledge she was standing on, and she couldn't see it down below. A warmth emanated from the mouth of the cave.

Stepping through the entrance, she was sheltered from the rain, but plunged into darkness. After a few moments her eyes adjusted, and she could see the walls around her, glistening with water. She began to make her way further inside, the ground becoming more and more uneven. Slipping on the wet rocks, she put her hand on the cave wall to steady herself. It sank into slimy wet moss and she withdrew her hand hastily.

Tamsyn began to doubt herself. Had the fawn merely wanted to guide her to the cave, to show her something? Was this merely a dead end, or would this cave yield some sort of an answer? Tamsyn was at a loss as to how she would find any answers in a dank, dark cave.

Water dripped into her hair; the sound of water on rock echoed along the walls. As she scrambled further into the cave, it grew uncomfortably warm. Tamsyn stooped lower as the cave ceiling began to slope down. There was barely any light; the entrance of the cave was now far away and behind a curve in the wall of rock. She squinted in the darkness, feeling her way with her hands over the slippery, smooth rocks.

This doesn't feel right, she thought to herself. Planning to retrace her steps, she was about to turn back when she saw a faint blue light coming from a gap in the rocks ahead. Her heart quickened. The deer had led her to something.

On her hands and knees, she crawled into the small opening. She felt the rocks cutting into her palms and shins where the water had yet to erode them into smooth, round pebbles. The angle of the slope was so steep that she feared she would not be able to crawl backwards. Paralysed with fear, she breathed hard as she felt the rocks closing in around her chest and waist. She could not turn back now; she had come too far.

Pushing her body through the hole, she was surprised and relieved to see that she had come to the entrance of a huge cavern. Stalactites hung like alabaster chandeliers, sparkling in the pale blue light. The cavern sloped downwards. Veins of pale blue water interlaced the black rocks, heading off inside the mountain, down through invisible cracks deep below.

The loose rocks shifted beneath her, and she put her hands out to stop herself falling. She skidded down the slope, gathering speed. She was falling faster, towards jagged black rocks, silhouetted against the ghostly blue light. She grabbed out, trying to catch anything she could to stop her fall; she felt her nails splintering. Seeing an oblong rock, she stuck out her foot, bracing for impact.

As she skidded, she saw that she had already reached the edge of the basin, where the serrated earth met the smoother surface below. Whatever fear she had felt crawling through the rock space was dwarfed by the claustrophobia she felt now.

Tamsyn was trapped in a cave deep within the mountain, surrounded on all sides by rock. Adrenaline coursed through her body, numbing the pain from any cuts or bruises. Turning with difficulty, she attempted to scramble back up the way she had fallen. But before she was halfway there, the loose earth crumbled away and she slid helplessly back down onto the cave floor. Her heart began to flutter frantically against her chest, like a small bird buffeting against the bars of its cage.

Taking a deep breath, she grounded herself. She was sitting in Ellis's front room. Her body was not here. Still, she felt the crushing weight all around her, trapping her like an insect in a glass.

'Ellis,' she said into the darkness, her voice shaking. 'Can you hear me? I think I messed this up.' She waited for an answer. Only the echo of her voice and the dripping sounds in the cavern returned her call.

Tamsyn scanned the basin. Was this what Ellis had warned her about? Her stomach turned. The stream was not the path. The fawn was not her spirit guide. She was lost— worse than merely lost. She would take being lost, out there in the open, any day. She thought about what Ellis had said, about the path being her lifeline.

Hands shaking, Tamsyn plucked her way through the labyrinth of rocks. She stared at the water, snaking its way through the cavern floor. Now that she was closer, she noticed that it glowed faintly, pulsating, dimming and then brightening slightly. The brook she followed must have originated from here. She lowered herself into the bowl, mesmerised by it. Bending down, she touched the water. Cautiously, she swept her fingers through it. It was luxuriously warm, almost hot. She stood for a moment, considering. That would explain the hot air coming through the cave entrance. 'It must be geothermal,' she said out loud. Yet in the forest down below, it had been almost icy to the touch.

Upon closer inspection, Tamsyn could now see that everything was smooth, as if carved out by water. There was nothing growing here as it did on the walls of the cave entrance. The water level must rise significantly, then, she thought. In that case, it was imperative that she find another way out, and sooner rather than later.

A thin shaft of light came from high above, streaming though the entrance she had squeezed through. It shone directly onto what looked like a stone monument in the middle of the basin. It was a large white mound, rising up amidst the small black rocks around it. She walked over to it, brushing the surface with her fingertips. From afar, it had appeared as a large white monolith, hewn somehow from the cave itself. Now she could touch it, she realised with surprise that it was a large piece of smooth, bleached driftwood, deathly white from years in the sun, despite now being enclosed in darkness. It was gnarled and ancient; she wondered how a chunk of wood had come to be buried in rock and earth.

She ran her fingers over the smooth surface, the various knots and bumps, and examined the lesions where there had once been branches. A creaking sound, like old bones crack-ing, shattered the silence of the cavern. The wood moved underneath her fingers. The hairs on her arms stood on end. She froze, too frightened to move.

Tamsyn took a step back, her foot slipping between the rocks into the warm water. The surface of the wood creaked again, and it began to split in numerous places. Tamsyn stared as one larger split near the top of the wood revealed a dull yellow orb. Other smaller openings, nine in all, appeared down the length of the wood, each revealing more spheres.

They began opening individually, shifting around. A pinprick of black appeared in the centre of the largest orb, growing steadily in size. The black dot stopped when it pointed directly at her, contracting again. With horror, she realised it was an eye. She stared at the other, smaller spheres —they, too, had black centres now. Moving around in their sockets, searching in the darkness, the smaller eyes now locked on to her too. She stood stock still, knowing that there was nowhere to run. The cave was silent, save for the constant echo of water dripping on stone.

'You have come again,' came a voice from the driftwood, reedy and hollow. Tamsyn studied it. There were no cracks in the bark, no jagged mouths below the beady yellow eyes. How was it communicating with her?

'I'm sorry,' she replied out loud. 'We have never met before. You must have mistaken me for someone else.'

'What is it you seek?' the voice said. Tamsyn suddenly realised she didn't know. Answers to why her grandmother had been killed? What had happened to her mother? Could she, or rather *should* she, trust whatever this was?

'I am lost. I am looking for a way out,' she said at last. It wasn't a lie.

'There is no lost. There is no way out.' The eyes searched her.

'What are you doing in here?' asked Tamsyn.

'I am the Seer. I see all. I know all.' The eyes remained trained on her, blinking independently of one another.

'You said we have met before, yet I have never been here. What do you mean?' This time, she did not ask aloud, instead, she closed her eyes and asked inside her mind.

'I am the gatekeeper of this realm. I am outside of time. I have seen all that is, all that has been, and all that is yet to come.' In the darkness behind her eyelids emerged a great tree, its huge branches bearing leaves, bathed in sunlight. She was standing at the base of its trunk, the same nine eyes staring down at her.

'You say we have met before? When?'

'You have visited me in different forms. I speak not of when.'

'And you can give me answers?'

The eyes merely blinked; some looked in different directions, as if trained on something, or someone, elsewhere. Other eyes began to close sleepily.

'There are no answers to that which you seek.' The voice seemed bored, but it had no discernible expressions on its surface, so Tamsyn couldn't be sure.

'I have come to find my grandmother, Sylvia Pride. Can you tell me where she is?'

'She has passed into this realm.'

'Yes. I know that. Can you tell me where to find her?' asked Tamsyn desperately.

'She does not wish to be disturbed,' the Seer replied. Tamsyn watched the eyes. She wondered if any of them were trained in the direction of her grandmother.

'She does not wish to see me?'

'She does not wish to be disturbed,' it said again.

Tamsyn opened her eyes again, adjusting from the daylight in her mind to the enveloping darkness of the cave. Stepping back, she considered the entity in front of her. She saw now that the arteries of blue water spread out from the dried roots of the wood, glowing slightly brighter now that it was awake, with a faint pulsating light.

'How long have you been trapped here? Inside this mountain?'

'I know not of where I reside. My existence is eternal.'

'But how can you see anything?'

'I am the Seer,' it replied simply.

Tamsyn looked at the glowing water again as it flowed placidly on through unseen cracks on the mountain.

'Are you connected in some way to the water?'

'Water is life. Water contains memory.' The eyes on the stump began to blink sleepily. One by one, they began to close.

'Wait! I need to get out of here. Please!'

The water that had been trickling down the cracks of the cave wall flowed more heavily now. It had been raining hard when she entered the cave; her time had already run out. The rocks Tamsyn stood on were already beginning to shrink.

Like a rat, she ran around the perimeter of the basin, desperately searching for footholds in the rock. Seeing a pointed outcrop, she untied her jacket from around her waist. She held the cuffs as she swung it up over the rock, a few feet higher than her head. The water lapped at her ankles now as she pulled on the arms of the coat, heaving herself up, feet scrabbling at any purchase she could find.

Once she was on the ledge, she began to climb, pulling herself from stone to stone, hand over hand. She had made it halfway up when she realised there were no more stones left. She crouched on a boulder that was barely wide enough for her feet. Clinging on to the wall, pressing herself against the stone, she looked down at the cavern. The water already covered a third of the white stump. It was completely inanimate; its eyes were firmly closed, as if she had imagined the whole thing.

A black outcrop of rock sat above her, over a metre away. Tamsyn placed her foot inside a crack in the cave wall, pushing herself upwards. Her fingers tried to grasp the stone, but she couldn't quite reach. She tried again, heaving herself towards it and using her momentum to swing up and forwards.

At last, Tamsyn's fingers brushed against the rock. She grasped it, but it was slick beneath her hands. She plummeted back down, hands and feet desperately scrambling for purchase. The rocks sliced at her hands and legs. Her head hit a rock on the side of the basin, and she tumbled into the water below.

Her ears rang; the cave slid this way and that, out of focus. Tamsyn put her hand to her head. She knew before she looked that there would be blood on her fingers.

She wasn't here, Tamsyn told herself again. Except she was. Her soul was here. Her mind was here. She would die here. Because she had left the path. Because, as usual, she had been utterly abandoned by her grandmother who *didn't want to be disturbed.*

She was sitting chest deep in water now. With effort, she stood up and began to splash through the water, running frantically around the perimeter, searching in vain for a way out as the water rose faster around her.

23
A PARTY OF CROWS

avin had encouraged Vivien to take the reins for the big event. He regretted it bitterly when he saw there were candles on every available surface, and flowers from the overly expensive florist in town. She'd even hired a band. He suspected she was doing it on purpose, to get a reaction out of him. He quickly rearranged the napkins and guest list when she wasn't looking.

He had said nothing to her all week about what he wanted to achieve this evening, taking special precautions not to mention the last piece of the puzzle by name. He didn't want her connecting any dots—not until he was finished with her, anyway.

Initially he had been pleasantly surprised, delighted in fact, that she seemed to be showing such interest. That is, until he saw the invoices. He had demanded to know why she wasn't able to get all this for free, like the steak from the butchers. She had merely shrugged, saying her power didn't extend *that* far, which he knew was a blatant lie.

'I will pull out all the stops to get you what you want,' she said. 'Once it has been achieved, you must set me free.'

He almost laughed. 'Do forgive me for being so blunt, Vivien, but I'm not sure you possess such bargaining chips.'

'You have stripped me of the ability to use my powers for anyone but you—not even myself,' she said. 'However, if you keep me here as your prisoner, I will do the bare minimum. I will fight you at every turn; you will have to sleep with your eyes open, wondering if one day the blood magic will wear off...' Although she stopped short of the threat, he could see it in her eyes.

'Or I can get you everything you want,' she went on. 'The land, ownership of the monuments, the things that you need to reconnect the ley line. I will serve them to you with a bow on top. Once you have access to that power, you will no longer need me anyway. You will not need *anyone*. My duty will be done, and I will have made recompense for attacking you that night. Even though you did not bring an offering to me. It is the honourable thing... the gentlemanly thing to do, Gavin.'

She was right, of course. He wouldn't need her once he had access to the infinite power of the ley line. It irked him that she was appealing to his honour, as if his status as a gentleman were even in question. He could think of no reasonable excuse to keep her captive longer than need be.

He reached out to her across the dining table, and they shook hands. The deal was set. He bid her goodnight.

Since that conversation, Gavin had seen Vivien very little. He paced back and forth, seeing new specks of dust on the armoire that hadn't been there a second ago. He obsessed over the seating plan, moving the name cards around the table over and over again until he thought he'd go mad. He wanted his guests to have a wonderful time; he wanted them to make conversation with new and interesting people with whom they had some common ground. He wanted them to admire him—no, he wanted them to writhe with jealousy of him. At the same time, he could not afford to place people of too much power next to one another. Especially people with too much money. What if they hatched their own plans?

He resorted to drawing the table plan out on two pieces of A3 paper, sticking them together and taping them onto a cork board. With toothpicks he made little flags, each with the name of a guest on it. He tried to speak to Vivien about it, but she simply waved him off, like a nuisance child that was getting under her feet. Like his mother sometimes used to do. He should never have made that bargain with Vivien, he thought crossly.

For all his bravado, Gavin was not actually sure of any of the details of his hold over Vivien. He had consulted numerous texts for information on blood magic. The practice, however, had been made illegal in Britain in 1666, after the last great plague in London. Thus, any information he could find on it merely contained warnings but no useful details.

Uneasy butterflies stirred in his gut. Was what she said true? Was he already losing control of her? Was it wise to allow her to mix with people at the party? He had no choice, he reminded himself. He needed her to cast whatever terrible magic she held over people, to convince them to do whatever she, or more accurately *he*, wanted them to.

Saturday arrived, and Gavin tried to busy himself to ease his nerves. Vivien had hired young women from the Girls' School to stand with trays of drinks and hand out canapés while the foyer of the Crow's Nest began to fill. He padded up the thin winding staircase to the door leading to the attic room and knocked softly.

'Vivien, dear, the guests are arriving,' he said to the cold, hard wood.

'Coming,' she called from inside.

He quietly unlatched the lock, and after a moment the door handle turned. The door opened slowly, and as his eyes fell upon her, he was taken aback.

She stood in a steel grey satin dress. Her dark hair fell in waves over her shoulders, so long it skimmed past her elbows. She had arranged the material so that it draped over her curves, clinging to her hips and descending into a lazy V between her breasts. The satin flowed down her torso until it draped around her feet, like a pool of dark water beneath a storm.

She had rouged her lips a deep, dark red. He had no idea where she had obtained lipstick from, but it stirred an ugly desire within him. He could hear his mother's voice: *Filthy little harlot.* His mouth was dry. He tried to speak, to tell her to wipe the lipstick off. But he just stood there, mouth agape.

Her eyes glittered in the light coming from the doorway.

He did not want the men downstairs seeing her like this, thinking the things he was thinking about her. But she was already walking past him, down the stairs.

Confusion swept over him as her scent enveloped him. He was rooted to the spot, and some still logical part of his brain screamed at him, *Don't let them see her before they see you. You are the man of the hour.* She stopped, looking back at him. She held her hand out expectantly, so that she might take his arm. A rush of blood deafened his ears as he walked to her.

He felt her hand slide into the crook of his arm. His pulse was racing; a white-hot fire raged in his head. He wanted to grab her, push her against the wall and hitch up her dress. Throw her back into the room and lock the door behind them.

The band started playing a different song, one that she must have instructed them to. They walked arm in arm to the top of the main stairs, her dress gliding over the carpet. Gavin almost tripped down the first two stairs. Between the balustrades he could see dozens of eyes staring, intently watching Vivien, in the same pathetic way they had that night in the Amber Room. She held him fast so that he did not fall. Just standing this close to her, he could feel her towering strength. She was rock, iron, water, all at once. He couldn't think straight. All he knew was that he needed to possess her, body and soul.

Vivien stopped halfway down the stairs. The band in the foyer fell silent. Gavin couldn't look directly at her; she was so intoxicating. The men below were still looking, though, their faces frozen, completely entranced. She looked at Gavin, waiting expectantly for him to say something. He was not prepared, however, and merely stood, frozen to the spot.

'Good evening, gentlemen,' she began, as he stood there dumbfounded. 'On behalf of Gavin Hardcastle, I would like to thank you for joining us on this special evening. Please make your way into the dining room. *Boneddigion nos da. Diolch yn fawr am ddod. Gwnewch eich ffordd i mewn i'r ystafell fwyta,*' she said. Vivien began to descend the stairs without him. As she did so, she nodded at the bass player. Like an automaton, he began to play again. The rest of the band seemed to rouse themselves from a deep slumber and joined him. The men below still stood there, breathing out of their mouths like animals at feeding time, clutching their champagne flutes and half-eaten canapés. After a moment the fog seemed to lift and they began walking towards the dining room, unwilling or unable to look away from her as she glided through the middle of them to the double doors.

Gavin trailed helplessly behind her. He was still elated by her touch, yet enraged that she had already stolen his night. As she placed her hand on one of the massive doors, he pushed in front of her, eager to get to the head of the table before she did. With a flourish, he opened the doors. The easel containing his seating plan was gone. As too were the place cards. Vivien stood at the entrance, warmly greeting each person by name before pointing to the place in which they should be seated.

Heart pounding, Gavin stood mutely beside her, feigning a smile as the guests filed past. He knew better than to cause a scene. Then, niceties done, he and Vivien made their way towards the head of the table.

Charlie Furth beamed as she approached. 'Love what you've done with the place—sorry, what's your name again?' he said.

'It's Vivien. Thank you, but I couldn't have done it without Gavin. He has been showing me the ropes. Where I come from, we don't do much entertaining,' she answered with a smile.

Charlie's eyes were alight, his dazzling grin stretched across his face. Gavin had seen it many times, usually when he was talking to attractive women. Even though he wore a wedding ring, it never seemed to dampen his chances at bedding whoever he set his eyes on.

Gavin looked around him; reluctantly, he admitted that the dining room did look marvellous. She had arranged it to utter perfection. The candles, the white flowers, sprays of eucalyptus, the silverware, napkins and china. Vivien had even embroidered the napkins with his initials, G.H., the delicate silver thread looping and curling. He imagined fetching them from the sideboard when she was long gone, idly wondering if she had ever really been here, or if it had all been a dream. He shook his head; he needed to pull himself together.

The guests took their seats. Teenagers from the local sixth form had been hired to walk round filling wine glasses, nervously fumbling in a way that displeased him.

Holding his glass, Gavin rose to his feet. 'Gentlemen!' he gestured to the room. 'Welcome to our first Annual General Meeting at the Crow's Nest. I am confident it will be the first of many. Please, raise your glasses to the AGM.'

'And cheers to you, Gavin, for organising it,' Vivien interjected.

'To the AGM. To Gavin!' everyone said in unison, raising their glasses.

Clinking ensued, and a brief murmur of idle chit-chat rose once again to fill the silence.

'Please, everyone, take your seats,' said Vivien.

What the hell was she doing? He was supposed to say that. Taking a calming breath, Gavin took his own seat and watched the guests chatting amongst themselves while they waited for starters, giving him the opportunity to speak to the men directly on either side of him. He had intended to be seated next to the mayor of Shrewsbury and Bill Rickerby-Clark, Shropshire's best property lawyer. However, Vivien's meddling meant that he was seated next to some dreadful unshaven millennial and Terence Buchanan, a mere farmer whose presence he had to endure every month at the council meetings. Vivien was sat next to Charlie Furth, who of course had his sweaty paws all over her.

He wondered whether she would be able to simply walk out with Charlie, if he asked her to. Even though his poor wife was sat at home with four children, he appeared to have not a care in the world. The way his eyes glinted at Vivien in the candlelight, one would believe he was a seventeen-year-old falling in love for the first time. A solitary bead of sweat slid down Gavin's temple as he watched them and gripped the stem of his wine glass. He stared at them until his starter arrived.

'So,' piped up the millennial, chewing with his mouth

open. 'You must be Mr Buchanan.' He held out his hand across the table.

'Yup. That's me,' Terence replied, his voice painfully gravelly from years of smoking. He sloppily forked partridge meat into his mouth.

Gavin snapped out of his reverie.

'Terence, this is Michael Schwartz. He owns a tech start-up in town.'

'Oh yeah? I.T., is it?' asked Terence with feigned interest.

'Of sorts,' said Michael. 'We are helping businesses around the world make the transition from office-based working into the virtual space.'

'You what?' said Terence, staring at him blankly.

'Many corporations and business owners are realising that there's a lot of money to be saved on overheads. Paying utility bills, rent for offices, the wasted time their employees spend commuting or going to unnecessary meetings. So, we have built a platform that allows people to work from home but still be part of the face-to-face office environment. Big meetings or one-to-one catch-ups with your supervisor can now be done wearing a headset in the comfort of your own home. And using our virtual headsets, workers will now able to jump into the office as and when required.' Michael took a sip of wine and smiled. Clearly he was required to repeat this spiel several times a day.

Terence and Gavin looked at him with a mixture of confusion and mild disdain.

'Companies want their employees to sit on their arses at home all day? Where's the sense in that?' Terence's voice reverberated inside his glass as he downed his red wine.

'Yes.' Michael laughed. 'Of course, it's not for everybody, but believe it or not, many people enjoy working from home and are finding, as a consequence, that they are more productive.'

'Maybe initially,' said Gavin. 'But as soon as the novelty wears off they will be sitting around in their dressing gowns watching TV and getting paid for the privilege. It is inhuman. Inhuman and wholly unhealthy to be sat at home all day, not interacting with anyone.' He took a sliver of partridge, using his knife to slather on the blackberry jus. In his nerves, he had forgotten to taste the jus earlier that afternoon. He was stricken as he realised that it was incredibly bitter, completely ruining the flavour of the partridge. He looked around the table, but the guests were happily eating, not even flinching as they shovelled the tart sauce into their mouths.

'That's the beauty of it,' Michael replied. 'They *are* interacting. We have built the most realistic virtual platform in the world. People are now able to fully immerse themselves into office life, to see lifelike avatars of their colleagues in front of them. We are expanding the business into leisure and gaming, of course.'

'You have a lot of clients for this thing, then?' asked Terence.

'Oh yes. In our third year of business, we are making a gross profit of one hundred and fifty million,' replied Michael.

Gavin turned his attention from the spoiled jus to Michael. 'Is that so?' He didn't know whether it was simply good fortune or one of Vivien's charms, but either way, she had seated him next to the right man after all. 'I wonder if I could pick your brain,' he said. 'I have a problem with this project I'm working on. You see, one of the strongest ley lines in the country exists in this very county. Well, it did until a few hundred years ago. Anyway, I have been working hard on re-establishing the monuments—some of which have been completely destroyed by newbuild developments and various other eyesores. One of the last pieces of the puzzle is the land at…' he spoke in a low whisper so Vivien couldn't overhear him, '*at Rosemount*. I need to raise the capital in order to buy the land.'

'I'm sorry. I don't buy land. As I said, I'm interested in virtual assets.'

'Ah, well. That's a shame. You really should speak to my Vivien after dinner. She's interested in all that… stuff.' Gavin smiled at the upstart millennial in his basic grey t-shirt and jeans.

'That Pride girl won't sell,' offered Terence, fishing a bit of meat from the back of his teeth. 'My great-great-great-grandfather gave the Prides that land after they cured their daughter of consumption. There will always be a Pride on that land, make no mistake.' He swayed slightly as he reached to the centre of the table for more wine.

'I'm sorry—your ancestors *gave* them the land? For free?'

'Aye. A small price to pay for a life.' Terence looked bleary-eyed at Gavin.

'Was there a signed agreement? Do you have a contract of any sort?'

'God, no. It were a verbal agreement. Probably the Pride women cast a binding spell to seal the deal. My family couldn't read or write. Had no need for it. But it was an understanding, passed down, that the Prides shall be left to live on that land until there are no more Prides left on this earth. Then and only then would a Buchanan be permitted to take back the land.'

'Fascinating. Thank you, Terence.' Gavin turned back to Michael, grinning as he sipped his wine. 'I don't think I will be in need of your money after all, Mr Schwartz.'

24
THE SEER

As Ellis watched with growing concern, the candles guttered as if in an unseen breeze, burning low and blue and threatening to be extinguished. He watched Tamsyn's face intently. In place of the calm, serene expression, her brow was now furrowed, her eyes moving erratically under the closed lids. He could not tell if she was frightened, in physical pain or both.

He had been trying to reach her for half an hour, calling her back again and again. He beat the drum harder, with an irregularity that had never failed to snap a student out of their reverie. She made absolutely no sign that she could hear him. Her hands were balled so tightly into fists he was sure her nails must be cutting into her palms.

Ellis's concentration was broken abruptly by the flapping of wings and the scraping of claws on glass. Alchiba the crow, his spirit guide, cawed and flapped, beating his body in incessant warning against one of the panes of glass in the bi-fold doors.

For the first time, Ellis noticed a hissing sound from the four corners of the room. The hiss erupted into a blast, as water began to spew out of cracks opening up in the plaster. He jumped up, shock and confusion rendering him momentarily useless as he watched pools of water flowing into the centre of the room, sweeping forwards from all directions. He watched the rug turn dark as it permeated the threads. The water rushed towards Tamsyn, who still sat motionless, pale and shaking.

'Tamsyn! You must come back,' he shouted. He was half commanding her, mostly imploring. Clearly she had strayed from the path, either willingly, innocently, or… Had she had been taken by force? He had not thought it possible, but something ominous hung over her and he had no experience of what that would mean in the Other Realm.

Alchiba cawed again, his large black wings beating against the glass. Ellis was loath to leave Tamsyn even for a second, but he knew never to ignore Alchiba. He, splashed through the thin film of water covering the floor and yanked open one side of the bi-fold doors.

Alchiba flew in, his large wings slightly folded. He landed on a side table near Tamsyn, his beady black eyes surveying her. Craning his head back, he opened his beak, cawing once.

Ellis rushed over to them and sat down next to Tamsyn. He looked from Alchiba back to her, then back to Alchiba. The raven stared back at Ellis. He cocked his head to one side. Tamsyn was dithering now, her lips turning a deathly shade of blue.

Ellis closed his eyes and took a deep breath, and now he saw through Alchiba's eyes. The bird was flying over a dense canopy of trees. In the distance, he saw a high stone peak. The bird dived down, and in a moment Alchiba landed on a stony outcrop. This was a part of the Underworld he had never seen before. It was true that each person experienced the place differently, but there was always a familiarity to it. That said, Ellis always stuck to the rules and never left the path, and so he had no experience of what happened when you ventured into the wilderness. Alchiba looked into the mouth of a cave, then flapped his wings, flying into it as far as he dared before the opening became too small for him to fly. He landed on the floor of the cave, then hopped on a little further. Through him, Ellis could hear the roaring of water, echoing somewhere inside the mountain.

Ellis opened his eyes. Alchiba's head bowed slightly as he surveyed Tamsyn with his glittering black eyes. Ellis took Tamsyn's hands. They were clammy and cold.

He closed his eyes again and muttered under his breath.

'Hear my words, Tamsyn. Hear my voice. I cannot pull you back. But I know you can overcome whatever is binding you. You do not belong to that world. You are here, with me.'

The water continued to rush in, sweeping over several candles that were on the floor and knocking them over; the wicks hissed as the flames went out. The flames of the others, situated at higher points, blew wildly back and forth until they too toppled over, spilling wax down the table tops.

Tamsyn sat slumped on a rock, blood pouring from the cut on her forehead. The water raged around her, bubbling and frothing around her chest. The icy cold took her breath away and she felt her chest contracting as she began gasping for breath. The light that had streamed from the cave entrance was dim now. She realised with desperation that the sun must be going down.

As the water continued to rise, she could see no way out. It was almost up to her neck now. She tried desperately to control her breathing, but it came in short, sharps bursts as she frantically inhaled the thin air and began taking on gulps of water. Her heart hammered, and she felt herself hyperventilating uncontrollably.

She jumped off the rock and began swimming desperately towards the white stump. Only its uppermost eyelid was visible above the water line, still tightly shut.

She reached out and clung to the divots in the bark to try and gain purchase. Maybe if she could get to the top of the stump, the water would not reach her and she could wait for it to recede.

She dug her nails in, her feet trying to find purchase on the wood below. Her shoes merely scraped along its smooth surface, slipping again and again.

The water bubbled and foamed over the last eyelid.

This is it, she thought. *Does your spirit simply stay in the Underworld if you die here?* Her chest felt like it was going to explode. The water raged. White foam and waves whipped up, splashing over her head before she could catch her breath.

She tried desperately to cling onto the wood; the water was rippling around the lip of the basin now. A wave hit her, prising her away from her anchor. As the water took her under, she gulped in a mouthful as she fought to swim to the surface. All had gone dark, but she opened her eyes anyway.

For a moment, far above her she saw a flash of light, warm and golden, before it was gone again. Her lungs were screaming now. She kicked towards the place she thought might be up.

As she broke the surface, the force of the water spun her around. With horror, she realised that the basin was acting as a whirlpool as water streamed into it from all sides. Tamsyn barely had time to take a breath before she was plunged under the surface once again. *This is futile*, she heard herself say. *You're going to die here.* With her last breath she propelled herself towards the piece of wood. She held on to it once more, forcing herself to open her eyes underwater.

Again, she saw light, caught a glimpse a sprawling meadow. Beside her stood the gigantic tree, its colossal branches reaching up into the sky. But now, where once it had been covered with lush green leaves, its naked branches were shaking in the wind. She stood underneath the huge tree in a vast meadow filled with wild flowers. She breathed in the crisp air.

In an instant, she was underwater again. Was she dying? She willed the meadow to come again. She let go of the stump, allowing herself to be battered away by the raging water. She heard the voice of the tree.

I know not of where my body resides.
Mountains and valleys rise and fall around me.
I travelled by waterways.
I died and became the Seer.

Mountains and valleys rise and fall around me.

This place exists outside of time, she realised. She felt the water filling her nose and mouth, entering her lungs. She struggled violently one last time, and then everything went dark.

~

Tamsyn's body went limp. Ellis caught her before her head hit the water. It was ankle deep now, but the urgency with which it flowed had ceased.

She was deathly white, her lips entirely blue. Moments before, her breath had been ragged, gurgling. Now she lay there with no signs of life. Swiftly, he picked her up and placed her onto the sofa. He could see no other way to keep her out of the foot or so of water that now filled the room, although it would make CPR difficult. He linked his hands, finding the correct place in the centre of her breastbone, and began to pump. He counted the compressions, panic rising in his own chest. His body shook as he reached thirty compressions. Hands shaking, he tipped her head back. Pinching her nose, he gave two deep breaths into her mouth. Tamsyn lay there motionless.

'Tamsyn!' he shouted, and resumed the chest compressions. 'Do something, for God's sake!' he barked at Alchiba, who was watching from a high beam close to the ceiling. His mind raced frantically. 'Get me something to make her sick. From the shelves in my office. Milk thistle—I don't know! Just anything from the second shelf down!' He had lost count now of how many compressions he had given. He counted another ten, hearing bottles crashing and breaking down the hallway from his office.

Alchiba swooped back into the room, a small vial held precariously in his claws. The crow was not one who liked to carry out errands, even in life-or-death situations. He dropped the glass bottle on the sofa next to Tamsyn.

'Broom flower?' Ellis said, exasperated. 'It will have to do.' Alchiba flew back up to the rafters and turned his back, making it clear he had done as much as he cared to do.

Yanking the cork from the vial, Ellis took one of the dried flowers and crushed it between his fingers. It released a pungent scent. He prised Tamsyn's blue lips apart and placed the flower as far back into her throat as possible. He closed her mouth again, uttering the first purging spell that came into his head.

Time stood still as he watched her face, now grey in the moonlight that streamed through the windows. Nothing. Struggling with her limp torso and arms, he gathered her up and placed her in an upright position, then bent her head between her legs. How long had she been without oxygen? He should have dialled 999, but how would he tell the police that she had drowned in his living room? What would happen if a coroner were to perform an autopsy on this 'drowned woman' and they found no water in her lungs?

Tamsyn's back straightened as her muscles began to convulse. With an almighty retch, she began to throw up. To Ellis's surprise, she expelled water and bile out onto the sofa.

In panic, Tamsyn flailed her arms wildly, gasping for air as she threw up again.

'It's okay! It's okay! You're safe. I'm here.' Ellis sat beside her and slapped her on the back, rubbing in circular motions, feeling the wracking coughs through his palm.

Tamsyn did not speak. Breathing as deeply as she could, she started to splutter and cry, tears streaming down her face. As her cries turned into an anguished wail, he stopped patting her and held her to him.

'It's okay. You're here now. It's okay,' he repeated soothingly.

'It's not okay,' she said, with a terrible anguish in her voice. 'I am a failure!' she shouted. 'I couldn't even find the guide! I died there!' Ellis could feel the anger and shock rippling through her body. 'She doesn't even want to see me!' Tamsyn tried to stand on shaking legs. She buried her face into her hands. Wracking sobs filled the silent room. Alchiba cawed from above. He wanted to be let out. Ellis shot him an angry look. Lips pressed together, he got to his feet, strode to the bi-fold doors and flung one side open. As the flurry of black feathers flew off into the trees, Ellis watched as the last of the water spewed out of the doorway.

Tamsyn was still standing with her head in her hands, trying to control her anguished sobs.

Ellis walked over to her. 'You are not a failure. You are not responsible for the people who have let you down.'

'This was a mistake. I should never have gone into the Underworld. Have you ever known anyone so idiotic that they die on their first journey?' Gritting her teeth in anger, she wiped away her tears in frustration.

'Well, yes, I do now. But you're not idiotic,' Ellis said

matter-of-factly. Tamsyn hugged her torso, shivering uncontrollably.

'It's okay. You're okay. You need to rest and recover. When you're ready, we will talk through what happened.' Ellis gathered a dry blanket from the sofa and put it round her shoulders. He wanted to put his arms around her again, to comfort her. Instead, he headed to the kitchen and made her a cup of nettle and lemongrass tea.

When he returned to the living room, Tamsyn was sitting forlornly on the sofa, cocooned and shivering, staring out at the wreck of the living room from beneath dripping locks of hair.

'Oh my God. What happened to this place?' she asked shakily. Ellis handed her the steaming cup of tea. Tamsyn took it, hands trembling. She sipped her tea and tried her best to compose herself.

'It's just stuff. It will dry out,' he replied.

'But how? Where is this water from?'

'I think it brings us closer to answering why you were sent away from Much Wenlock. I think that when you're in danger, you're not in control of your power.'

She gave him a puzzled look. 'What is my power?'

'I'm not exactly sure, yet. But somehow, you bought the water from the Underworld into this world.'

'How is that even possible?' she said.

'I don't know. Not yet anyway.'

Tamsyn was silent a moment. Then, handing Ellis her teacup, she stood and walked over to her backpack. After an awkward moment of fiddling, she carefully pulled out the two halves of the coffee cup and walked back to the sofa with them.

'I made this happen, earlier today, when I was at the coffee shop. I didn't want to tell you. I guess I thought you might think I wasn't ready and... well, maybe I wasn't ready.'

Ellis held the two halves in his hand and didn't seem to be listening to her. He stared intently at what was left of the coffee cup and appeared to be in deep thought.

'I think we need to pay your grandmother's best friend a little visit,' he said at length, breaking the silence. 'What was her name?'

'Bridie.'

'Bridie, yes. I have a potion that should loosen the effects of the oath spell long enough to get answers. We'll leave first thing in the morning.'

PART THREE

Sabrina Fair,
Listen where thou art sitting
Under the glassie, cool, translucent wave,
In twisted braids of lilies knitting
The loose train of thy amber-dropping hair;
Listen for dear honour's sake,
Goddess of the Silver lake,
Listen and save.

—John Milton

25

A SHADOW

Vivien was climbing the walls. So insanely bored, angry, frustrated and out of her mind. There was no word for this turgid existence, locked in a tower devoid of any stimulus whatsoever. Sometimes, when Gavin left the Crow's Nest, she would watch him walk down the cobbled alleyways and then scream into a pillow until she felt her vocal cords shredding.

When she'd broached the subject of their agreement, Gavin's reply was that until he had secured the last piece of land, her end had not been fulfilled. Although she knew that nothing was permanent, she felt with a sickening certainty that she would be locked in this room forever. Even if she managed to walk out one day, to make her way down to the river, a part of her would remain here forever, trapped.

Why had Sabrina not come for her? Had she even noticed she was gone? Maybe she was punishing her for trying to attack this man in the first place. Perhaps her mistress thought she should have just answered his questions, thus avoiding all of this mess. And if she had done? He would just call on her again and again, or on some other poor river creature, until the inevitable... Men always wanted more. As soon as they saw a Siren, they made it their life's mission to own her.

Vivien had no reason to expect Gavin would keep his end of the bargain; regardless, she began jotting down every move he made and at what time. She watched everything he ate and drank, what time he took bathroom breaks. Things were getting desperate; this was her last-ditch attempt to look for a moment in which he might be weak. But she was still unable to commit any form of harm, magical or physical, against him.

After two weeks of watching him and surveying his property, she noticed a man sneaking in the side entrance every Sunday and Thursday at 10:30 p.m. It was always dark, but she could see him approaching each time, and something in the way he moved disturbed her.

The previous Sunday, she had watched from the window with all the lights turned off, waiting to see him. He had looked directly up at the window. Her heart had pounded in her chest as she slowly backed away so as not to create any sign of movement, and peered at him from behind the curtain. The man had stood there a while, immovable, eyes glistening. Watching. Waiting.

He usually crept away through the front garden and out again into the winding streets at one o'clock, but that night, he hadn't left until 3 a.m. She made a note in a half-empty notebook she had stolen from one of the drawers downstairs and then tucked it under her mattress.

When Thursday rolled around again, Vivien waited on her bed with only a candle for light, continuously checking the pendulum clock on the wall. At twenty-five past ten, she blew the candle out and crouched down by the window.

After a few minutes, the shadowy figure came ambling up the cobblestone street. Under his arm he looked to be holding a large book. Vivien assumed it was another spell book from the library. Maybe it had something to do with helping Gavin figure out how to get into Rosemount, she thought.

This time the man was wearing a long black coat. Vivien's stomach flipped. There was something about his gait and the way the dark fabric billowed behind him. She had seen him before. She watched him for a few more moments, her unease pinging at her like an alarm. Then it came to her: it was *him*, the one who had summoned her and warned her that a woman called Tamsyn Pride would seek revenge upon her for her grandmother's death.

She was breathing hard as she backed away from the window. Perhaps it was a coincidence that he and Gavin knew each other. For downstairs, she heard Gavin's hushed tones as he greeted him at the door. After a moment, the library door clicked shut. The house fell silent again, save for the pendulum swinging inside the grandfather clock.

26

THE RUNES OF ROSEMOUNT

G avin paid Bridie a visit, Vivien at his side. A dickie bird had told him that the old bat knew where all the defences to Rosemount were. When she opened the door her eyes widened when they fell upon Vivien. She stood fast in the doorway, as if she wasn't planning on letting them in, even though they both knew she had no choice in the matter.

Gavin noticed Vivien looking around Bridie's home with keen interest, although he couldn't understand why. The place was a filthy hole. He wondered who would have the unfortunate task of clearing the place once the senile old biddy had snuffed it. Maybe it would be that Tamsyn girl. She might even have to live with Bridie soon enough to take care of her until she shuffled off to meet her maker. He couldn't help but smile at the thought—it would serve them both right. He never had got his revenge on Sylvia and Bridie for meddling with the council when he was chairman. He'd eventually secure Rosemount for himself, though, and it was a real shame Sylvia hadn't lived long enough to see it.

Gavin pulled out the large tome that Colin had brought him a few nights earlier and dropped it onto Bridie's coffee table.

'Do you know what that is?' he said, reluctantly sitting down in one of the grotty armchairs facing the fire.

'Don't 'ave a clue,' she replied, which they all knew was a lie. Her beady eyes glistened as they fixed on to his. 'Who is this woman?' she asked him, raising a crooked finger in the direction of Vivien, who was fixated on a dusty wooden carving on a shelf.

'This is Vivien.' He looked over to her; she looked back at them, her face set in stone.

'That's not 'er name.' Bridie's bottom lip quivered.

'Of course it is,' he replied.

'It bloody ain't.'

'Oh, all right. Fine. That's not her name,' he said.

'Do I—know you?' Bridie asked, addressing Vivien.

'Of course you don't know her, you silly old witch,' Gavin cut in.

'What is she?' Bridie eyed Vivien warily. 'She ain't human, is she?'

Vivien looked at Bridie in surprise, but remained silent.

'Honestly, Bridie,' Gavin huffed. 'You can drop the act now. You deserve an Oscar. Just stop playing the innocent. You know she's a Siren. You knew damn well, from that moment I handed you the pen, what was going to happen. I'm not a fool. My mother always told me you had the Cunning. What happened in the vision, Bridie?'

Bridie turned to Vivien, ignoring what Gavin had said. 'You're one of Sabrina's handmaidens?'

Vivien nodded.

'I don't see everything!' Bridie said to Gavin, her voice betraying her fear. 'I only saw that she'd 'elp.' She shot a quick, nervous look at Vivien. 'An' she's 'elped, ain't she?'

'Oh, yes. But now I need your help, Bridie,' said Gavin.

But Bridie wasn't listening. Her eyes darted from left to right, as if she were searching for something. 'You have brought a darkness on us all,' she muttered.

Gavin leaned over and prodded the book. 'It took me a very long time to secure this. It's filled with meticulous notes on all of the oldest buildings here in Much Wenlock. Including dear Sylvia's home, Rosemount. What intrigued me the most was that the old heap of stone has reportedly survived many "attacks of ill-intent" due to its protective runes.'

The room fell silent again, though none of what Gavin had said seemed to make the slightest impression on the old lady.

'Let's get down to it, shall we?' Gavin said, standing up. 'It's no secret that I have secured all the land I need. There's just one plot missing. You know how to break down the protective spells, don't you?'

'I won't help you.' Bridie crossed her arms over her chest and stuck her chin out.

'You will. My friend here is going to make you. I have paid for the land. It belongs to me, by law.' Gavin fished a piece of paper from his inside pocket and handed it to Bridie.

She pushed it away. 'Have with it, will ya? I don't care what the damned thing says.'

Gavin ignored her. 'Terence has kindly allowed me to purchase the land at a reasonable rate. You are going to come with us and help me disarm the protective runes surrounding the walls. Unless you want everyone to know you've been reading their futures and meddling in all our lives for the past God knows how long.'

Bridie's lip quivered. She looked at the fire grate. Gavin could see the rusted old cogs grinding away.

'It's no use trying to think your way out of this one,' he said conversationally. 'You're lucky I don't get Vivien here to kill you.'

'You wouldn't!' Bridie half-laughed.

He smiled thinly. 'I don't think you want to find out what I'm capable of.'

She thought for a moment. 'And what's to stop you killing me as soon as I've helped you?'

Gavin pondered for a moment. It was true; he had been planning to get rid of her. She knew far too much. It would be so easy to make it look like she had died in her sleep.

'As long as you prove useful to me, you can stay alive. Mum's the word, though, about our Vivien, eh? I know you love to gossip, and I don't feel like being dragged into some boring hearing about it all. I have very important work to do.' He got to his feet, brushing his hands together. 'Right. Shall I come and get you first thing in the morning?'

'Do I have a choice?'

'Of course not. But it's nice to be asked anyway, isn't it?'

Vivien watched as Gavin paced up and down Bridie's front room, almost tearing out the three hairs he had left. He had been obsessing about the last piece of land he needed and had become paranoid that the old woman would figure out a way to outdo him.

When Vivien had first caught sight of Bridie at the door, she had known immediately that there was an immense strength to her, even if her outer shell was practically dust. The old woman's house was captivating. There were vessels and devices here and there, used in magical practices that had not been performed for hundreds of years. She wondered where this woman had procured such rare and unusual items. Clearly Bridie held to the traditional beliefs that mortals and witches would be cursed if they fraternised with anything supernatural or immortal. And there was something else—a brief moment when Bridie was looking at her and Vivien caught her eye. She had felt as though she were in a deep well, a dark chasm, plummeting down through the earth, before the old woman snatched her glance away.

The next morning, as arranged, Gavin and Vivien went round to Bridie's to collect her. They struggled to navigate the heavy metal wheelchair, laden with Bridie's rotund body, over the uneven terrain. She was stuffed into a huge red-brown fur coat and matching hat; Vivien was sure they were made from fox. The old crone barely fit into the chair; the rolls of fat made her coat bulge like a sheaf of furry sausages as she sat with her jaw set.

'I don't do outdoors! It's bloody freezing!' Bridie said indignantly. She complained the whole way to Rosemount, insisting still that she could not lift the protection spells placed by her dear old dead friend Sylvia. Gavin merely barked at her now, emboldened by the knowledge that he held a bargaining chip over her.

'The sooner you get on with it, the quicker you will be back at home, shoving your face full of custard creams.' They came to a stop at the old wall. Vivien looked at it with interest; she thought she recognised this place. Gavin blew into his cupped hands as he tried to fend off the cold by rocking from one foot to the other. Bridie's lips pursed, completely disappearing into her deeply lined face.

'I wouldn't goad her, if I were you,' Vivien whispered to him. Gavin shot Vivien a warning glance. *Such impertinence.*

They watched on as Bridie held up her bony hands, eyes closed in concentration as she whispered incantations through her dried lips. Her limp white hair blew this way and that in the chill air. Orange-red runes began to glow within one of the ancient stones. Vivien studied it: it was a complex version of the Algiz rune. Whoever had created this magic was someone who lived in fear of the outside world, desperate to protect what lay inside these walls. They had clearly spent years perfecting these beautiful and intricate spells.

As the rune burned brighter, it began to singe at the edges. It turned black and then, like a lit fuse, it disintegrated, leaving a black scorch mark on the stone.

It took Bridie almost two hours to do just a few stones by

the entrance, after which she fell back in her chair, shaking uncontrollably, her lips still moving with the last of the incantations.

'We need to get her inside,' Vivien's voice hissed into Gavin's ear. He held his hand up to stop her speaking.

'Shh. I'm trying to listen to the words. She's nearly finished, I think.'

Vivien could not feel the cold, but she could tell the old woman was suffering. She shoved her hands into the pockets of the brown tweed overcoat Gavin had given her to wear. Her fingers brushed something inside. Turning slightly away from Gavin, she stealthily withdrew it. In her palm lay a small packet wrapped in green and blue paper that housed a silver foil, twisted tightly on one end. Only the letters LO remained. She discarded the mint packet, surreptitiously crunching it under her foot, and felt in the other pocket. In it was a screwed-up piece of paper. Still keeping her hands hidden from Gavin, she unfolded it. It was covered in faint pencil lines—the blood magic incantation Gavin had used the night he had enslaved her at the river. Quickly, she buried it inside the pocket again.

So he *had* intended to enslave her all along. That was why he hadn't brought an offering.

Vivien fought down a tide of rage; her blood surged through her veins. She wondered if Gavin's mother had ever seen a glimpse of the monster he would become. Had she played a part in it, either inadvertently or deliberately creating a sociopath who would resort to using blood magic to control women?

Vivien looked over at Gavin, who was still watching

Bridie at work. Only she, and now this old woman, knew of what he had done. She shuddered inwardly. What would become of them all if this despot connected the ancient ley lines and became the most powerful druid since Merlin?

Ten minutes passed before Bridie finally looked over at Gavin, giving him a weak nod of her head. The old woman wouldn't look at Vivien, still trying her best to pretend she wasn't there.

'It's done,' she said weakly. 'But I cannot get you inside.'

'Don't worry. I have found other means to get into the house,' Gavin said casually.

Bridie's arms slumped into her lap from exhaustion. Her breathing was ragged.

'We need to get her to a hospital,' said Vivien.

'She'll be fine. We'll drop you off at home, okay, Bridie?' he said airily.

Bridie didn't seem to hear him.

27

RETURN TO ROSEMOUNT

The November morning threatened rain as Tamsyn and Ellis set out on the return trip to Rosemount. Tamsyn watched Ellis's cabin receding in the rear-view mirror, feeling a pang of sadness when it finally disappeared through the trees. She had barely slept, and the adrenaline from the night before was finally beginning to subside.

They drove in silence until they crossed the bridge, leaving Anglesey behind.

'Thank you again, for all of your help and for letting me stay with you,' she said.

Ellis looked ahead as the rain began hammering on the windscreen, obstructing the view beyond.

'No need to thank me. Anyone would do the same. When someone needs help, you help them,' he replied.

'Most people don't.'

'I like to think that most people are good people, when it comes down to it.'

'I used to think so. Now I'm not so sure.' Tamsyn

checked to see if the wipers would go any faster as rain began to pool on the windscreen. 'So now you've seen me dead. And having a breakdown. I'm not sure which is worse.' She turned off the radio, which was struggling to find signal.

'I'd say seeing you die just about pips it to the post,' he said drily.

'Well, if you don't mind me saying, I feel like you know an awful lot about me, and I know nothing about you. Also, I'm incredibly nosy, and it would make the journey go faster.' Tamsyn smiled while keeping her eyes on the road.

'There's not a lot to tell. I grew up in Anglesey, on that same plot of land Ravenscourt now stands on. When I was a teenager, I couldn't wait to leave. As soon as I turned eighteen, I left to go to a university in Scotland.'

'What did you study?'

'I furthered my studies in Druidry and Magic.'

'There are universities for that?' Tamsyn asked, genuinely surprised.

'There are only three. In Scotland, Wales and the South of England.'

Tamsyn felt her stomach sink. She couldn't bear to think about how much Sylvia must have kept from her.

'After I graduated, I did everything I could to avoid living back at home. I travelled to Tibet, Mongolia, South America. I was away for many years, working, studying magic. Eventually, though, I returned to Anglesey to look after my father, and I got a job at the university,' he said simply.

Tamsyn knew he was intentionally leaving out any mention of the child she had seen in the photo at his home, and she did not wish to pry.

'So that was your parents' house?' she asked.

'No, God no. I bulldozed their house two weeks after my father died, and had the cabin built.'

'Did you find it hard, bulldozing the house? I've tried to sell my grandmother's house, but I just can't seem to. Maybe that's some kind of spell too, on either me or the house. Likely both.'

He glanced at her, but let the comment pass. 'It wasn't hard at all. I almost shed a tear of joy watching it being torn down.'

'You didn't have happy times there?'

Ellis shrugged. 'They weren't the worst. But I certainly wouldn't describe them as happy. It was the usual story. My parents were completely incompatible, but they stayed together anyway. My mother told me it was for my sake. My dad said it was because my mother was incapable of looking after herself, let alone providing for a child. They were miserable, and they in turn made me miserable.'

'What happened to them?'

'My mother died of cancer when I was twenty-three. When I was in my thirties, my father developed dementia, so I returned to care for him. He died two years later. I saw him as little as possible, but if anything, dementia made him a bit softer. I think he must have forgotten how much disdain he had for me.'

'That's rough. I'm sorry to hear that.'

'It is what it is. I can't change the past. All I have is now.'

Tamsyn felt the churning of shame in her stomach. What must he think of her, whining over her dead grandmother and complaining about feeling unloved? As if her situation was any different or worse than so many other people's.

'Yes. You're right. Sometimes it can be hard to see the wood for the trees when you feel so... lost. Pardon the cliché.'

'It's a process. I had a lot of times in my twenties where I was angry. I still am angry, I suppose. But I'm not going to waste my life dwelling on shadows.'

'And, you've always lived alone?' she asked sheepishly.

'No. I had a wife, for a time. We have a daughter together. My wife took a very different path, and she no longer wanted me to walk with her along that path. So she took my daughter to live with her.' His voice remained level, but Tamsyn could hear the thin fault line underneath threatening to crack.

She stayed silent, her mind racing. How long since he had seen his daughter? Had he tried to contact her, to follow them?

As if reading her mind he said, 'I have tried everything. She told me she was going to visit her family in America. I couldn't go. I had work commitments. Then one night she called, said she wasn't coming back. I called her family, and they told me she had not even visited them. Who knows if she even stepped foot in America. I have tried everything. I flew over there, took pictures of them to all the places I thought they might have been to see if anyone recognised them. I was unable to file a missing persons report, since my wife is an adult, and the authorities won't tell me where she flew to. The police gave me the distinct impression they thought she might have been fleeing from me.' He looked out of the window.

'How long has it been?'

'Five years,' he answered. She could hear the anger simmering, threatening to boil over.

'My mother disappeared when I was two,' said Tamsyn. 'I went to live with my grandmother, who wouldn't allow me to speak of her, and preferred to act as if she had never existed. When I was growing up, children used to whisper about it behind my back, or sometimes to my face, if they were feeling particularly mean-spirited that day.'

'Kids can be so cruel,' he said.

'One girl told me that her parents said my mother was dead. Some others used to tease me that she went to become the leader of a cult in Ghana.'

'Oof. I can't imagine what that must have been like.'

'I just want to know the truth. That's all I ever want to know. The truth is what drives me. Yet everyone around me only seems to want to bury it.'

Ellis let out a short laugh. 'Yep. That's the magical community. In fact, I hear the non-magical community is exactly the same. I hope you don't mind... I took the liberty of bringing a few things with me. In case people aren't willing to talk.'

'Guns? Knives?' Tamsyn teased.

'Both,' he laughed. 'Just a little truth serum and various herbs and leaves I've collected over the years that I've found to be quite useful.'

'To use on my grandmother's friend Bridie? To get her to talk?' Tamsyn felt uneasy.

'Only if we need to. And only if you want to. If Bridie is unable to divulge information to you because she signed some sort of oath, but she *wants* to tell you what she knows… I have something for that.' He kept his eyes straight ahead.

They drove in silence for a while, which Tamsyn could tell was a welcome reprieve for Ellis—and for her, come to that. Her body ached; her face felt drawn. The overwhelming urge to sleep gripped her.

'Are you okay?' said Ellis after a time. 'You look a bit pale.'

'I'm just tired,' she replied. 'Could you take over for the last hour?'

Ellis's eyes went wide for a moment, before he nodded in acquiescence. The rain had ceased, and as Tamsyn pulled over in a lay-by, the sun began to shine on the wet fields beyond.

Tamsyn slept until the sound of grinding roused her. They were nearing a roundabout she recognised, and Ellis grimaced as he wrestled with the gearstick, wrenching it hard into second.

'This is a ridiculous car,' he spluttered. 'Why would you buy something that's thirty years old? Do you not like to feel safe?' He was perspiring. Tamsyn could see that he had not driven in a very long time, and if he had, it was in an automatic.

She winced as he attempted to come down to first, repeatedly jamming the stick as it refused to slide into place.

'You're being too heavy-handed. You need to press the clutch all the way down.' She covered her eyes as the gearbox made horrible noises, fighting against her own instincts to stop herself from shouting at him.

'The clutch *is* all the way down!' he snapped as they coasted around the island a little too fast, the G-force pulling their bodies to the left.

'Is your foot down now? Here...' She put her hand over his, guiding it into second, then into third. 'It's okay. We're not far now,' Tamsyn said soothingly. 'Take a left at the next island.' She put her hand back in her lap. His skin was surprisingly warm and soft to the touch.

The trees lining the road were in the last throes of autumn; some were clad in vibrant reds and oranges, while others had already given in to the encroaching winter, standing naked against the biting cold.

'It's very beautiful here. It reminds me of Anglesey,' Ellis said.

'We are very fortunate to live in such beautiful places.' Tamsyn smiled. 'I spent my whole life trying to get away from here. I think that when you're young, you don't see beauty. Beauty is meaningless. You just want to feel safe and loved. I have come to appreciate it a little more now, though.'

Ellis was quiet for a moment, and Tamsyn knew he must be thinking about his daughter.

'Yes, I think you're right,' he said at length. 'I used to be so consumed with thinking I had to play a role. The working man, providing for his family. And as time goes on you don't even realise that you have prioritised your career over your relationships. You're on autopilot, "getting things done", while your little girl is waiting for you to play a game or just to really notice her.'

'I'm sure she knew you loved her—oh, it's right here. The gap between the stone wall,' Tamsyn said.

She was relieved to be returning to Rosemount with someone who knew magic much better than she did. Perhaps Ellis could find a way to make sense of it all. Either way, she would settle for being rid of the threat of the spectre. Even better if she could get some answers as to what had happened between it and her grandmother. Once that woman was gone, Tamsyn decided there and then she would never again let herself lie around all day. She was going to dedicate all her time to re-learning magic, but properly this time. Then no one would have the upper hand over her ever again.

The ash trees lining the road to Rosemount were beginning to turn a deep shade of purple.

'Wow. These ash trees are huge,' Ellis said, craning his neck to look up at them. 'They must be at least five hundred years old. I thought they only lived for about two hundred years.' He marvelled out of the window as he carefully manoeuvred Fig up the driveway.

'They have always been here, according to the records kept in the house,' said Tamsyn.

Ellis nodded, and then glanced sharply at her. 'Um… I don't want to alarm you, but has your house been part of a crime scene?' He looked back at the road as they rounded the driveway.

Following his gaze, Tamsyn saw the yellow tape. Flapping in the wind, it stretched from one end of the house to the other, disappearing around the side. She opened the door as the car was still moving, jumped out and bounded up the steps. She pulled the tape up and ducked underneath, staggering to the front door. Planks of wood had been hammered haphazardly over it to prevent anyone from entering. A laminated page had been pinned to one of the planks. She snatched it off, barely able to focus on the words in her haste.

'What does it say?' Ellis said, coming up behind her.

The paper shook, either from the wind or from her hands; she couldn't tell.

'It says this site is due for demolition on the twelfth.' Her voice trembled in confusion and disbelief.

'What? That's ludicrous! They can't demolish your home. I thought the Prides owned this land outright...' Ellis took the notice from her and began to scan it with a furrowed brow. 'This makes no sense. It says here that the house and all of its contents are being repossessed through lack of payment. Let's go now and speak to the council. There's a number on here.'

From the way Ellis was looking at her, Tamsyn could tell that he was wondering whether she had fallen behind on her rent and was now being evicted from a house she didn't own.

'No. We can't call the number,' said Tamsyn. 'I don't want to go in unprepared. We need to know what we're up against. We need to go and see Bridie.'

28

THE OLD LADY WHO
SWALLOWED A FLY

The rain finally slowed to a drizzle as Ellis and Tamsyn pulled up at Bridie's grey-white terrace house. It was early evening. Tamsyn strode up the pathway, Ellis beside her. The grimy net curtains in her front room twitched. Tamsyn was fully expecting to see the old woman's face peering out. Instead, two pointed ears, followed by a pair of glowing amber eyes, stared out at them. Winnie nudged the window with her nose and miaowed silently behind the glass.

'Winnie! I've missed you so much.' Tamsyn pressed her finger on the other side of the glass where Winnie's wet nose had left a mark. The cat narrowed her eyes to show her displeasure and gave another insistent silent miaow to let Tamsyn know she should hurry up and get her out of there.

Ellis rang the doorbell, which sounded off faintly inside. They waited.

'Maybe she's gone out?' Ellis ventured.

Tamsyn looked at her watch.

'No. She rarely goes out any more. She wouldn't leave the house in the evening.' Tamsyn rang the bell again, pressing it three times. 'Maybe she's fallen asleep.'

After a few more minutes of waiting, and Winnie desperately clawing at the window, Tamsyn turned to Ellis.

'Can you use magic? To unlock the door?' Tamsyn asked.

Without hesitation, Ellis stood back and launched his body weight against the door. He tried twice with no success, and then reared back and aimed his foot at the lock. The rusted screws gave way, and the old wood splintered and cracked.

'If I used magic for breaking and entering, there might be questions from the coalition. At least this way there'll be less interrogation.'

The smell hit them immediately. Putrid, hot and thick. Tamsyn retched as she ran through to the sitting room. Bridie sat in the chair. Her eyes were closed. Her mouth hung open; the skin on her face drooped in peculiar ash-purple folds. Her hair was wild, standing on end this way and that.

'Bridie? Bridie?' Tamsyn held her hand over her nose and breathed through her mouth. With the other, she touched Bridie's hand gently. She was cold. 'Bridie!' Tamsyn shouted while shaking her arm and trying not to be sick.

Bridie's chest heaved, her eyes flickering underneath their lids, her breath ragged.

Tamsyn instructed Ellis to gather blankets from Bridie's room. She noticed as she lay them over her that the old woman had not been able to move from the chair to go to the toilet. She wrapped the blankets snugly around her and rubbed her hands and arms.

'We should call a doctor,' Ellis said to Tamsyn. 'Do you have the number?'

'She's on speed dial. Number 2. Dr Anita Palgrave. The phone is in the kitchen.'

'Who—?' Bridie managed between breaths.

'Bridie, it's me, Tamsyn. I brought Ellis Rowlands. He's come to help.'

'Row—land?'

'Yes, Bridie. Please, save your strength. Dr Palgrave will be here soon. Do you have medication?'

'Spray.' Bridie's eyes darted to the large side table in the corner of the room. Tamsyn went over and pulled open the stiff, heavy drawer, wondering how someone as weak as Bridie ever managed to open and close it. A white spray bottle was inside, and a golden vial, half-empty, clattered to the front of the drawer.

'Here.' Tamsyn rushed back over to Bridie and handed her the vial. 'I think it's one of the ones Sylvia used to make for you.' Bridie opened her mouth and lifted her tongue, too weak to administer it herself. Tamsyn leaned forward and let the liquid drip under her tongue until there was no more left.

Bridie breathed deeply and closed her eyes, waiting for the effects from the golden-coloured medicine to kick in. Tamsyn held her hand beneath the blankets as she looked around the room. There were cups and glasses with varying amounts of old liquid in them, plastic take-away containers, their contents half-eaten, on the floor next to the armchair.

Winnie sat in the corner of the room, staring daggers at Tamsyn. She looked rather scrawny and worse for wear.

'I'll be back in a second,' she said to Bridie.

Tamsyn walked through the door to the kitchen, and Winnie got to her feet and ran after her, making the sound that existed halfway between a purr and a guttural rumble. Tamsyn found the cat food in a cupboard. She emptied a whole pouch and some dried food into a bowl, and as she placed it to the floor, Winnie whipped out a paw and scratched her hand. A line of blood glistened red and bright.

'Ow, Winnie!' Tamsyn scolded. But she couldn't help but think she probably deserved it. She had known Bridie might not be the best person to leave Winnie with, but really, there had been no other option. And of course, she hadn't considered that Bridie would fall ill like this. The cups of tea and TV dinners lying around told her that Bridie had definitely managed to feed herself, meaning she had simply neglected to feed the cat.

A pile of plates and crockery lay balanced in a heap in the sink. The bin hadn't been taken out. Left with food inside, it now sat in its own dark juices that had pooled on the floor.

In one corner, Ellis was finishing up his phone call to Dr Palgrave. 'Great, thank you. See you soon.' He put down the receiver and turned to Tamsyn. 'The doctor will be here shortly. How is she?' he said quietly.

'She doesn't look good,' Tamsyn whispered. 'She hasn't moved from the chair in days. She's been sleeping in it, by the looks of things.'

Ellis nodded in understanding.

'Well, we definitely can't use a truth serum on her while she's in this state,' said Tamsyn.

Ellis thought for a moment. 'Mugs?' Tamsyn pointed to the cupboard. Ellis took the last mug from the shelf and opened the fridge, only to find the bottles of milk had curdled. Regardless, he filled the kettle and put it on to boil. He added coffee powder to the mug, then added boiling water and three spoons of sugar, cooling it with a splash of cold water from the tap.

'There's nothing in the serum that will cause her harm… it's merely nectar and oil of snow lotus, wolfberry and pasque flower and vervain. I don't wish to be blunt, but if we don't do this now, you may never get a chance to know the truth. What if she doesn't make it?'

'You're sure it won't hurt her?'

'Positive. The remedy simply undoes the effects of the seal she signed. Anything she has sworn to keep secret, she will now be able to tell us. Only if she wants to, of course.'

Tamsyn looked at him uncertainly. 'Okay,' she said after a moment.

Ellis took a round potion bottle from the inside of his jacket. The dark maroon liquid could easily have been mistaken for wine. Stirring it into the black coffee, somehow it made the liquid devoid of all light—a swirling black hole in the mug. 'Once we have heard what the doctor says, perhaps I could set a bed up for her down here?' Ellis offered.

'I don't think Bridie will let us. If we can get back into the cottage, I will insist she stay with me until she feels better.'

As they made their way back to Bridie, Ellis didn't seem to notice the state of the room and he didn't baulk at the smell. He was far too polite and Tamsyn suspected he had seen similar things when caring for his father. He handed the mug and its precious contents to Tamsyn and excused himself to fetch something from her car.

'Here Bridie, drink this.' Tamsyn held the mug to her lips, her hands slightly shaking. She waited with baited breath as Bridie took a sip.

'Urgh! I can't abide black coffee!' Bridie grimaced.

'What happened, Bridie? How long have you been feeling unwell?'

Bridie ignored her. 'G-Gavin.'

That name caused Tamsyn to shudder.

'Gavin Hardcastle? What about him, Bridie? What did he do to you?'

'Rosemount,' Bridie said, barely managing to open her mouth. 'Took… Rosemount…'

'Gavin took Rosemount? But… how is that even possible? How did he get past my grandmother's defences?'

Bridie looked stricken, and Tamsyn knew right away.

'You? Why, Bridie? Why would you do that?' Tamsyn sat up straight, trying to quell the urge to shout. 'Why would you do that, Bridie?' she repeated, feeling the anger come all too quickly to the surface. Bridie looked up at her now, her eyes full of fear.

'Had—no—choice,' Bridie managed. She closed her eyes again, breathing heavily from the effort of speaking.

'Here, drink some more coffee,' said Tamsyn. She held it up to her lips, while Bridie slurped. Even though she was angry, she hated seeing Bridie suffer like this.

Ellis returned with their bags from the car.

'Hello, Bridie. I'm Tamsyn's friend, Ellis. How are you feeling?' he asked.

Bridie eyed him warily.

'Here, have some more coffee, it will make you feel better,' Tamsyn said before setting down the coffee mug on the table between them. Ellis and Tamsyn stood watching her in silence. Bridie squirmed uncomfortably under their gaze.

'I had seen a vision.' She stopped, unsure whether to continue. She looked over at Ellis; the twinkle was long gone from her rheumy blue eyes.

'It's okay. Go on,' Tamsyn urged.

Tamsyn reached once more for the coffee mug, and as she did so, Bridie's hand darted from beneath the blanket, grabbing Tamsyn's.

'What did we always tell you, Tamsyn? Not to trust anyone but yourself.'

'Clearly you were absolutely correct,' Tamsyn said, pulling away. 'Because I should never have trusted you—or my grandmother. She poisoned me so I wouldn't remember that I'm a witch, and you have helped to take my home from me. Just tell me what in hell your game is?'

The old woman considered for a moment. 'Much Wenlock is a place of immense history and tradition. Sometimes there are people who upset the balance. They have to go. For their own sake.' She seemed surprised that the words were finally able to come from her mouth.

'Like me? What did I do that was so terrible?'

'Sylvie made me swear. To keep you safe. That meant keeping secrets. We took an unbreakable oath, sealed by magic. All of us.'

Ellis suddenly turned his back to them. Tamsyn could tell he was angry, trying to keep his emotions under control.

'What did I do that was so awful?' she demanded, turning back to Bridie.

'I—I don't know. I wasn't there. Sylvia wouldn't discuss it, but the council told her you had to go. That you were dangerous.'

'Right...' Tamsyn said, feeling she was coming to another dead end. 'What about Rosemount? How on earth has Gavin Hardcastle taken possession of my land?'

'Rosemount was a gift. From the Bradshaws,' Bridie said cryptically. 'Gavin has a strange woman with him. I think I've met her before.' Her lips were turning purple.

'How long until Dr Palgrave gets here?' Tamsyn asked Ellis with concern.

'She said ten minutes at the most.'

'I—I'm fine. I don't want her here.' Bridie waved her hand dismissively.

'Why is he so hell-bent on getting Rosemount?' Ellis cut in.

'The ancient ley lines,' Bridie said, wheezing. 'He believes there was once a powerful line, connecting us directly to Stonehenge, that was severed over the years. Since he was a young boy, he has been using divining rods to seek them out.' She stopped for a moment, taking deep, slow breaths before continuing.

'His mother believed he was destined for great things, and they convinced themselves this was his great destiny. Rosemount sits directly on top of an ancient barrow. He thinks this is why the Pride women are so powerful.

Getting Rosemount was the last piece in his puzzle, and I helped him succeed.' Bridie hung her head forlornly, but Tamsyn was beginning to question her actions in a whole new light.

There was a knock at the door.

'That will be Dr Palgrave. I'll get it,' said Ellis.

Bridie watched him leave, her hand shaking as she reached out to Tamsyn.

'I—I have to tell you something I have never told anyone. Well, except Sylvie.'

'What is it?' Tamsyn asked.

'It is the best-kept secret in Much Wenlock. You cannot tell a soul!' she rasped.

'You can tell me.'

'I have the Cunning. It runs in my family. I have to tell you now. I am not long for this world, Tamsyn. This is why I do what I do. What I have always done for this village. When I touch people, I have visions.'

Tamsyn tried to pull her hand out of Bridie's, but the old woman's grip was surprisingly strong. Bridie's eyes were searching hers.

'I have to go with what my foresight shows me, see? It doesn't always work out the way I would want it to, but somehow, it always works out in the end. So now you see? I was just trying to help. He was going to tell everyone. Then they would send me away too!' Bridie was attempting to whisper, but as the words came, frantic and hoarse, Tamsyn feared she wasn't being as quiet as she thought she was. Bridie pressed harder on the skin between Tamsyn's thumb and forefinger.

'When you see her, don't tell her she's passed on,' Bridie whispered.

'What? Who?'

'Sylvie. When you speak to her. She won't understand. If you tell her, it will cause her great suffering.'

Ellis and Dr Palgrave came into the sitting room, and Bridie let go of Tamsyn's hand. Her lips were blue. Dr Palgrave hurried over to her, urging Ellis to call an ambulance.

29
THE FIRST SNOW

Tamsyn and Ellis sat on the bed upstairs in Bridie's tiny spare room. Winnie was still disgusted about being abandoned; however, she had put aside her distaste for now and sat curled in Tamsyn's lap. Her claws latched painfully into her jeans to ensure that she would not attempt to move or leave again. Tamsyn scratched the cat's neck at the back of her ear until Winnie's purr was low and ferocious.

'I had a quick chat with the doctor before she left. Naturally, she was very wary of me. When I told her that I was here with you, her demeanour changed,' said Ellis.

'Oh yeah?'

'I think they're scared of you. She didn't say why, of course. She is subject to the oath. But she made it clear that they—' He stopped, unsure of how to proceed.

'Want me out of here, as soon as possible?' finished Tamsyn. Ellis nodded glumly. She looked down at Winnie. For a second, she felt nothing. She told herself it was okay.

Even so, after a few moments the weight of it all began to bear down on her. Her pulse began to race.

Gavin had taken Rosemount. Closing her eyes, she saw her fingers brushing along the papered walls of Rosemount's hallway. She felt the rough texture. She walked over the wooden floor; it still creaked in all the same places. The air smelled of dust, old wood and paper.

She imagined walking down the couple of steps on the landing, and looked down the hallway to her grandmother's room. She felt her hairs stand on end. A figure stood in the doorway. Tamsyn tried to look at it, tried to focus. It morphed and shifted, like a figure in a dream, and turned towards her. Tamsyn tried to speak, but no sound came out. It was the woman: the woman she had seen at the pool. Not dead and decaying now, but alive. Alive—and strikingly beautiful. They locked eyes. Tamsyn opened her eyes with a start.

'Where were you just then?' Ellis was watching her intently.

'I—I was thinking about Rosemount. I saw someone there. In the doorway of my grandmother's bedroom. It was the woman, the dead woman that tried to kill me, who I think killed my grandmother. But she looked very much alive.' Her heart thudded in her chest.

'I don't think you were merely thinking of Rosemount. I think you were projecting,' said Ellis.

'You mean she's actually there, right now, in my house?'

'Yes. Well, it's a theory. Though if she is there, why would she be helping Gavin Hardcastle?'

Tamsyn shifted uncomfortably on the ancient mattress.

'I don't think I've ever done anything like that before, but... do you think that is why everyone is afraid of me?'

'I think there's more to it than that. There are things that happen around you, things that I've never experienced before. The water pouring into my living room from nowhere while you were Journeying, for example. It's unprecedented.

'It could be a form of elemental magic, or perhaps you're bending time and space. I don't know the answers. And if the people here have taken an unbreakable oath never to speak of it, we will not find answers here.'

Ellis stood up and glanced down the hallway. 'There is one other thing.'

Tamsyn's stomach knotted. 'What?'

'Before we left, I went to find Alchiba. He had been a little off since the night you drowned—he's not the biggest fan of drama; he prefers a quiet life—so I gave him some fuss. It turns out he had been watching us that day I asked you to imagine an apple. Remember?'

'I remember.'

'Well, there was an apple. A real apple. On my table. It was there, with a bite taken out of it. And then it turned rotten. Eventually, it disappeared.'

'You think I did that?'

'Yes. Perhaps that's why people here were scared of you— and still are, I think. Maybe it has something to do with your grandmother, and why she went to such lengths to wipe your memory. The only way we can get answers is through her.'

Tamsyn stared at the faded roses on the wallpaper. Her mind went back to her grandmother's diaries; oddly, they had rarely mentioned Tamsyn at the time she was sent away. It occurred to her suddenly: what if her mother had been sent away for the same reason as Tamsyn had?

It was safe to assume Sylvia had taken the oath, like everyone else. And that would have rendered her incapable of writing down anything regarding Tamsyn or magic. Tamsyn had scoured the writing desk numerous times in the past few months, fetching every single piece of paper out. She had even felt along the empty drawers for some hidden compartment, all the while knowing somehow that there would be nothing there. And as a child she had searched the house as often as she could, in the same way, looking for information about her mother, Annalise Pride.

'We have to try, one more time,' Ellis said, cutting into her thoughts. 'You need to find her in the Underworld. Whatever oath she was under in this world will be rendered void there,' he said softly.

'After last time, I don't think that's such a great idea. She has made it very clear she does not want me to find her.'

'It is fear that is holding you back. The fear that you are not wanted. Self-doubt is what made you stray from the path. This time you have to believe that you will find your spirit guide, that you are worthy. And they will come. Through them, you will find her.'

Tamsyn sat in silence, Winnie's claws still painfully pricking her thigh.

'You are enough,' Ellis said. 'Just you. You don't need her permission, or anyone else's. And who knows, maybe your grandmother will be at peace knowing that you finally know the truth.'

'But what happens if I flood Bridie's home? Or worse…

set it on fire?' she asked.

'Then we'll fix it.'

A bitter wind struck Tamsyn's face as she climbed out of the empty grave and into the Underworld. Powdered fresh snow collapsed underneath her fingers as she heaved herself up, the delicate snowflakes melting beneath her palms.

She stood for a moment, bracing herself against the cold air. She remembered what Ellis had told her about the apple, how she had conjured it out of thin air.

Closing her eyes, she saw herself wearing a long down coat. She had owned it years ago, and had given it away when she found it too hot and bulky on the Underground. But now, she imagined sliding her hands into the arms and pushing them down into the deep, silky pockets. She could still smell the old perfume she used to wear, lingering on the collar. She reached behind her shoulder, pulled the large hood over her head and opened her eyes. Her heart quickened as she looked down at the familiar deep-green coat. She hugged it around her body as if greeting an old friend.

The path ahead was narrow, barely visible under the thick bank of snow that had gathered on the forest floor despite the protective canopy of the fir trees. The light amidst the dense trunks was starting to fade as twilight approached. Tamsyn could hear twigs snapping underfoot, and somewhere in the distance a fire crackled. She was entirely alone in the growing darkness, yet could smell wood burning, and the gamey smell of meat singeing on an open flame.

Stopping momentarily, Tamsyn thought she heard voices carrying through the trees.

She continued on. She did not remember the path winding like this. The trees were also different. This path led through squat, immensely fat trees, their branches gnarled and growing in impossible directions. Some she had to climb over or under to stick to the pathway.

Eventually she came to a stretch of river. She looked around, puzzled. This was about the same spot where she had encountered the fawn last time. But now, instead of a brook, there lay a waterfall, encased in thick slabs of ice.

She looked up to the top of the falls, wondering what lay above. Would the tree with nine eyes still be there? Would it now be standing tall above the waterfall? Or would it still be entombed in its cave? She shuddered at the memory of it.

The buzzing of flies plagued her, just as it had the last time she was here. 'Flies in winter?' she wondered. She forged ahead, jumping over snow-capped boulders and making her way across the frozen water. On the other side, the path meandered down, away from the water's edge.

She stopped dead when she thought she heard the sound of muffled voices again. Dogs howled in the distance, yelping to each other and their owners. Nearby, unseen animals responded with sounds of fear. She started to run. The buzzing followed her, getting louder and louder.

She looked down to see where the noise was coming from. A large bee had attached itself to the breast of her coat. She could just about make out its iridescent wings, vibrating so quickly now they became almost invisible.

A bee. She could not believe she had not realised it before.

Bees were synonymous with memories of her childhood, her grandmother, and Rosemount. She recalled the day she'd stood at the kitchen sink. She had been on the phone with Sarah and the bee was batting against the window. She had felt the urgent need to flee. It had been warning her.

Once again, the bee's wings began to vibrate. It let go of her coat and took off, flying away from her down the path. Tamsyn picked up her pace in order to keep up with it, her heart in her throat. What if this was another mistake?

The path was quickly disappearing among the trees, drifting over with snow. She watched the bee intently as it weaved this way and that. An answering flutter of wings beat overhead. Tamsyn risked looking up at the canopy for a second. A small peregrine glided between the gaps in the trees. It must have been following them, gliding noiselessly. It was beautiful. She heard a snap of twigs behind her, accompanied by the howl of a wolf. The bee buzzed loudly now and began moving frantically. Tamsyn felt her skin prickle with goosebumps: the falcon, and whoever it belonged to, was a threat.

She continued to run after the bee, not stopping to look again. Her mind was whirling with doubts. Perhaps the bee was the threat, and the bird was her spirit guide? Or perhaps it belonged to another druid or witch? Maybe it was a hunting bird, accompanied by the howling hound, tracking her through the woods. Her breathing quickened. She heard Ellis's voice: *Self-doubt is what made you stray from the path.*

The voices grew louder. The yapping turned into guttural snarls. She saw two glowing red eyes between the trees. A low growl emanated from a mouth rimmed with sharp teeth. The hound stepped forward. It was bigger than a wolf, completely white except for its red ears and glowing red eyes. Foam dripped from its bared fangs as it approached her. She backed away from it. Behind her, she could hear its companions gaining on them.

She picked up a large branch from the undergrowth and shouted, '*Inge gehennae!*' And the end of the branch burst into flame. She held it to the ferns, setting the ones behind her alight. She thrashed the flame back and forth in front of the hound. It backed away. As she ran down the path, she set the forest aflame behind her.

The farther she ran, the more the sound of the yapping hounds receded. The forest returned to its peaceful state, full of the fresh scent of pine and terpenes. Slowing to a brisk walk, her breath heavy from running, she doused the flaming branch in a pile of snow. The bee landed on her once more, its tiny legs hooking into the front of her coat. Tamsyn looked down at it. She felt an odd sensation: sparks igniting inside her, like a cascade of energy through her very molecules. She felt her skin fizzing for a moment, then easing off to a steady static in her fingertips before subsiding completely.

She smiled, relieved with the knowledge that she had finally found her guide. She thought back to the buzzing she had heard the first time she saw the fawn. The way she had batted away what she thought was a fly as she decided to follow the deer downriver.

Please help me. Please help me find my grandmother. It was merely a thought, a plea.

The bee remained motionless for a moment before taking

flight once more. It weaved slowly, left to right, then right to left, moving steadily along the path so that she could follow.

Tamsyn walked for half an hour; the snow became deeper and more treacherous, and Tamsyn began to worry that they had somehow left the path. But the bee flew steadily on.

Eventually she came to a crossroad. She stood uncertainly, looking in each direction in turn. Ellis had not mentioned that it was possible for the path to diverge like this. A wooden signpost stood at the corner, four wooden arrows pointing in the four different directions. The writing carved into each one was worn down to an illegible set of dashes and disjointed curves.

The bee meandered lazily, hanging in the air as if dizzy or drunk. After a moment, it began to head in a north-westerly direction.

Twilight had faded to darkness half an hour ago. The path was now lit only by the faint light of the rising moon, still hidden by the canopy. The pathway became overgrown with huge nettles that poked through the snow. Tamsyn thought of the garden at Rosemount, how it had almost succumbed to the weeds that had engulfed it while she lay in her fugue state. She felt the sick twist of guilt in her stomach, a warning or maybe an admonishment—but she stopped the thought from going any further. She could not afford to sabotage herself with self-doubt again.

But as she carried on walking, Tamsyn felt the knot of nerves grow in her stomach. Would they really find Sylvia? And if they did, what would she say to her? Adrenaline coursed through her, making her hyper-alert.

The trees were thinning; the terrain felt different underfoot. Rubble lay strewn across the earth; large stones lay in heaps where an ancient wall once stood. Fresh snow peppered a pile of blackened wood, the traces of a fire that had long burned out. The huge blue moon was climbing in the sky now, its light lending an eerie pallor to the already grey landscape.

Following the pathway, Tamsyn saw remnants of raised flower beds, the wood decayed and the hardened soil spilling out. Further on, the path plunged straight through a thicket of brambles, grown so wildly out of control it now stood towering over her. She followed the bee through a small gap in the mass of thorned vines. As she weaved her way through them, the thorns pricked her jacket and the legs of her jeans, trying to hold her back.

Tamsyn followed her companion as it navigated her through the dense maze. Whenever she thought they had reached an impasse, the insect would somehow lead her through another way, until finally she saw the white snow on the other side. Pushing on, she felt the thorns piercing through her coat, ripping the lining.

At last, Tamsyn stepped out into the moonlight.

The bee had slowed significantly, and now, exhausted, it dropped to the ground. Tamsyn knelt, holding her finger out on the snow. The bee languidly crawled on. She gently held it to her jacket to let it rest there.

Rising to stand, Tamsyn felt suddenly light-headed. A thick, familiar aroma filled the air. Closing her eyes, she thought back to one summer when she was eight years old. Sylvia had given her a jar, a piece of gauze and an elastic band and shooed her out of the house. Tamsyn had spent hours down by the pond, catching tadpoles and examining them with her magnifying glass. She would draw them as she sat in the shade on the porch, before trekking back through the unrelenting heat to release them. But on one particular occasion, on the way back, she'd dropped the jar, and... And what? The memory seemed to stop here.

What had made her think of that?

She stumbled on further, breathing through her mouth and covering her nose to shield it from the pungent scent.

Tamsyn walked through snow and dead vegetation. She could see rows of stalks, covered by a blanket of white. She felt her legs grow heavy. That smell—it was valerian.

Sylvia had always kept a small amount of valerian in the Poison Garden. Now she remembered: that day, in the heat of summer, she had gotten too close to the garden and the smell of the plant had overcome her, making her drop the jar. It had made her sick for three days. When she went back for the tadpoles, they lay shrivelled and dead in the grass.

Tamsyn coughed and tried to hurry forward. A distant light weaved and bobbed crazily in her vision, but she stumbled doggedly on.

Her foot caught something and she fell, striking her head hard against the ground.

Tamsyn's ears rang and her vision juddered as the ground met the sky. It was still dark as she struggled to stand, head throbbing from the fall. The ground was littered with ash, glass and shards of wood. Mystified, she looked up to see the smoking ruins of Rosemount.

30
THE WINTER CRONE

The charred remains of Rosemount were now completely enveloped in dense vegetation. Brambles topped with snow fought to gain purchase over the remaining structure in a bid to entomb it. The roof of the veranda had completely caved in. What was left of the floorboards was dusted with frost, curled leaves and dried mud. The windows were black gaping holes, the glass blown out, their singed curtains billowing in the wind.

To the right of the house, Tamsyn saw a neat row of bee hives. The little white houses were silent, devoid of life and scorched with black soot, their roofs capped with snow. Remembering, Tamsyn looked down at her coat, searching for the bee. It was gone.

Tamsyn heard the dull sound of flutter-beat-flutter-beat. A large moth was battering itself mindlessly against the glass of the porch light, even though the glass was smashed and the bulb inside was dead. Somewhere off in the distance, she heard the rumbling sound of water.

A warm light emanated from underneath the heavy wooden door, blackened with soot but still complete. Muffled music swam through the thin, cold air. Tamsyn couldn't quite make out the song that was playing. Head and heart pounding, she staggered towards the door. Her hand shook as she twisted the doorknob.

The warmth from inside hit her face, stinging her cheeks. Inside, the front room was alive. She recognised aspects of the house, but somehow it looked different to the Rosemount she knew.

A roaring fire crackled in the same carved wooden fireplace, but this version of Rosemount had bookshelves lining every wall of the sitting room, like they had before Sylvia moved them upstairs. Piles of papers and photographs, teetering on the brink of collapse, covered every available surface, even spilling onto the floor. A gramophone whirred at the opposite end of the room, warbling Glenn Miller's 'Moonlight Serenade'. Tamsyn looked around in confusion. She cleared her throat, speaking up over the music.

'Hello?'

In the centre of the room, an upholstered wing-back chair sat facing away from her and towards the fire. The chair was almost exactly like the one Sylvia had favoured, except the pattern was somehow blurred. Its colours seemed slightly off, too, and the more Tamsyn tried to focus on it the more the pattern morphed under her gaze. She breathed deeply in a bid to calm herself.

'Grandma?'

Tamsyn heard the familiar click-clack of knitting needles. She closed the door behind her to the snow and dark outside and stepped further into the room. She rounded on the chair, heart and stomach in her throat.

Sylvia, rotund and small, sat placidly knitting, bright pink wool working between her crooked fingers, spilling out over her lap and onto the floor. She looked up from her work and gave Tamsyn a curt nod and a smile. Tamsyn's heart thudded so violently she thought she might collapse.

A small wooden chair sat by the fire, one she'd used as a child. Tamsyn pulled it up in front of Sylvia, just as she had done all those years before.

She was relieved to see Sylvia's face was not the death mask she had grown accustomed to in her waking memory. It was still the shining, plump face with the shrewd, glittering eyes that pierced if you stared too long. The more Tamsyn tried to take her in, the more her grandmother's face began to warp, slipping away once more.

'Would you like tea and biscuits?' Sylvia did not look up from her needles to wait for an answer.

Looking around the room, Tamsyn could see that tea and biscuits were not an option. There was no end to the wall of books, no way out of this room other than back out into the cold.

'No. No thank you, Grandma,' she said warily.

Sylvia went back to her knitting. Tamsyn watched for a moment as the needles worked, making no progress along the line.

'Grandmother, I've come to see you, to ask you some questions.' Tamsyn fell silent again; she had no idea of how to proceed. She looked out of the window. The night was black, huge clumps of snowflakes fell steadily. Now that she was here, she couldn't think straight. All the questions she wanted to ask floated in the corners of her mind, swimming away when she tried to grasp them. She remembered Bridie's words: *Do not tell her she's dead.* She felt lost in a fog.

'Why did you send me away?' she managed finally. 'Why did you make me forget everything?' She watched Sylvia, but like a reflection in water, her grandmother's expression melted away in ripples.

'It was the will of the council. A compromise we had settled on years before.' Sylvia's voice was light, almost happy.

'Why would you do that to me? Your own flesh and blood? What did I do that was so terrible?' Tamsyn could feel tears rising, angry and hot.

'I couldn't very well exempt my own family after we had done it to so many others. Has the spell worn off, then? I have an extra bottle, y'know, down in the basement.' Sylvia continued to knit.

'You did this to others? How many others? Why would you do such a thing? And more importantly, *how* could you do such a thing?' Tamsyn had never been permitted to speak to her grandmother in such a way. She felt decidedly uneasy, panic rising, as though she were caught in a dream that someone was trying to wake her up from. She was suddenly terribly aware that this could all melt away.

'When we were sixteen, Bridie had a vision,' Sylvia began, seemingly oblivious to Tamsyn's tone. She smiled inanely at her knitting as she continued. 'She saw that I would be stripped of my powers, and sent away to live and die in the woods like the other poor things. That's what they did in our day if you didn't conform, or had powers beyond the natural order. If you were lucky, they would banish you into the woods, where you were no longer part of the community of witches. And as we both well know, the normal folk would as soon have any lone woman hanged as to look at her!' Sylvia shook her head mournfully. 'These women were shunned, and they would die of terrible illnesses, alone in the woods.'

'If you were *lucky*? And what if you were *unlucky*?'

'Oh. That was very rare. Very rare indeed. But… if you were of a particularly powerful persuasion, they would drown you in the river. So you see now? I did what I had to do. I never stepped out of my bounds. I was careful never to stray from the path of hedge-witchery. Never!' She raised her finger. 'And after a time, it was easy. I was never strayed from the path by using any elemental or dark magic. I became a pillar of the community,' she said proudly.

'So what did you and Bridie do, when she had this vision?'

'Very gradually, over time, we were able to get people on our side. We joined the council. We convinced some of the members to get the rules changed. In the last forty years we made sure that any witch or druid deemed to be a deviant, or a disrupter of the rules, was merely sent away and made to forget about their abilities. The forgetting part was essential: that way we would all avoid any silly ideas of retribution that they might have. Gradually, we finessed the spell so that family members could still see their loved ones. We just took away the memory of magic. Isn't that clever?' Sylvia beamed with pride. There was an innocence to her simple smile that fought hard against the anger swelling inside Tamsyn.

'The last forty years? So before that… were you responsible for drowning women?'

Sylvia's expression dropped momentarily. 'They were very different times.'

'No. No, they weren't.' Tamsyn couldn't believe what she was hearing.

But it was all too late. It had always been too late, always too impossible to argue with her. Tamsyn felt a knot tighten in her stomach as she realised that this version of Sylvia in front of her was a fragment, a shard among others that made up the whole. The part of Sylvia's consciousness that inhabited this husk was not fully aware of her situation. Tamsyn would never be able to repair their relationship now, although that felt impossible to accept.

'That way, you could all lead a happy life,' Sylvia continued, 'with a family, without the knowledge of what you had left behind. And you are happy now, aren't you? With your boyfriend, down in London? What's his name again?'

Tamsyn paused, trying to think through all of the possible answers.

'Dominic,' she said. 'Yes… we're happy,' she lied, defeated. She hated that she couldn't tell Sylvia about everything that had happened, everything she'd learned. That she needed help. That she'd lost their ancestral home—the one thing in the world that really mattered to Sylvia. She hated that she could not grab hold of this moment, tie up the loose ends and feel some sliver of satisfaction.

'Maybe you youngsters can change things again one day.' Her grandmother's hands continued to work, getting nowhere. 'There is ancient magic in Much Wenlock that

273

needs to be protected. We've always done what we had to do to protect the old magic, at all costs.'

'Grandma,' Tamsyn tried again. 'What did I do that was so bad that you felt you had to send me away?'

There was silence. The only sound came from the record player, the soft hiss and crackle of the needle tracing the grooves of the vinyl as it moved on to the next track.

Sylvia stared at her. When 'The Pied Piper's Dream' started to play, the same look of blissful detachment returned to her face. She put her knitting on her lap and tilted her head to one side.

'You were always a fiery thing. Just like…' She stopped.

'My mother?' asked Tamsyn.

'Yes,' answered Sylvia gravely. 'You were a young teen without a mother and father. Granny-reared, we used to say. You never quite fitted in at school. You grew very sullen and angry.' Her brow furrowed slightly as she looked off into the far distance.

'I thought a firm hand was what you needed. But it was like fighting fire with fire. Strange things started to happen.' Sylvia looked troubled, the serene expression cracking with the memory of a fear just out of reach.

'Strange things? What strange things?' Tamsyn was perplexed as to why she still had no recollection of any of these events.

'At home. Things would disappear. I would get very cross with you. I thought that you were turning out like… you know. Her. Thieving things.' Sylvia looked at her in desperation. Speaking of her daughter seemed to be too much to bear.

'What happened? Please, Grandma.' Tamsyn put her hand on hers. There was neither warmth nor coolness to the skin. No familiar spark of magical energy. She thought of the time she'd posed with the wax figures at Madame Tussaud's; their shiny skin had felt like Sylvia's did now.

Sylvia looked up at her now as though she had made a decision. 'You caused a terrible accident on the school bus. It was history repeating itself, really. Girls were being girls, as usual. Y'know, the catty things they do to one another. You were so beautiful. You still are so beautiful. And sharp as a whip. You were different from them, and they didn't like it. Well, I think that one day you'd had enough.'

Tamsyn tried to recall the bus. The last bus trip she remembered was when she had been around sixteen. She had been at the front of the bus, with her only friend at school. The popular kids had been terrorising them, but that was nothing unusual. One of them, the clown of the group, had made her way up to them and spat chewing gum into her hair. A fight had ensued.

'You didn't know what you were doing,' Sylvia continued, 'and by God, I had tried to help you control yourself. When I got there, afterwards, I saw it. The back of the bus, sticking out of a huge ravine. It had just opened up in the middle of the road. The poor driver. He'd slammed his brakes on, but there was no avoiding it. The bus went into it, this huge crack in the tarmac. Some of those poor kids were badly hurt, you included. I knew it was you as soon as I saw it.'

'How did you know it was me?' Tamsyn asked angrily, wary as always of any summation her grandmother gave of her, or anybody else. Sylvia merely laughed bitterly.

'You did strange things all the time at home. If I told you off, great holes would open up in the garden. All my veg would fall inside. You've got to laugh, I suppose,' Sylvia said.

'I don't think it's funny at all,' said Tamsyn.

'One time I nearly ended up in one of those fissures when I wouldn't let you stay at your little friend's house. Well, can you blame me? With you doing things like that? Your face would go blank, like you were sleepwalking. It was very odd. You couldn't seem to control it. And when you were angry, sad, afraid, things would just happen.'

'So what happened, after the bus incident?' asked Tamsyn.

'It took them hours to get you all out. Terrible it was. Anyway, with the help of the council we managed to make the police and the locals believe it was a random sinkhole. They don't like asking too many questions, the folks down at the station. As long as we deal with it and make it go away.' Sylvia's tone was laced with the familiar disdain she had had in life. 'It sealed the deal, though. I had kept the secret for as long as I could. But some council members had been feeling these bursts of energy. They began to monitor them, and eventually one of them realised they were coming from you.'

'I don't suppose that was Gavin Hardcastle?'

'No. It was that busybody, Colin, from The Snooty Fox. He fancied himself as a bit of an amateur sleuth and desperately wanted in with that toad Gavin Hardcastle. I always told Bridie he was a bad egg, but she wouldn't hear of it. Colin had taken it upon himself to monitor this energy, gathering up the data to hand to Gavin. Then Mr Hardcastle presented it all at the meeting, and I knew you had to go.

Once you're in that man's sights he will stop at nothing. They wanted to put you in the river! Said you were far too dangerous, even for the Binding Spell!' Sylvia shook her head bitterly, tutting as if she were merely recounting some bad news she'd just read in the paper.

'And that Colin. Nothing whatsoever special about him. He wanted so badly to have magic. That's why he became Gavin's little ferret, you see. After that, I would always go to Colin's café with Bridie, to keep my third eye on him.' Sylvia tapped the middle of her forehead with a crooked index finger.

Tamsyn was silent for a few moments, digesting what she had just heard.

'I need a way to stop Gavin, Grandma. Please, will you tell me what I should do?'

'Now, now. Don't be silly, Tamsyn,' Sylvia chided. 'Pride women do not stick their necks out. We do what needs to be done under the radar. You, though—you always want to go against the grain and put a target on your back.' She *tssk-tssk-tssked* in the same way that had always infuriated Tamsyn as a teenager.

The needle was skirting the edge of the record again, the track long since finished. The room was dark and growing cold; only the dim embers of the fire were left in the grate. Outside, the snow was heaping up against the window. Sylvia's knitting needles began to slow.

'Grandmother. Do you remember a dark figure? Coming to the house?' Tamsyn tried hard to focus on Sylvia's eyes. The old woman's lids were heavy, almost closing.

'Someone here? In Rosemount?' Sylvia asked, yawning.

'Yes.'

'I don't let people in.'

'But did you see an apparition? In black? Did you go to the garden? Did you collect wolfsbane?' Tamsyn's heart raced as the last sliver of moonlight coming through the window disappeared behind a heap of snow. She was running out of time.

Sylvia's brow furrowed, as if she were remembering a bad dream. 'You must never touch the wolfsbane. You know that, Tam.' Sylvia hadn't called her Tam since she was a little girl. Sylvia's right hand instinctively covered the left, rubbing it gingerly as if she were wounded.

'I'm very tired. I think I'll go up to bed for a bit.' Sylvia sighed and closed her eyes. The snow outside must be the height of the door, Tamsyn thought. As Sylvia's chin rested against her chest, the corners of the room began to ebb away, leaving the burned-out shell of Rosemount visible.

Tamsyn knew it was time to leave. But how? How could she leave her grandmother, knowing that this was the last time she would ever see her? There was so much she wanted to say, but those moments had passed years ago, when she'd sat in her lonely flat in London, completely unaware of the truth.

'I love you, Grandma,' she said simply. Hot tears fell down her cheeks. It was not something that they had ever said to each other. But she knew it was now or never.

Without opening her eyes, Sylvia smiled a little. 'I know, dear.'

31
BLOOD CURSE

For days, Vivien had watched and waited as Gavin doggedly researched hundreds of old runic texts. Eventually, he had emerged from his study, grey-faced and bleary-eyed. He informed Vivien that he had found a spell he was sure would demobilise the runes carved over Rosemount's door. It was the last key to getting inside. Unfortunately, Gavin explained to her, the hex required to break the protection spell had a rather steep price. And as he loathed getting his hands dirty, the price would be hers to bear.

The night before, he had ordered Vivien to go to Bradshaw's farm and collect blood. Any live animal would do, he added. She had simply stared at him in silence. If looks could kill, flames would have engulfed him, incinerating him bones and all.

Vivien went to the field as instructed. She saw a cow, alone and grazing. Carefully, she had approached it, shushing it as it considered backing away. She exerted her will over it, lulling it into a stupor. Its chewing slowed; the domes of its big brown eyes stared sadly at her. It wasn't sad at all, of course.

'You are such stupid things,' she said to it softly. 'You always have that sad look in your eyes,' she said soothingly as she patted the old girl on the head.

She had taken a knife from the kitchen. Her pull over the sow was so strong, even the sight of the blade didn't faze it.

Vivien placed a bucket on the ground between them. She took out the screwed-up paper she had found in Gavin's tweed jacket. On one side, written in shaky pencil, were the words he had used to summon her. On the other, in perfect ink-blue cursive, he had written the blood curse. He'd told her it had been in self-defence, that he had been forced to use it in order to protect himself. Now she had proof that his using the blood curse on her had been premeditated. He had planned to bind her to him all along, not that anyone would care.

She bought out the knife, holding it aloft. Wincing, she read the words he had penned. She had altered them, in hope it would reverse the curse.

Sanguis meus sanguine tuo
Servus liberetur
maledictionem hanc mihi depone!

At the last moment, she looked away and slashed the blade across her wrist, swearing at the pain. He had sent her to collect blood from Bradshaw's farm; he'd said any animal would do.

After watching her blood, mingled with the remnants of Gavin's, drip into the bucket for as long as she dared, she grasped her forearm tightly, stemming the flow. Wiping the blade on her shirt, she held her hand over it. She was able to summon enough magic to heat the metal, until it burned white-hot. She held it against the wound; the pain of the seared skin made her head spin. Gasping, she collapsed to her knees, oddly satisfied by the excruciating pain. She felt invigorated. Letting some of his blood out had removed at least a portion of the toxins from the blood magic that he had used to subdue and control her. She laughed as she sat there in the mud. The cow was still standing in the field, chewing the same piece of grass. As she watched, the raw, cauterised skin was already fading as she healed. Drawing the blade high, she plunged it into her leg. She wanted it gone.

When she returned to Gavin's house, she was deathly pale, and had a haunted look in her eyes. Luckily, he thought it was because she was traumatised from cutting an animal's throat. The smear of dark red blood on her cheek and the splattered spots flecking the tweed coat added to the illusion. She could see he was savouring every moment. As she handed him the basin of blood, he took the opportunity to remind her how she had made him look that night they'd held the party at the Crow's Nest.

∾

Vivien watched nervously as her congealed blood was smeared across the ancient oak door of Rosemount. Gavin read aloud from a tattered book. She assumed it was the same text she had seen the shadowy figure carrying along the alleyway to the house. She had never had the displeasure of hearing the language before, but she understood perfectly the intention. Gavin held his breath as he tested the doorknob. It swung open, unyielding.

Inside, Vivien saw the flash of an old woman answering the door. She looked terrified, mouth opening to a scream. Then she was gone.

Rattled, Vivien followed Gavin into the front room. The beauty of it was enchanting. She felt the history of the place seeping into her pores. She could sense the women who had lived there previously, each creating her own impression on it.

Methodically, she ran her fingers over every well-worn dent and groove, feeling every surface alive with memory. She found the switches to the honey-gold Tiffany lamps. On the mantlepiece there were matches. The fire was stacked neatly with wood, paper twisted and prodded into the gaps, ready for the owners' return. She struck a match and lit the kindling. Warmth slowly began to return to the cold, silent home. Vivien felt a longing, a distant call from a long-buried memory.

Gavin watched her like she was possessed. He reminded her how sorry he was that he had to tear the whole thing down.

'So this is the inner sanctum of the old crone. I thought it would be so much more impressive,' he said as he searched for the library. 'Why wouldn't you keep your books in the parlour?' he muttered crossly, looking around the receiving room that had once housed Rosemount's library.

'Knowledge is power. That is why you hid your books from me, is it not?' she called after him.

She touched the arm of the chair facing the fire, then recoiled sharply. She thought she had felt something, fleshy and cold. A chill ran down her spine.

It was a great shame, thought Vivien, that such a detestable, unworthy worm of a man had stepped foot on such hallowed ground. The longer they spent here, the more Vivien felt the energy of the cottage rising within her, fortifying her. She could almost hear voices in the walls, angry, snarling, warning. It set her nerves on edge. *Can't make an omelette without breaking some eggs*, he had said to her that morning, as he finished talking to the contractors. They would be arriving to bulldoze Rosemount at 8 a.m.

Vivien headed to the kitchen. She traced her hands along the countertop where generations of women had kneaded, chopped, ground seeds and herbs with pestle and mortar. She felt a desperate longing. What she would give for this house.

Running her fingers along the ancient dresser, she marvelled at the matching china set. Proudly on display were four plates patterned with pale blue and white forget-me-nots. There were three matching teacups, but the fourth was different. Instead, this one was pink and blue, with intricate lacework and a gold rim. Vivien reached for the handle.

The smell of freshly turned soil filled her nostrils. The taste of earth filled her mouth. The face of an old woman appeared, contorted, eyes bulging, screaming silently. The same woman she had seen at the door.

She jumped, dropping the cup. She watched in horror as it smashed on the flagstone tiles.

'Started demolition already?' Gavin called from another room.

Hands shaking, her heart pounding in her ears, Vivien made her way to the pantry. Her eyes lit up when she saw the rows of bottled remedies, dried herbs and unguents. She scanned them quickly, pulling down anything she thought might be useful.

She yanked out three strands of her hair. Hands working feverishly, she bound the hair with dried knotweed and horse hair she found on a shelf. Plaiting them together and binding them together with twine, she focused her intention on casting a protection spell. It was a last-ditch attempt, a sort of good luck charm that she hoped would hasten her chances of getting away from him. Holding the charm in her hand, she hurried back to the living room.

As she singed the hair in the fire, she circled around the room, creating a fog around herself.

Gavin watched with disdain as Vivien pranced around the room holding a rolled and smoking piece of something that stank to high heaven. The smoke it created was thick and white, swirling around her, as if attracted by some unseen force.

'What the hell are you doing? Are you burning sage?' he said mockingly.

'I would never do such a thing. Burning sage is cultural appropriation.' She did not stop to look at him as she continued wafting the smouldering bundle through the hallway and into the kitchen.

Since the incident with the cow, she had grown increasingly bold, barely able to disguise her contempt for him. No matter, he thought. He was so close now. Soon, he would no longer need her. The smoke reached his nostrils. It was hot, singeing his nose hairs and catching at the back of his throat. He coughed uncontrollably.

'You didn't answer my question,' he said through fits of coughing. 'Satan's arse, what is that smell? Why are you cleansing the place when it will be rubble tomorrow?'

'There is someone here. In that chair.' She pointed at it.

He curled his lip in contempt. 'Don't be stupid. Just hurry up. As soon as you've finished, come and help me look for the blueprints. I need to know where the source of energy comes from.' He made his way to the carved oak staircase.

Vivien poked her head out of the kitchen doorway. 'Are you sure you want to go up there? Before I've cleansed?'

'If there are spirits here, you can see to them for me. As long as you're operating under my will, you can overpower anything. Well, almost anything.' He continued up the stairs, stomping his meticulously polished brogues on the worn wood that had only ever borne generations of Pride women.

He made his way to the old crone's room. *Aha*, he thought. There was the library. The books of utter nonsense she kept were astonishing. He perused them one by one, gathering speed, flinging them from the shelves as he looked for something that could tell him exactly where Rosemount's power came from. He turned to her drawers and began to rifle through the old woman's belongings, throwing silk blouses and enormous underpants over his shoulder. Hearing a noise, he looked up to see Vivien watching him, arms folded and leaning against the door.

'Don't just stand there! Help me look!' he spat.

'I'm feeling a bit tired, I'm afraid. Last night really took it out of me,' she said, standing in the doorway and smirking.

Vivien continued to watch him with contempt. Silk underwear, dresses, jewellery and papers were strewn across the floor. They were in the home of someone who had kept the place like a museum, but that clearly mattered not a whit to Gavin; the man had no respect for anyone or anything else.

She heard a creak behind her and turned to see a woman standing in the hallway, a pretty young thing with light brown hair and green eyes. She looked sort of like the old woman who had lived here, only much younger and prettier. Vivien felt like she had seen her before. The girl looked frightened, and then in a second, she was gone.

32
UNDONE

Hours had passed. Gavin searched Sylvia's bedroom as Vivien lazily poked and prodded various things around the room. He watched her with suspicion as she idly lifted books off the shelves, picking up pieces of paper he'd already discarded, before letting them float back to the floor. There was a knock at the front door. Gavin's eyes met Vivien's in surprise.

'Sounds like the cavalry's arrived,' she teased.

Gavin held up his hand to silence her. Despite owning the house, he couldn't help but feel like a trespasser who was about to get caught.

'Who would be coming to save you? Your beloved Sabrina?' he whispered scornfully.

That seemed to wipe the smile off her face. In a moment, she'd disappeared down the hallway before he could stop her.

'Stop! Wait!' he yelled after her as she flew down the stairs, her long, dark hair billowing behind her. 'What is happening? Why aren't you doing as I tell you?'

Vivien unlatched Rosemount's heavy front door.

'What is wrong with you? Stop doing that! Don't let them in!' he shouted down the stairs.

With a huge effort, Vivien pulled open the door. The light from inside illuminated two faces.

'Please, I need you to—' Vivien stopped when she saw who was standing at the door. She leaned against the wall for support, confused, unsure whether to fight or flee like a cornered animal.

Gavin watched as she slid down the wall, panting for breath. She had defied him, he thought. Something had to be done.

Vivien looked up at the young woman's face, then at the face of the man who stood beside her. One moment, she had been looking at them standing at the door. The next, she was screaming into dark water. Bubbles were escaping from her mouth to the surface as she kicked and fought against black tendrils that tightened around her body.

Vivien cradled her head in her hands. A searing pain ripped through her brain.

'It is you,' the woman said to her. 'He sent you to kill me.'

'I—I don't know what you're talking about. Who are you?' Vivien replied.

'You know damn well who I am. My name is Tamsyn Pride. I am the one you tried to kill. In the water, beyond the walls. You were here. The day my grandmother died. She put wolfsbane in your tea. In her haste, she had no time to get her gloves. The poison entered her body through a cut on her hand. Is that about right?' Tamsyn glared down at her.

'I don't remember!' Vivien wailed as images flashed painfully through her mind. Steaming black tea in the cup with the forget-me-nots. Bitter leaves mixed with sweet almond to mask the taste. Vivien struggled to her feet. She pushed past them and ran out of the door.

Rounding the front steps, she began searching the weeds that stood high against the side of the cottage. The nettles pricked like needles, making her hands throb. She kicked them away, and then she saw it. Lying dirtied amidst the long grasses and weeds was the fourth missing teacup from the dresser, patterned with the same blue forget-me-nots. She bent down to retrieve it.

She saw strobing images. She had been here. She had walked out of the door and poured the tea on the ground, before flinging the cup into the bushes. She had looked back and caught her own fragmented reflection in the diamond-pane glass. She was cloaked in black. The face that had smiled back at her was partially decayed, showing teeth and skull. She knew the old woman was inside the house, and would soon be dead.

Tamsyn tried to calm her breathing. She rounded on Gavin, who had made his way down the stairs and now stood in the front hallway, regarding her coolly. 'You really want Rose-mount that badly, that you sent this woman to kill my grandmother? And how did you get in here in the first place?' Her voice caught in her throat. She tried to step into the cottage, but something prevented her.

'I used a strong magic to get in here. Rosemount belongs to me now.' He smirked. 'Ah, Ellis Rowlands,' he said smoothly, turning to him. 'It's been a while. What brings you to Much Wenlock?'

'Hello, Gavin. I can't say it's nice to see you again. I was here to help Tamsyn with a problem. I see you've already dealt with it… to a fashion.' He looked round with consternation at Vivien, who was standing out in the driveway with her back to them.

Gavin furrowed his brow. 'I have no idea what went on between Sylvia and Vivien. That's their business. *Was* their business.' He grinned.

Ellis continued to stare at Vivien, his eyes searching in confusion.

Gavin turned his gaze back to Tamsyn. 'But yes, Miss Pride, going back to your original question, I did want Rosemount that badly. You women have been sitting on top of this particular seat of power for too long. You think you are all so naturally gifted? I think not. In fact, I know that it's the magic of this place that has afforded you those powers. Now tell me, where is the source, Tamsyn?'

'The source? You'll have to be a bit more specific… My brain isn't what it used to be. After the… you know, binding potion.' Tamsyn cocked her head slightly and tapped her temple.

'I want to know where the source is!' he screeched like a petulant child. 'I will raze this place to the ground to find it.

Just tell me where it is, and maybe I won't have to demolish this hole brick by brick!' He was red in the face now. 'If you'd just sold it in the first place, we wouldn't be in this mess!'

She looked at him, deadpan. 'Okay. Are you done screaming now? I have no idea where the source is. Sorry, I can't help you.' She made no effort to hide her disdain for him. She wanted to smile, seeing how wound up he was, but she also wanted to rip his head off, walk past his decapitated body and enter her own home. Of course, she knew exactly where—and what—the source was. It was the water that flowed through from the Frog Well in Acton Burnell, all the way to the statue of Hecate in Rosemount's garden. It gave unnatural energy to everything from the house to the garden. That was why the Prides had always had their peculiar innate power: it came from the food they consumed and the water they drank. Yet all those years, they had had to make themselves invisible. Generations of women hiding away, making themselves as small as possible.

She wondered if the magic she possessed would enable her to rip Gavin Hardcastle limb from limb. She realised she was clenching her fists so tightly her nails were embedded into her palms. She breathed deeply. How long would it take him to figure it out? Rosemount would be a pile of rubble before he realised it wasn't some ancient hoard of treasure, or a sacred burial ground beneath the earth.

'So be it!' spat Gavin. 'The contractors are coming at eight a.m. We'll start with the house and the barrow it sits on. You're more than welcome to come and watch. Vivien!' he shouted over their shoulders. She stood there, unmoving.

After a moment, she turned and headed towards them, her eyes never leaving Tamsyn's as she walked past them.

'You're lucky,' Gavin seethed at Tamsyn. 'If it had been up to me, you'd have been drowned in the river at birth. You're a freak. You spent too long in this house, absorbing its energy, casting unnatural spells that go against the laws of nature.'

With that, he slammed the door in their faces.

'Do you do that, then?' Vivien asked, her voice flat.

'Do what?' Gavin replied absentmindedly.

'Drown people in the river.'

'It was just a figure of speech. We certainly wouldn't drown *babies*.' He laughed, tossing papers and books around.

'We? You don't deny drowning women, then?'

'Oh, for pity's sake, will you shut up with these stupid questions?'

'Who was I?' Vivien asked as she watched Gavin rifle through the writing desk. 'Never mind. I think you know. You know everyone who comes and goes in this weird little village.'

He didn't look back at her.

'You're a Siren. I named you Vivien,' he said disinterestedly.

'I was someone before I belonged to Sabrina.' Vivien looked around the room. 'I have been here. In this house. That girl, Tamsyn—she said something about a binding potion, one that makes you forget. Is that what you've done to me?' Vivien wanted to run. She wanted to kill him first. But she also wanted answers. Answering the door against his wishes had taken every last bit of energy from her. She hadn't drained enough blood, she thought desperately. There must be some part of the spell, clinging to her blood. Multiplying again like a cancer.

'Stop with all these bloody questions and *sit down*,' Gavin spat.

Vivien sat heavily in the armchair in front of the fire. It was too hot, but she could not disobey him. 'Who's the man in the long coat that visits late at night?' she asked.

'Christ, Vivien. Just some mule from the village. He runs errands for me. I needed a book. You really shouldn't spy, y'know. It's very unbecoming.'

'I'm leaving now. I have fulfilled my end of the bargain.' She stood, swaying, looking desperately towards the front door.

'Stop.' He turned to her, holding up his hand. 'I don't want you to leave.'

Vivien felt a pull, deep in her chest. 'You have no power over me.' She reached for the figure of Hecate on the fireplace. It was astonishingly heavy. She held it up high over her shoulder as a warning. He looked at her quizzically, before the realisation dawned in his eyes.

'You know,' he told her, 'I didn't think that spell I found would be strong enough to open the door. A cow's blood, especially an old one's, was a bit of a gamble. But you used your own blood, didn't you? You silly thing.' He put one hand on her shoulder, taking the statue away from her with the other. She tried to run for the door, but her legs felt like lead.

'Is this why you've been so disobedient?' He *tut-tut-tutted* with his tongue. ' The problem with that is,' he called over his shoulder as he walked to the kitchen, 'you'd have to drain every last drop. And that would kill you. Bit of a predicament, really… So, we are stuck together forever, it seems.'

He came back to her, holding a knife and length of witch's twine, which Sylvia had made from her own hair with the fur from a black hound and dried thistle stems. She shuddered as he stroked her hair. He grabbed her face, and kissed her hard. She bit down on his lip.

'Argh!' He reeled back, blood already dribbling from his mouth. He slapped her, much harder than he had the first time. The shock was immediate, and she was sure her eardrum had burst.

'I don't have time for this! If you won't be mine, you will die. Do you hear me?' He shoved her powerless figure back into the chair, then worked the twine to bind Vivien's feet to the chair legs and her hands behind her back, cutting it with the knife.

'You'll have to kill me, then!' she screamed.

Tamsyn watched helplessly through the window as Ellis tried various incantations to open the front door.

'Who do you think she is?' asked Tamsyn.

'I couldn't find anything in my research. There are various reports of missing women, bodies found in the river. But most of the records have been sealed, or destroyed. I fear she is one of a number of witches the Much Wenlock council put to death before they started using the Binding.'

'She couldn't remember *me*, could she?'

'I don't think so. Sirens are extremely dangerous. Gavin probably forced her to drink the Binding potion. But there's more to it than that... From what I can tell she seems to have no autonomy. And when she does do something of her own accord, it takes every ounce of strength from her. I fear he has used some very dark, illegal magic indeed.'

'So he made her kill my grandmother?'

Ellis nodded. 'I believe so, yes.'

'Then we have to help her. How do we get in?' Tamsyn stared through the window at the woman Gavin called Vivien. Her mind scrabbled frantically, trying to fill in the missing pieces.

Tamsyn could barely see them. She could see the back of the chair, and the top of Vivien's head poking above it. She saw Gavin bending down, tying her legs and wrists with the witch's twine.

Tamsyn banged hard on the window. 'Stop! I'll tell you!' she shouted. 'I'll show you where it is.' She picked up a rock and hurled it at the window. It merely bounced off like it was made of rubber, clattering onto the ground.

As Gavin finished binding her arms, Vivien felt nothing but a vague sense of pity for him. He was a truly desperate creature, searching for some form of recognition that would forever elude him.

'I am sorry about this, Vivien. If only we had had more time together, I think you would have come around.' Light glinted upon the knife in his hand.

'What are you doing?' Vivien's eyes bulged wide as her feet tried to scramble backwards. The chair scraped the floor as she bucked wildly. She had thoroughly underestimated him.

'No! No, no, no, Gavin, please! Please don't do this! I am more useful to you alive!'

'My hold over you is waning. I know you will try to kill me the second you have the chance. I am really, truly sorry, Vivien. But you can rest easy in the knowledge that you made a difference. I will make this village, this county, great again, and I won't forget your contribution.'

'If you kill me, your soul will be blackened! The hounds of hell will drag you away! You idiot!' Vivien closed her eyes tightly. Her whole body tensed to breaking point as she felt the hopelessness of escape. The fire crackled in the grate, spitting out sparks.

'My soul is already blackened. So many witches had to die to protect this community. That is *my* contribution,' he said sadly. 'I do hope that when my deeds are weighed, they will be judged as acts of altruism. I hope I will be looked upon kindly. I have come too far to go back now. I am sorry. Truly.'

Gavin paused. Vivien opened her eyes. For a moment she thought he couldn't go through with it, or get his hands—or jeans—dirty.

'Wait,' she implored. 'If you are going to kill me, I just want to ask you one more thing. Please, will you answer my question?'

'Yes, of course. How could I say no to that beautiful face?' His voice was soft.

'Was Sylvia Pride responsible for my death? Or did you set her up? Did you make me believe she had done it so that I would kill her?' she asked.

Gavin seemed confused, then amused.

'Oh no, that was real. I keep all the documentation in the church... We all signed off on it. Sylvia, Bridie, Bradshaw, Roy, Daisy, Anita, Leila... all of them. Truth be told, I didn't even remember you. Then I saw the odd article here and there. Strange sightings. "Suspected Siren Spotted". So, I dug out the old records. I mean, did I doctor them a little? Yes, maybe I'm guilty of that. I needed you to see only Sylvia's name. But it wasn't a lie. She did have a hand in your death. She put pen to paper and signed her name. I put it in a jar with all those disgusting offerings so you would see it.'

'Who took me to the river? Who sent me to my death?'

'Oh, just some idiot from the village, the chap who does my errands. His name is Colin.' Gavin held his hand over her mouth. 'Enough now. No more questions.'

He bent over her and sank the blade deep into her stomach.

Searing pain, unlike anything she had ever felt before, sent powerful distress signals to her brain. She tried to scream as she looked at him wide-eyed. He pressed his hand harder over her mouth and nose.

'Goodbye, my beautiful Vivien.' He kissed her on the forehead.

He watched with mild interest as her blood, a deep scarlet red, began seeping through her white blouse. The log in the fireplace exploded, scattering pieces of wood onto the carpet and over Gavin. He cursed, murmuring something that sounded so far away. The world went dark.

33
BURN

Tamsyn and Ellis stood beside the statue of Hecate in Rosemount's garden. They watched in silence as the water trickled down her body, retracing the new black trails Tamsyn had observed weeks before. Fine rain began to fall. Tamsyn shuddered when she thought of how recently she had stood before Rosemount in the Underworld. The memory of snow, ash and the small part of Sylvia that refused to leave her home was still too fresh to process.

'What do you think he's going to do to her?' Tamsyn asked.

'I dread to think. We have to act now. Sylvia told you when you were younger that fissures appeared in the ground when you were upset. I saw the water flooding into my house when you were drowning in the Underworld. I think that when you're in distress you're able to bend the space around you. And when the force reaches breaking point, it splits the fabric of this universe, spilling into another.'

Tamsyn knew Ellis was looking at her, but she couldn't meet his gaze.

He continued. 'And when you distort space, because our world lies directly between the Mirror World and the Underworld, they are able to seep into one another.'

Tamsyn thought again about the day on the bus when she was sixteen. Her mind wanted to protect her from the memory, but she pushed harder. They had been driving back through the village after school. The group of girls at the back had been sniggering at her, as usual. They wore their school ties short and their skirts even shorter. Leah, the girl who had been her best friend in primary school, had come up to Tamsyn's seat and spat her chewing gum into Tamsyn's hair. And when the bus had begun to slow down for their stop, Kayleigh, the dumb one, had spat at her as they walked past. They'd all laughed. Tamsyn had watched them as they neared the steps to climb down out of the bus. Her fingers had begun to tingle horribly. She'd felt sick and numb, her stomach rolling over and over in powerless anguish as she felt the warm glob of saliva sliding down her cheek.

She'd had no idea what was happening. The driver slammed on the brakes, then cranked the wheel sharply to avoid something in the road. Craning her neck, Tamsyn had seen a huge hole in the tarmac. It had come from nowhere. And then the bus plummeted into it. She could hear kids screaming, but all she felt was the blunt force of the seat in front hitting her head.

'But how does that help us now?' she asked Ellis.

'Gavin's coming,' he said urgently.

They watched as Gavin ran wildly from the house. He

stumbled, fell to the ground and rolled about. His shirt smoked as he thrashed around in the grass. Ellis and Tamsyn raced over to him.

'Where is she?' asked Tamsyn. 'Where's Vivien?'

'She's inside. Tried to set me on fire, the little minx!' He sounded angry, but Tamsyn could tell he was enjoying it. 'Show me where the source is, and I'll let her go,' he demanded.

Tamsyn shot Ellis a look. He nodded in recognition.

'It's there.' She pointed to the statue. 'The water runs from the Frog Well, in Acton Burnell. That's where the source of Rosemount's magic comes from.'

Gavin got to his feet, brushed himself off and approached the statue, tentatively touching the side of Hecate's cheek where the water fell, tracing the flow down her torso. There were large singed holes in the back of his shirt.

'We've done our bit. Now how do I get into the house?' Ellis asked him angrily.

Absently, Gavin tossed a screwed-up piece of paper from his pocket onto the ground. He continued examining the statue, while Ellis snatched up the paper and ran back to the house to get Vivien.

'The Frog Well?' Gavin said, still examining the statue. 'That's just a silly old wives' tale.'

Tamsyn shrugged. 'Whether the water is imbued with power from Satan himself or not, it does *something*. Sylvia used it in all of her remedies, and that's why they worked so well.'

He nodded. 'She grew her own produce, I see.' He circled

around the statue, crushing the plants that grew around it underfoot.

'So, what are you going to do now?' Tamsyn asked. Gavin rubbed his fingertips together, before sniffing at the black mould he had lifted from Hecate's breast. He flicked it off his fingers onto the ground, before touching the statue again to taste the water. Tamsyn grimaced; he was truly repugnant.

'If what you say it is true, that Acton Burnell is the source of the water, then I was correct. It is indeed the direction of the ley line, running straight through here,' he said, patting Hecate's backside. 'I will have access to one of the oldest seats of power. Shropshire will no longer be at the mercy of the archbishop. It will be as it was hundreds of years ago, where *we* called the shots. We will make our own laws, negotiate our own deals. In a nutshell, I will have a seat at the table. Maybe even at the head of the table.' He could not contain his elation.

'Right… so now you know. There's no need to destroy the house looking for it,' said Tamsyn, completely uninterested in his game plan.

'Oh dear,' said Gavin. 'Speaking of that, I'm afraid there may have been a little… accident.'

Tamsyn heard banging, then shouting from the front of the house. A few seconds later, Ellis came running towards her, shouting 'Fire, Rosemount!' into his phone.

'I can't get in,' he said breathlessly, shaking his head at Tamsyn before grabbing Gavin with both hands.

'You killed her! You sick bastard!' He punched him and wrestled him to the ground.

Tamsyn ran to the front of the house; black wisps of

smoke were escaping from under the front door. She ran to the window and peered in. The front room was ablaze. The rug and the chair were already engulfed in flames.

Tamsyn picked up a terracotta plant pot from the veranda. Standing back, she hurled it at the glass. The red clay smashed into smithereens. The window remained completely undamaged. She kicked at the hinges as hard as she could, screaming. She tried the door again in vain, even though she knew Vivien was likely already dead.

After what she had seen in the Underworld, Rosemount going up in flames now seemed like an inevitability. But having to watch a woman burning alive inside while they stood and watched, unable to help, was more than she could bear. Tamsyn's pulse throbbed inside her head. She tried to breathe but her lungs constricted, tighter and tighter. She pounded on the window, screaming.

Turning, she saw Ellis drag Gavin to the front of the house. He hit him again, harder this time. Gavin slumped and lay prone in the tall grass.

She pounded on the window again, but the heat burned her palms. She screamed in horror as she watched the fire spread across the room and up the wooden beams to the ceiling.

'Why would he do that to her?' she screamed at Ellis. 'I told him! I told him I'd tell him where it was!'

'Get back, Tamsyn! Get away from the house!' Ellis was pulling at her arm, dragging her away.

'We can't leave her in there!' She struggled against him.

'She's dead, Tamsyn!' Ellis shouted.

He threw his arms around her and dragged her away as

the curtains went up in flames. She could still see it, seared into her retinas—the lone woman sitting in the chair. Burning. She stood staring at the house, at the window ablaze with fire.

'The fire brigade are on their way. And the police.' Ellis held her as they watched the cottage going up in flames. Behind them, they heard muffled laughter.

'No use calling the police,' said Gavin mockingly. 'I'll tell them it was you. That rather than letting me have your beloved cottage, you committed arson and assaulted me. If I were you, I'd run. Get a little head start. Or you can sit here and enjoy watching the whole thing burn before they come and arrest you.'

There was an explosion followed by a tinkling sound as the front windows to Rosemount shattered. The glass sprayed out over the porch, huge fragments bursting into the darkness. They seemed to slow before her eyes, disintegrating into thousands of tinier pieces. As they fell to the ground, they sparkled like snow.

Tamsyn's breathing slowed. She closed her eyes. All the sounds—wood cracking, flames shooting up into the night sky—fell away.

When she opened her eyes, she found herself sitting by the brook where she first saw the deer. The winter landscape that had been there the night before had turned to spring.

The bee was back. It hovered for a moment, circling above her head, before it turned and zig-zagged downriver. She stood and followed it, passing through the trees, until she found herself at the edge of an immense lake.

'Would you mind if I gave you a name?' she asked the

bee. 'What about Nashira?' The bee had landed near her feet, on the large yellow head of a dandelion. She studied it. 'It means bearer of good news.' She waited for something; she did not know what. She closed her eyes once more, enjoying the cool breeze and the spring sun on her face.

Through the lids of her eyes, she saw that the light turned from pink to orange. The birdsong ended abruptly, giving way to the low rumble of fire consuming brick and wood. She knew she was back again, standing in front of her home as it burned.

34
THE RECKONING

Tamsyn stood with her eyes still closed, feeling the heat from the blazing inferno radiating across her. In the garden, the face of the maiden cracked. The fissure spread, moving first down her left cheek and then to her torso. A great rumbling shook the ground. The statue of Hecate exploded violently, splintering in half. Where she had stood, a huge column of water burst upwards.

For the first time, Tamsyn was in control.

She whispered, *Sabrina appello, ut terram scindat, servus tuus te indiget!*

She couldn't see it, but Tamsyn could feel the immense power of the water. She focused upon it. A huge wave rose from the back of the house, curling and crashing over the cottage, spraying them all with wet, hot ash. She opened her eyes. Water seeped over the earth, filling the space as if the lake she had seen in the Underworld were spilling into the land around them. Gavin and Ellis looked around in confusion.

'What the hell is this?' Gavin was already ankle deep in water. 'Is this from the source? Did you do this?'

Tamsyn didn't answer. She watched the remaining flames that still burned on Rosemount's ruined façade. She watched as the water that had seeped inside the cottage overflowed from the broken windows and front door.

'Are you doing this?' Gavin shouted. Ellis held him back as he tried to get to her. 'The power from the source will be lost forever!'

'Tamsyn,' Ellis said, gently. 'It's too late. Everything inside Rosemount will already be gone.'

The flow of water had already begun to subside, merely bubbling up now from the plinth where the maiden had stood.

'You said a house is just stuff.' She shrugged. 'You were right. Rosemount belongs to Mr Hardcastle now. Let him have it.' As the water receded, Tamsyn saw that it had not just come from where the statue had stood.

There was a large crack in the ground, almost like a crescent moon, around the cottage. She had caused a huge rent, but this time, she had meant to.

Suddenly Tamsyn froze. Both Ellis and Gavin turned to see what she was staring at. The door to Rosemount was open, and in the doorway was the outline of a woman with dark, dripping hair. They watched as, against the smouldering embers of Rosemount, the figure flickered. She began drawing closer to them now, the shadow of her form shifting as she moved. They squinted against the low light, watching her body grow and writhe. She moved unnaturally, slithering across the ground, making up the distance in no time at all.

Tamsyn looked up at her in awe. She towered above them, standing against the swirling smoke behind her: half woman, half serpent. She was beautiful and terrible to behold. The huge tail, muscular and thick, lashed back and forth, cutting through the sludge on the ground. Fear kept all three of them rooted to where they stood, hearts in their throats. Twigs cracked as she neared them, and Gavin stared at her, his eyes betraying his sheer terror. He opened his mouth to scream, but no sound came.

The creature reared up, one massive hand grabbing his neck. Her mouth was contorted with snarling hatred.

'We meet again.' Vivien didn't contain her rage as she crushed his windpipe harder. 'I told you Sabrina would come for me. She gave me life when you took it the first time. And now she gives me life again.' The Siren let go of his neck. He crumpled to the ground awkwardly, wailing hoarsely in pain and terror.

'Do you remember me now? Who I was before you had me murdered the first time? I had a family. Children.'

'I—I don't know what you're talking about! I never met you until that night at the river!' he rasped, rubbing his throat.

'Before Sabrina named me Ophelia, my name was Grace Piper. I was an elemental witch. I used my magic once. *Once*, to save my son from fever. You had that little man—Colin? Was that his name?—strangle me and throw me in the river.'

Gavin tried to shuffle backwards, his hands sinking into the mud.

'What? No, I—Vivien, please stop!' he pleaded.

'Ophelia.' She advanced towards him. 'Grace might be

dead. But I am Ophelia, handmaiden of the goddess of the River Severn.'

Tamsyn tore her gaze away from the Siren and turned sharply to Gavin. 'You and this... Colin... murdered witches?'

'No! It was something that just happened back then. And we *all* did it! Bridie, Sylvia, Roy, the lot of them! We all signed off on it.'

'How many?' asked Ellis through gritted teeth.

'I—I dunno!'

'How many?' Ellis shouted.

'Bloody loads! Dozens! There are records in Old Chad's!' Gavin cried. 'Please don't kill me! I will do anything.' He got awkwardly to his knees and began to grovel.

Ophelia ignored him and turned to Tamsyn.

'I didn't kill your grandmother. I merely wished to torment her. I appeared in the form of a drowned woman; all I wanted to do was scare her. I thought that she was solely responsible for what had happened to me.' She gave Gavin a sharp look. 'I knew there would be grave punishment if I killed a mortal, and I could never betray my mistress. Alas, Sylvia was so afraid that she tried to poison me with monkshood. I drank the tea. I knew exactly what she had done. It grows in many places near the river, and so I have a high tolerance for it. I won't say I'm sorry for her death.' She turned to Tamsyn. 'But I *am* sorry for trying to hurt you. I believed you had come to avenge her.'

'My grandmother played her part in all of this. As did Bridie.' Tamsyn looked over at the smouldering house, and then back at the figure in front of her. 'You have suffered enough, Ophelia. I just wanted to know the truth.'

Gavin was sobbing now, his head in his hands. He looked up at Tamsyn and Ellis. 'Please,' he blubbered to Ellis. 'Help me.'

Tamsyn couldn't bear to look at him. She felt Ellis's hand on her arm.

'Tamsyn,' Ellis said gently. 'He must stand trial for what he has done. We need information. Names of all the women.' He tried to catch her eye, but she looked away.

The Siren slowly wound her tail around Gavin.

'Don't do this, Ophelia,' he warned.

'There is no justice to be had in this world,' said Ophelia.

'He has to answer here. He has to answer to all those he has wronged,' Ellis pleaded with her.

'If I had more time, I would take him somewhere. Torture him where no one can stop me,' said Ophelia, relishing Gavin's fear. Her tail was coiled tightly around him now. Somewhere beyond the trees, they could hear the faint wail of police and fire sirens.

Gavin looked from Tamsyn to Ellis, wide-eyed. 'Help me! By God, please do something! Don't just stand there!' he pleaded. 'I—I will tell them everything! I will make sure they know you're not arsonists. I will tell them I set the house on fire. Anything! Anything! Just don't let her kill me!'

'You can rest assured, your death will be agonising,' Ophelia spat. She lifted him with her tail clean off the ground.

'Stop! Stop this now!' shouted Ellis. 'Tamsyn, we have to do something!'

'I'm sorry, Ellis,' Tamsyn said softly.

The Siren squeezed. They heard Gavin's legs breaking. His guttural scream filled the smoky air. The tail coiled up and around him, tighter now, a hideous crunching signalling his ribs shattering. His mouth gaped open as he gasped for air, blood spilling from his mouth. For a terrible moment he hung there, like a fish silently suffocating. And then the tip of Ophelia's tail wound around his neck, snapping it in two. Gavin's head flopped limply to the side, his eyes wide and glassy.

Police cars sped up the driveway, the flashing lights blinding them. Tamsyn and Ellis squinted, watching the red and blue lights illuminate the form of Ophelia as she disappeared through the trees.

EPILOGUE

Gathering her thoughts, Celia Mosley let out a sigh as she hung her coat on one of the pegs. Unsure of how to handle the meeting, she had concluded that forgiveness and a 'water under the bridge' approach would perhaps be the easiest option. Her mind had wandered back countless times to the last time she had been in this room. The night she'd looked upon the faces of the people she thought were her friends, who had, as one, raised their hands in the air in a vote of no confidence. She wasn't sure she could, or even wanted to, forgive them.

She tried her best to remind herself that they had had their ears and minds bent by Gavin Hardcastle. With their livestock under threat, and fearing that Tamsyn Pride would unleash her power, they had allowed him to sow his plans of greed. Like knotweed, it had spread throughout every last one of them. She wondered which one of them had approached the others with the idea of asking her back. It couldn't have been easy. She imagined their conversations as they tried to come up with some other candidate—any other candidate, really—for the role of chairman.

Pride swelled in her chest, along with another, more sinister feeling, a growing urge that she desperately wanted to push aside: the feeling that she wanted revenge. However small and petty it might be, she could not shake the feeling that, in some way, the members who had voted against her needed to be reminded that she was not someone to mess with.

Celia took her seat at the head of the table. Methodically she placed her coffee cup, notepad and pen on the table in front of her and then sat, waiting, in the heavy silence.

A murmur of voices echoed in the hallway as the old doors to the library banged shut behind them. The conversation drew nearer, and Celia breathed in through her nose and out through her mouth as the butterflies intensified.

The door opened, and the shocking pink tea-cosy hat of Daisy Cartwright appeared, followed by Roy, permeating the room with the smell of mothballs. They shuffled in as they always did, like nothing had occurred.

'Evening, Celia! Bit nippy out,' said Roy as he rubbed his paper-thin hands together. Daisy smiled and nodded with that dimly happy expression she always wore.

As the pair took their seats, Leila Ahmadi arrived, followed by Dr Anita Palgrave. They ceased conversation immediately when they saw that Celia was already in the room.

'Hello, ladies. Glad you could join us,' said Celia. They didn't look at her as they made their way across the room, selecting the chairs as far away from Celia as possible. Clearly these two weren't in agreement with the others about her return, then. Whatever happened to women looking out for each other? But Celia expected nothing less from those two harpies. She opened her notebook, jotting down the date and time of the meeting.

After a few awkward moments of silence, Terence Buchanan and Farmer Bradshaw entered the room, sheepish and red-faced. Terence had been asked to sit on the council after Gavin's untimely demise. Everyone sat quietly, coughing, wiping noses, twiddling their thumbs or looking around the room, until they heard a familiar voice, followed by something hard banging into the door.

'Satan's beard, Colin! Watch me foot, will ya?' Bridie was wheeled in, pushed by a po-faced Colin, who delivered her to the usual spot and then disappeared into a corner, desperate not to be looked at.

Celia glanced at her watch, waiting. As soon as the second hand reached its mark, she proceeded.

'I think that's everybody. First of all, I'd like to thank you all for coming today. I know it can't have been easy for some of you, asking me back here.'

'Well, no one else wanted the job,' said Peter Bradshaw, matter-of-factly.

'Quite so.' Celia looked at them all, trying to conceal her loathing. 'Nevertheless, I'm sure there was reluctance from some members to see me back here.' She looked pointedly at Leila and Anita. 'However, I'm sure you know me well enough by now. I take this role extremely seriously. I am here to ensure that standards are upheld, and that the procedures enacted by this council are fair and just. I have been reflecting of late on the sordid history of this council. On the deeds that have been carried out against witches and druids, particularly under the tutelage of Gavin Hardcastle.' She paused, her eyes scanning their faces.

'I have been trawling the archives these past few months. There are many things that we as council members need to rectify—even if *some* of us were not responsible for these acts directly. I was perplexed to find, in my scouring of the records, that much of the paperwork has been destroyed.' She watched their faces for any tell-tale reactions. They stared at her blankly.

'Someone has removed all the pages that held the signatures. So, it might take a little longer to prove who signed those documents. But believe me, I will find them. In the meantime, this will no longer be a meeting where you just show up, do nothing, and then expect tea and biscuits.'

The council members shifted uncomfortably in their chairs. Daisy glared at Roy. Tea, biscuits and gossip were the only activities they enjoyed be partaking in.

Celia placed her round spectacles on the end of her nose and read her notes. 'First on the agenda, our ex-chairman's funeral arrangements. Now that he is back from the mortuary, I vote we have a very, *very* small service, conducted at the Old Church. No driving him through the centre of town in a horse-drawn carriage. I don't care what his last will and testament say.' The others shrugged in agreement.

'Fantastic. Item two. PC Thompson has informed me that the questioning of Ellis Rowlands and Tamsyn Pride has concluded for now. They are free to go, with the caveat that they may be called back at any time for further questioning.'

Some of the members gasped in disapproval.

'How can they possibly let that menace roam the streets? She killed Gavin!' Leila exclaimed, sitting up in her chair and trying to rile the others up.

'Well, all I can say is that the police found no evidence of that. They both have alibis; they were with Bridie all night. Item three—'

'Have they left already?' said Dr Palgrave, in shock. They all turned to Bridie.

'Yep,' she said.

'Well, where have they gone?'

'That Ellis went back to Anglesey. Tamsyn… damned if I know. She won't tell me anything. Took that horrible cat with her an' all.' Bridie said it as a joke, but Celia could tell she was terribly sad.

'Well, the police have their contact numbers, so let's move on, shall we?' said Celia.

'Did they not leave together, then?' asked Colin nosily. 'Thought you said there was a bit of tension there?'

'Nope. They went their separate ways,' said Bridie. They all sat in silence, waiting for more.

'Well… where did she go?' asked Terence Buchanan.

'I said *damned if I know!*' said Bridie bitterly. 'She wouldn't tell me. She…' Bridie trailed off, thinking for a moment. 'She just said she was going somewhere she could learn to control herself. To learn more about magic.'

The others looked at each other, unsure what to do or say.

'And she left Rosemount like that? That girl has no pride! Ironic, really.' Daisy smiled, seeming pleased with herself.

Celia could practically feel the steam rising from Leila

and Anita. She looked back down at her papers. 'As I was saying... let's move on to item three on the agenda. As you know, Daisy, Roy and I have spent the last month trawling through the minutes from these meetings, as well as documents that have been sealed up at the Crow's Nest, spanning decades. It was extremely laborious.' Celia sat back in her chair, watching the faces of the council members as it dawned on them. 'Some of you have been around long enough to have been witness to the debased, grubby dealings of Gavin Hardcastle. Some of you may even have had a part to play. I am not here to point the finger. But we shall atone. I have made a start in tracking down every witch and druid who has been excommunicated from our community. Bridie has kindly handed over the restorative tincture that should help to bring back at least some, if not all of the memories that have been robbed from them.'

Shocked murmurings rippled through the room, as Celia watched them with an anger that she fought to keep under control.

'No doubt it will be extremely uncomfortable and difficult for some of you. There may very soon be people coming back into our community who are old friends, exes, family members or rivals. People who you had a hand in sending away. You may have to answer to them personally, but I am sure that, together, we will get through this, and welcome them home with open arms, should they wish to return.'

Dr Palgrave looked ashen. 'How many have you found?' Her voice was remote, her fingers trembling as she twisted them together.

'Unfortunately, it has been extremely difficult. Currently,

I have found seven witches and five druids. It is hard to know just how many there are. But I am hopeful that, in time, I will find them all.' She smiled.

'Y-you can't,' stammered Leila, putting her arm around Dr Palgrave. 'They were dangerous. You are putting this whole community at risk!'

'That may be the case. And if that is the case, we will have to deal with them properly, through the law. And with the help of the High Council. As I'm sure you can appreciate, it has been difficult to determine who was sent away justifiably, and who were the victims of jealousy and competition. People who were too powerful, more talented than you, people your husbands took a shine to...' Celia watched them coolly, proud of herself that she was so expertly hiding how much she was enjoying this.

The council members, relieved the meeting was over yet unable to stop themselves from grumbling, made their way out of the room.

Colin, who had been staring at his phone in the hope no one would catch his eye, stood up and walked over to Bridie.

'Actually, Colin,' Celia said, meeting him halfway, 'I wouldn't mind a quick chat with Bridie... in private.'

Colin rolled his eyes and looked over at her.

'I'll give you a shout. Off you trot,' Bridie said, waving him away.

Celia waited for him to close the doors. 'It really is a

shame Tamsyn Pride left so quickly,' she said, turning to Bridie. 'I thought you should be the one to tell her.'

'What do you mean?'

Celia's eyes grew wide.

'We found her mother.'

DID YOU ENJOY THIS BOOK? YOU CAN MAKE A BIG DIFFERENCE.

Reviews are the most powerful tools in an author's arsenal when it comes to getting attention for our books.

An honest review of my book will help bring it to the attention of other readers.

If you've enjoyed this book I would be very grateful if you could spend just five minutes leaving a review (it can be as short as you like) on the book's Amazon page.

Thank you very much.

Book 2 in the Arcane Tales of Tamsyn Pride Series.
Coming in 2023

Sign up to my newsletter to be the first to know:
www.NatashaBache.com

ACKNOWLEDGMENTS

First, I'd like to thank my cover designers Micaela Alcaino and Stuart Bache—it's the highest honour to have two of the best designers in the industry create such a beautiful cover. It truly inspired me to keep going, right up to the finish line.

Thank you to my editors Kerry Barrett, Charlotte Ledger, Jennifer McIntyre and David Brawn for your invaluable advice and input. Also, a special thank you to Carwyn Tywyn for translating the Siren's song into Welsh.

Finally, this book would not exist without the love and support of my husband, Stuart. Thank you for giving me the confidence to find my way again, and for the unwavering love you show us every day.

ABOUT THE AUTHOR

Natasha Bache studied English Literature and Philosophy at Keele University. After completing a Masters degree at Warwick University, she became an Editor at HarperCollins Publishers where she worked with estates such as Agatha Christie and J.R.R. Tolkien.

In 2015, she co-founded a design agency with her husband called Books Covered, where they specialise in designing market-leading book covers for both traditional and self-published authors.

Natasha lives in Shropshire with her husband and two children.

facebook.com/NatashaBache

twitter.com/Natasha_Bache

instagram.com/natashabache_author

tiktok.com/@natashamariebache

Printed in Great Britain
by Amazon